"YOU'RE GOING TO HAVE TO DO BETTER THAN THAT."

Martok coughed, spitting black spots out onto the snow, though the lung puncture might be the least of his worries. With each passing second, strength drained out of him and he felt a strange, unaccountable pressure in his chest around his heart.

Off in the distance, another creature howled; more of Gothmara's pets on the prowl. Almost as if it could not control itself, the Hur'q before him threw back its head and howled in response and Martok knew he had his chance.

When the distant voice echoed across the plain again and the beast before him lifted its head to respond, Martok struck. If not for the deep snow and his shattered leg, the blow would have been perfect, but as it was all he did was slash the monster's jugular. Blood jetted out as its heart pumped the Hur'q's life out onto the snow, but life did not flee its body. Snapping its head forward, the beast launched itself at Martok, who was ready for it. He aimed to deflect its attack, to give its heart time to finish the job, flutter and fall silent, but the edge of the cliff was too close and his body too battered.

The pair of them, monster and warrior, scraped to a halt at the lip of the precipice and, for a brief, thrilling moment, Martok thought he might be able to keep the blade pressed against its nose, to hold it, just long enough. Its eyes grew dim and he could feel its breaths coming shorter and shorter. Death would come. Its head would drop onto the ground and Martok would climb up over the corpse, find his communicator and Pharh would get him out of there before the other Hur'q found him. He would be warm again and there would be medicine and food . . .

. . . And then the ice shelf crumbled from beneath them both.

STAR TREK
DEEP SPACE NINE®

THE LEFT HAND OF
DESTINY

BOOK TWO

J. G. HERTZLER & JEFFREY LANG

Based upon STAR TREK® created by Gene Roddenberry
and STAR TREK: DEEP SPACE NINE
created by Rick Berman & Michael Piller

POCKET BOOKS

New York   London   Toronto   Sydney   Singapore   Qo'noS

An *Original* Publication of POCKET BOOKS

POCKET BOOKS, a division of Simon & Schuster, Inc.
1230 Avenue of the Americas, New York, NY 10020

STAR TREK is a registered trademark of Paramount Pictures.

This book is published by Pocket Books, a division of Simon & Schuster, Inc., under exclusive license from Paramount Pictures.

ISBN: 0-671-78494-3

First Pocket Books printing May 2003

10 9 8 7 6 5 4 3 2 1

POCKET and colophon are registered trademarks of Simon & Schuster, Inc.

For information regarding special discounts for bulk purchases, please contact Simon & Schuster Special Sales at 1-800-456-6798 or business@simonandschuster.com

Cover art by Cliff Nielsen

Printed in the U.S.A.

*For my dad, Col. J. G. Hertzler, USAF,
and my mom, teacher of Latin, French,
and life*

J. G. H.

"For the Andorian Girl. She knows why."

J. L.

ACKNOWLEDGMENTS

Firstly, I am ever thankful for the patience and talent of my editor, Marco Palmieri. I am no less grateful for the heart and wisdom of Ira Steven Behr, Executive Producer of *Deep Space Nine;* for the words of Ronald Moore, poetic soul of the Klingon Empire; and for Gene Roddenberry, the sine qua non of this grand adventure called *Star Trek.* And most humbly, I must bow to the boundless talent and craft of my cowriter, Jeffrey Lang.
—J. G. Hertzler

I'd be remiss if I didn't acknowledge the producers, writers, and actors who made the Klingons into the rich, highly nuanced culture we know today. In particular, I'd like to pay homage to the work of Gene Roddenberry (naturally), Michael Ansara, Ira Steven Behr, Hans Beimler, William Campbell, Shannon Cochran, John Colicos, Kevin Conway, Gene L. Coon, Michael Dorn, Ronald D. Moore, Marc Okrand, Robert O'Reilly, and no doubt many others whom I omit only out of ignorance. Special thanks to the good folks at the Klingon Language Institute—in particular, Lawrence M. Schoen, Alan Anderson, Roger Cheesbro, and Lieven Lieter—for their help, and to editor supreme Marco Palmieri.

My thanks also to friends and family who have been so supportive during the "Klingon project," including

Tristan Mayer; Joshua Macy; Helen Szigeti; Annarita Gentile; my wife, Katherine Fritz, our son, Andrew; and, yes, even the dog (hi, Buster!). More than anyone, however, I owe a debt of gratitude to Heather Jarman—friend, advisor, sister in spirit—I literally could not have finished this one without you. May the next one have fewer words in italics and less raw food.

Last, of course, a bent knee and a fist in the air to my comrade and collaborator, J. G. Hertzler, without whom I wouldn't have been on this journey. *Qapla'* to the Chancellor and *kai* to the General.

—Jeffrey Lang

PART ONE

"Sometimes fate plays cruel tricks on us."

I

THE FUTURE

Angry Fire from Star's fair daughter / Scorches earth with icy fingers / Wielding flame and cold, She hails their doom . . . The ancient Trill rune-verse cycled through Ezri Dax's memory like an errant two-year-old child in the aisles of a market on a festival day, getting in the way of unwary travelers, pestering, nagging, demanding attention. *More . . . important . . . things to think about,* she reprimanded herself. *Focus, Ezri—* Inhaling too much of the foul, smoke-choked air, Ezri hacked and retched, wishing she could stop for a moment and slide on the helmet to her EVA suit, but those were precious seconds she could not afford to lose. A wave of dizziness threatened to capsize her.

At least she had thought to activate the magnetic soles of her boots, which meant that she could keep her feet under her, more than any of the others on the *Rotarran*'s bridge could claim. She glanced over her shoulder and saw Worf clinging to the main weapons console and Alexander right beside him, valiantly trying—but failing—to keep his footing.

A Klaxon blared. Drawing on Dax's memories of time spent on Klingon ships, Ezri "recalled" that the alarms, coded by duration and intensity, helped crew members specifically identify the danger the ship faced. This one indicated a major coolant leak in the secondary hull, the kind that would result in a warp-core breach without quick action. More by sound than by sight, Ezri knew that the two damage-control engineers who had come onto the bridge at the beginning of the battle had abandoned their stations and headed for the lifts. Bridge repairs were secondary to what was happening back in the engineering section. All Worf's clever plans would be for naught if the core breached.

The deck slid to the left under Ezri as she lifted her left foot to take a step toward tactical. Her right ankle twisted and she fell hard, her right hip and shoulder crashing into the unpadded floor. The heavy Klingon spacesuit—more like a suit of plated armor than any EVA garment she'd ever donned before—prevented her from cracking either her collarbone or pelvis, but even as it was, Ezri knew she would ache in the morning—assuming there was going to be a morning.

All right, then, Ezri thought, slapping on her right thigh the patch that deactivated the magnetic boots. *If I can't walk, I'll crawl.* She slapped another patch on her left thigh and the knee magnets pulsed to life. A limp, bleeding body she recognized as the navigator Ortakin slid past her as the deck seesawed. A gaping wound in his chest destined him for certain death. Ezri looked on helplessly, unable to attend to the dying man. Another buck and the body vanished from view. Since the filtration units had ceased spinning, the bridge was submerged in greasy smoke billowing from the sizzling and sparking environmental control panels. Fire-control foam that had been gushing from a nozzle in the floor sputtered and died and the flames guttered, then flared. *As if we weren't burning up enough atmosphere as it is, dammit. Might need the helmet after all.*

She reached around and felt to make sure the helmet remained attached to her equipment belt. It was difficult to be sure, since she couldn't feel it bang against her hip, but, yes, there it was. Almost as an afterthought, she strained to extend her reach a little farther, patting along her back to make sure the other package—the whole reason they were in this stupid situation—was there, too. She found it right where she had strapped it on.

Leskit, the pilot, regained control of the ship, leveling out the *Rotarran*. A throb raced through the deck under her hands and knees and, moments later, Worf and Alexander cheered exultantly. *A hit,* Ezri thought. *Good for them. Now all we need is about twenty more of those and we might survive. . . .* The deck bucked up underneath her and Ezri's arms and legs collapsed. Her ears rang, tiny lights flashed behind her eyelids, and her chest throbbed as though someone had picked up the starship and slammed it into her ribs. She imagined she could feel the symbiont squirming inside her and pictured the new tenant of an unexpectedly raucous hotel slamming on the ceiling to quiet the upstairs neighbors. *Another one like that,* she thought, struggling to remain conscious, *and Dax is going to need a new host.*

The cloud of gray, grimy smoke dropped lower and Ezri lost sight of Worf and Alexander, though she could still hear them impassively discussing what to do next. Strangely, through all the background noise and the blare of the Klaxons, it was difficult to tell when the father spoke and when the son. The timbre of their voices was entirely different, but the pauses, the cool, gruff starts and stops, were remarkably similar. She wondered if anyone else had noticed this, then realized that her mind was wandering. *Oxygen deprivation,* she decided, and reached around behind her for her helmet, realizing that Worf and Alexander had been speaking through breathing masks. Her fingers felt clumsy, and not just because of the thick gauntlets. *If I don't do this soon then wielding flame and cold She hails their doom . . . STOP THAT!*

"My old teachers would be thrilled I could still remember after all these years," Ezri muttered to no one in particular as she fumbled with the helmet's clip. "Never mind that the distraction might get me killed. . . ."

As she slid the helmet down into the suit's neck ring, another shudder rumbled through the deck, but this one didn't feel like either a weapons strike or an internal explosion. Ezri twisted the helmet into place and heard the connections click into their slots. Cool air rushed into the helmet and Ezri felt her head clear almost immediately. Status lights flickered into life, no doubt signalling something important about the suit's status. When Ezri relaxed and concentrated, she could call on her past hosts' extensive repository of matters Klingon to keep up with such details, but not under the current circumstances. Instead, she tapped the sequence Worf had showed her on the gauntlet's control set and checked the HUD on the upper left corner of the faceplate. The reading troubled her.

Ezri learned that she had used up a considerable amount of oxygen during her spacewalk. Yes, she was carrying a supply meant for an adult Klingon and her Trill physiology was not nearly as demanding; as she had expected, her air supply was sufficient to last until the current crisis had played out. On the other hand, her dangerously low battery power threatened to run out before she asphyxiated. A suit this large and heavy would be impossible to move without servomotors and she had been relying on them—much more than a Klingon would. Checking the status display, Ezri found she had ten, perhaps twelve minutes left.

Damn. Not good. Oddly, this knowledge did not alarm her. In fact, she felt quite calm, much calmer than she should have. Ezri wondered briefly which part of her many-faceted nature was responsible for that, then realized she didn't give a damn. She may never have planned on being joined, but she wasn't going to question the benefits, whether consciously utilized or not. *Best get to work, then.*

Having lost her orientation in the dense smoke, Ezri crawled until she ran into a console. Dragging herself up to her feet, she found that her aim was better than she could have expected, having crashed into tactical. The station appeared to be intact with most of the controls still functional. *Where in the hell are we, and what the hell is going on?* she thought, trying to coax the console into action. A quick check revealed that the main sensor grid was offline. If she could pull a visual reading from off of auxiliary feeds, she might be able to ascertain the

Rotarran's position relative to their attackers. The main monitors had gone down during the first wave of the attack, but the backup grids should be able to provide a visual. . . . *Yes, there we go,* she thought, grateful for the time her symbiont had spent on Klingon vessels. She tapped in the command that directed the feed to the closest functioning monitor.

The smoky gloom suddenly became brighter at one end of the bridge. *The computer must have directed the visual feed there,* she thought, squinting through the haze. Ezri was too far away to make out details, so she half hopped, half staggered the few meters to the glowing monitor, praying fervently that it was still keyed to main exterior camera and not some useless auxiliary view. Somewhere behind her, seemingly an eternity away, she heard Worf shout, "Torpedoes—fire!" So, at least two other people were still alive, unless Worf was issuing himself orders.

The bottom edge of the monitor image was shot through with fine spiderwebs from one of the direct hits to the *Rotarran,* but it otherwise appeared to be functional, though the picture made no sense. Ezri had expected to see either the black of space dotted through with glowing blobs when a ship decloaked and fired or the white arc of the planet below them. But this—a crackling white rush—the visual feed must be malfunctioning.

No. It isn't. Ezri staggered away until she collided with the navigator's console, then grabbed it with both hands, as much for reassurance as to steady herself. She wasn't looking at static, but at ice.

The flaming *Rotarran* was plummeting toward the icy surface of the planet Boreth, and they were already much too close for the ship to pull away.

Angry fire from Star's fair daughter, she thought, mouth agape. *Scorches earth with icy fingers . . .* The silver-white peaks of mountains winked in the sun as the ship spun in, down, down, and the edges of the image reddened with the heat of their passage. *Wielding flame and cold, She hails their doom.*

2

THE PRESENT

Ezri Dax gave the shuttle's thrusters a nudge, easing around the edge of a medium-sized asteroid, and thought, *This may well be the stupidest thing I've ever done. That, in and of itself, is remarkable, because if I add up all the stupid things I've done in my lives, I'd end up with a monumentally large pile of stupid.*

The shuttle was called the *Wardrobe* and it was, well, in a word, adorable. Obviously meant to be a vacation craft, the trim, tidy little rental was the kind of ship Ezri would have hired if she were planning a quick run back to Trill and didn't want to have to be at the mercy of a Starfleet ship's schedule. When she had asked the agent, a human named Riku, why he called it the *Wardrobe,* the pleasant old man had replied that he had permitted his eight-year-old daughter to name his three new ships and the other two were named the *Lion* and the *Witch.* Then, laughing in a manner that suggested Ezri should understand the joke, Riku had handed her the ship's papers and the key card and asked that she return to the station by Thursday next week.

Ezri hated to lie to him, hated knowing that the *Wardrobe* would likely never return home, but she still retained enough latinum in her personal holdings to cover the cost of replacing it, so Riku would not be out a shuttle. Plus, his daughter would have the fun of naming a new ship something just as baffling. *It's precisely this sort of little lie that permits us to do the things we must do,* she thought, mentally shading her words with her best counselor's tone. Over the past few days on her journey to this remote corner of Klingon space, she'd repeatedly used that rationalization to prevent her from changing her mind.

Part of her (the part that believed that the Klingons had brought this latest catastrophe on themselves) thought that Admiral Ross and Colonel Kira could help far more effectively than she could. But Ezri had known from the moment she'd read Worf's one-word message to her that his, and therefore Martok's, situation was desperate. On the surface, his message had been simply "now," but Dax had understood what had not been said: *The House of Martok has need of you.* And part of her (not exclusively Jadzia and Curzon, surprisingly) knew she would honor her obligations or die trying. Dax was nothing if not loyal.

Sighing, Ezri popped the thruster and initiated another passive scan. She watched the panel patiently, hoping that this time she'd obtain a different result. When the scan pinged nothing resembling a Klingon starship, she sighed again. *Worf, I'm going to throttle you. . . .*

* * *

The conversation with Kira, predictably, had not gone well.

"I have to take emergency leave."

"Why?" Kira had asked in her best *I'm going to be reasonable* tone.

"Because there's an emergency."

"Where? Back home? Something we can help with?" She spun her desk viewer toward her and began to check for debarkations in the direction of Trill or Sappora VII.

"No, not back home. Elsewhere."

"Elsewhere? Where elsewhere? Elsewhere Earth? Elsewhere Alpha Centauri? Give me some help here, Ezri."

"Elsewhere *elsewhere,* Colonel." Dax said, sitting straighter in her seat. "I don't believe I'm required by protocol to tell you my destination, only when I'll return."

Sinking back into her chair, Kira narrowed her eyes and replied, "No, *Lieutenant*. You're not required to tell me, but I guess I'd like to think that I've earned some trust."

Ezri almost gave in then. She desperately desired to tell *someone* about the mission she was about to embark upon, but Worf's message—though terse, in the typical Worf style—had been clear. He needed her to drop everything and join him immediately. *Klingons. What is it with them, anyway?* True, it had been Jadzia who had sworn the oath, but as Worf had made clear, Ezri had inherited all the privileges and responsibilities inherent in being a member of House Martok. Admittedly, Ezri would be lying to herself if she didn't confess a degree of curiosity and excitement, but it didn't make the corresponding compromises any easier.

"I . . . appreciate your offer, Colonel," she said. "But I have to respect the wishes of . . . others in this regard."

Kira puffed through her nose, which Ezri interpreted as a sign that she could go, but the sigh, it turned out, was simply the colonel's way of mustering her strength to bring out the big gun. "Have you told Julian where you're going?"

For a terrifying moment, Ezri imagined she was sixteen again. She was sitting in her mother's office being quizzed about who was taking her out that evening, where they were going, and did she know what time the curfew was? It was almost enough to make her race for the door screaming, but she fought down the urge. A fleeting image—one of Jadzia's memories—bubbled up to the surface and she remembered a time when she and Kira had talked late into the night about the intricacies of their respective attachments, Jadzia's to Worf and Kira's to Odo. Both of those relationships were over now, the first irretrievably and the second, well, time would tell, but they had agreed that the essential ingredient in those relationships was trust. *If Kira can use a big gun,* Ezri decided, *then so can I.*

"Julian trusts me," she said quietly. "As you should."

Kira opened her mouth to respond, but no sound came out. She pressed her lips together, opened her mouth again, then closed it a second time. Finally, she said, "You've read the latest reports coming out of the Klingon Empire?"

"Of course," Ezri said.

"So you know how chaotic the situation is already and how much worse it's likely to become. They took over *embassies.* Being a Starfleet officer isn't going to carry any weight. In fact, if half of what we've heard about this Morjod is true, it could work against you."

"*If* I were going anywhere near the Klingon Empire—and please note the use of the conditional—what makes you think I would even mention the fact that I'm a Starfleet officer? Being on leave means I'm just Ezri Dax, civilian."

Kira almost smiled at that. Almost. She appeared to have more to say on the subject, but while she had been among those to question most stridently Jadzia's decision to uphold Curzon's blood oath six years ago, if there was one thing Kira understood, it was personal necessity. "Go," she said. "Be careful."

Ezri rose and walked toward the opening office doors, trying hard not to move too quickly. "I will," she said.

"Say hello to Worf for me."

"I will," Ezri said, then stopped midstride on the threshold, abashed. "If I see him," she continued, then stepped through. The doors hissed shut before she could hear Kira's response.

Drifting at a constant velocity near one of the larger chunks of undifferentiated rock, Ezri dozed as the *Wardrobe*'s sensors delicately scanned the asteroid field. Her charts did not name the formation, but listed it as one of many medium-sized, unremarkable clusters that studded the Klingon outmarches. Ezri had already considered sending in several new names to the chart makers, except, alas, she suspected they would object to her more colorful sobriquets, especially since many of them used less than polite anatomical references.

"So help me, Worf," she said after checking the coordinates for the third time in an hour. "You'd better not have gotten yourself killed already." Worf had piggybacked these coordinates onto the transmission he'd sent her on DS9, obviously counting on her knowing him well enough to check. She stared out the shuttle's main viewport and wondered if she could slink back to the station without anyone noticing she had left. (*"Me? Away? What gave you that idea? I've been here the whole time."*) Probably not.

It was possible, of course, that Worf was in the vicinity, but there was no way her little shuttle's sensors would detect a cloaked ship. If he *was* nearby, though, why wouldn't he attempt to contact her? Assuming he was still alive, the most likely answer was that he was waiting for some sort of sign or password. The remaining members of the House of Martok—however many of them there might be—would be feeling mighty paranoid. Perhaps the direct approach would be best.

Tuning the *Wardrobe*'s tiny little subspace transmitter to all channels, Ezri sent the message "Worf, I'm here. If it has to be 'now,' then you're going to have to come find me." She had hoped the reference to Worf's single-word message would give him the reassurance he desired, but she wasn't expecting it quite so suddenly.

The *Wardrobe*'s sensors beeped furiously as five Klingon vessels simultaneously decloaked around her, three birds-of-prey and one *K't'inga*-class battle cruiser. The communications monitor flickered to life, and Ezri was shocked by how Worf looked even more grim and careworn than usual. "*Hello, Ezri,*" he said, his expression melting a bit.

"Do you have any idea how long I've been waiting for you out here?"

Worf glanced off-screen, then looked back at her. "*Two hours and forty-two minutes.*"

"Why didn't you say something?"

"We could not risk revealing ourselves until we were certain it was you."

"You don't have sensors?"

"Many of these asteroids contain trace amounts of kelbonite," he explained. *"It makes it difficult to scan."*

Ezri knew about kelbonite. Not only did it inhibit sensor scans, it made it nearly impossible to get a transporter lock. "So I'm going for a spacewalk?"

"A short one, yes. Do you have an EVA suit?"

"Yes," Ezri quipped. "A very stylish one with large purple flowers on it. You'll love it."

As usual, Worf was not certain how to respond when Ezri joked with him. He gave her a quizzical half smile, then said, *"We will turn the ship at your stern so that our airlock is pointed toward yours."*

"That would be great, Worf. And have a nice warm drink ready for me. Spacewalks always make me cold."

"I will see to it. Come as soon as you can."

"I will. Oh, and Worf?"

"Yes?"

"It's good to see you."

Worf glanced over his shoulder, obviously checking to see who was in earshot. Reassured, he looked back at her and said, *"It is good to see you, too, Ezri. The House of Martok is honored by your presence."*

"You tell the House of Martok it has a lot of explaining to do."

3

All of the Klingon ships—including *Ch'Tang, B'Moth, Ya'Vang,* and *Orantho*—were familiar to Ezri, all having visited DS9 either before or during the Dominion War, but it was into the *Rotarran's* airlock she slipped, though only after the other four had taken up defensive positions around it. *Wardrobe's* docking port wasn't compatible with its Klingon counterpart, but once Ezri had sidled alongside the *Rotarran,* stepping from one ship to another across the void was the work of seconds. Worf awaited her outside the inner hatch, his expression carefully neutral upon seeing her purple-flower-covered EVA suit. "I might be able to find you something more . . . suitable later."

"What—it's not warriorly enough for you?" Ezri said, uncoupling the light helmet. He helped her climb out of the suit, then directed her to the door.

Memories of the *Rotarran*—not her own, but

Jadzia's—overwhelmed her as soon as they stepped into the passage. In comparison with Starfleet vessels, the air was more humid, the lighting dimmer, and the ratio of oxygen to nitrogen in the atmosphere slightly higher, making Ezri feel a little giddy. And there it was—a smell both Curzon and Jadzia had associated with Klingon vessels, an odor unique to their culture that they probably didn't even notice or maybe did and just liked.

Every time she came aboard a Klingon vessel, Dax noted it. She smiled at the memory of Curzon trying to explain it to a young Ben Sisko: "It's something between the smell of frying bacon, old-fashioned petroleum oil, and the yeasty smell you get off truly exquisite beer." Only two of those smells (bacon and beer) were even in Ben's sensory vocabulary, and since he had never been much of a beer drinker, let alone an *exquisite* beer drinker, combining their smells hadn't made sense to him. And petroleum oil was a concept wholly lost on a modern twenty-fourth-century lad. Benjamin might have been unable to truly appreciate "essence of bird-of-prey," but it never failed to evoke a response in Dax. Damned if it didn't make Ezri wonder when was the last time that she had eaten. Either her stomach was growling or, again, maybe it was the symbiont.

Walking up from the stern of the ship toward the bow, Ezri took longer strides, threw her shoulders back, and breathed in more deeply, partly in an effort to keep up with Worf's long-legged stride, but also because this was how she imagined the crew of this ship must all walk.

And then she noticed that there was no one else in the corridor.

Observing her questioning expression, Worf said dourly, "We are spread rather thin."

"So I see. How many?"

"Among the five ships: approximately fifteen hundred."

Ezri whistled ominously. Struggling to remember the complements for the various warships, she asked, "That's about . . . half strength?"

"Closer to one-third."

Ezri winced.

"But they are the finest soldiers of the empire."

"They'd have to be to keep these ships in operation." She almost asked, "When do you all sleep?" but then she saw, even in the low light, the dark circles of fatigue etched under Worf's eyes. There was a light there, too. A touch of fever? "How is Martok taking all this?" she asked.

From the low murmur of annoyance, Ezri knew this was precisely the sort of question Worf did not want to discuss, but she was feeling rattled and fell back on her counselor's training, part of which was collecting intelligence.

Worf must have been even more exhausted than she thought, because he snapped, "Jadzia would not have asked such a question. She would not have had to."

Stopping in her tracks, she retorted, "Jadzia isn't here. I am. And though I can call on Jadzia's memories of Klingon inter- and intra-familial politics, it would be tainted—yes, *tainted*—by her view of things. Jadzia *loved* Klingons. She had a very romanticized view of all of you. So did Curzon. I, on the other hand, do not. You summoned me *knowing* that *I* think there are some fundamental flaws in Klingon philosophy, or, at least, in how it's being expressed currently. *I* would *not* make the mistake of walk-ing into a room full of warriors who are looking for a way to prove how valuable they are to their chancellor without first getting a sense of said chancellor's mood. *Am I making myself clear?*"

Worf stared at her, his bushy eyebrows so high up on his prodigious forehead that they looked like they were ready to crawl up into his scalp. Finally, after several seconds, they both crept down to form a level horizon and he nodded once. "Yes, I understand. This is *your* way." Ezri knew that the words and concepts Worf attempted to form in his mind were not things that came easily to him. While Klingons enjoyed, even indulged themselves in, their passions, they were not, culturally speaking, a species that enjoyed discussing same. "Martok is . . . resistant. He does not seem to understand that he must embrace the destiny that has been laid out before him."

"Maybe he doesn't *want* that destiny."

Worf shook his head impatiently, then looked down at Ezri as if he was once again reminded to whom he spoke. "One does not want or not want one's destiny. One accepts it . . . or not. Not accepting one's destiny creates strife and disharmony."

"For that person or for everyone else?"

"Both."

"Worf," Ezri said. "I might not have every detail about Klingon culture at my fingertips the way my last two hosts did, but I have to say I don't remember ever hearing any of this before. Is there some cache of Klingon wisdom that you've been hiding from outsiders for all these years?"

Now Worf stared deep into Ezri's eyes and, looking back, she was able to study more closely the thing that she had thought was a glimmer of exhaustion-induced fever. *No,* she realized. *Not fever, not exhaustion: exultation.* "Worf," she said breathlessly. "You've been having visions, haven't you?"

He smiled—not so rare a thing for Worf as he might like to think—but there was a note of something in it that Ezri could only describe as beatific. *I am in so much trouble.*

As she walked, she was continuing to ponder what confluence of events might have brought Worf to this place when she nearly tripped over something—no, make that someone—lingering in the narrow hallway outside the conference room: a Ferengi of Nog's approximate age, but, from the look of his long, gangly arms and legs, about half again his height. Without getting a better look at him, it was difficult to say exactly how large this utterly unexpected figure was, but he was doing his best to make himself as invisible as possible. Stopping where she stood, she blinked, shook her head, and blinked again, but the knotty little ball of Ferengi wearing a shabby gold-and-green-striped suit didn't vanish as she expected a hallucination should. The knotty little ball waggled a few fingers in her direction; she waggled back. She glanced over at Worf, who seemed to be reading her mind, but the only explanation he offered was a quick roll of his eyes. *Later,* he was saying. *When we have time. Lots and lots of time.*

A few paces down from the Ferengi, they paused before a door long enough for the security sensors to scan and clear them. Ezri understood that this was standard procedure on many Klingon ships, but she recalled that Martok held such practices in disdain. "If I cannot trust the least of my crew," he had said once, "then I do not

21

deserve to be their captain." Obviously, times had changed.

The door slid open and they stepped into what passed for a conference room on a Klingon ship. Unlike the large, comfortable work areas on Federation starships and certainly nothing like the Cardassian-designed cavernous spaces on Deep Space 9, this cramped, narrow room was obviously meant to be as uncomfortable as possible, a room where orders were issued, not where options were discussed.

Looking around the room, studying the occupants' faces, Ezri was not surprised to find that nearly every person exuded a profound discomfort. As a rule, Klingons despised *meetings*. Why discuss when a warrior should act? This, Ezri believed, was part of the empire's problem: an unwillingness to examine the situation at hand and choose the proper course based on the situation's specifics. Instead, most Klingons believed battle-fever-infused decision making to be superior to logical decision making. To be faced with the present dilemma, one that required measured discussion, analysis, and planning, must be disquieting for the lot of them. Few, if any of them, knew precisely how they'd arrived at this moment; fewer still had any inkling about what the future held.

Seated at the center of the long, crescent-shaped conference table was Martok, wearing neither his chancellor's cloak nor even a general's regalia, but the simple garb of a Defense Force soldier. Rather than looking like he was in charge of the meeting, to Ezri's eyes he evinced the posture of a caged *Tika* cat, eager to flee the room for the bridge the moment Sirella took her eyes off him. *He must absolutely hate having to sit here. To be* political *in a crisis must be repugnant to him,* she thought. Restless to the point of fidgeting, Martok periodically twisted from side to side, drilling his gaze on the tabletop or at his open hands, but rarely into the eyes of the others in the room. *Something terrible has happened,* Ezri realized, her counselor's training coming to the fore. *He's blaming himself for whatever has happened to the empire. He's even trying to punish himself—wearing a common soldier's uniform—but none of the others is allowing him to suffer the way he thinks he ought.*

Studying his posture more carefully as they approached the table, Ezri sensed a frosty zone of uncertainty and shame radiating from Martok's back toward Sirella. While Ezri had never met the imperious lady of House Martok herself, Jadzia's experiences with her before her wedding to Worf were among the most indelible memories of Dax's previous lifetime. Sirella stood as tall, straight, and proud as she had on the day Jadzia—the supplicant daughter-in-law—had greeted her at the door of Dax's quarters, but there was a palpable sense of fatigue around her. *No wonder,* Ezri thought, *considering what she's been through.* There had been scant information from Qo'noS since Morjod had destroyed the Great Hall a week before, but if the small amount they had was to be believed, Sirella had been captured and held prisoner until Martok and Worf and a small contingent of warriors had rescued her a few days ago. Ezri could only hazard a guess at what might have passed between her and Martok that caused this icy animosity. If half of what Worf and Ben Sisko had told her about the Martok marriage was to be believed, the single word that best defined their relationship was "heat," whether the heat of battle or the heat of passion.

Seated on Martok's right was his son Drex, a young warrior whom Ezri had only met once or twice in passing during the war. From Jadzia's recollections as well as her own impressions, she believed Drex to be what she considered the personification of the contemporary Klingon warrior—arrogant, fearless, quick to anger, and, most of all, proud. He possessed none of his father's patience or humor and very little of his wisdom, though Drex had always seemed to enjoy the high esteem of his fellow warriors, which was, Ezri thought, precisely the problem. While Martok and Worf possessed most of the qualities that represented whatever greatness remained in the empire, Drex embodied the attributes that hastened its ruin.

Beside Drex was a bowed, white-haired figure that Ezri recognized as Darok, *gin'tak* to House Martok. He and Jadzia had shared a warm, open friendship based largely on the fact that Darok had known Curzon in his youth. Consequently, they shared an understanding that endured long after the old Klingon could no longer tolerate the blustering and posturing of the young. Ezri had first talked to Darok during the rocky adjustment period following her joining. Recalling the encounter, she was certain that he had been puzzled by her own confused sense of "knowing, but not knowing," if not outright annoyed. Still, when Darok caught sight of her standing beside Worf, he inclined his aged, gray-maned head at her in a nod of greeting.

On Martok's left were two empty chairs, obviously meant for Worf and herself, and then, beside these, was

Worf's son, Alexander Rozhenko. Surprisingly, rather than looking stressed or uncertain (his usual expressions), Alexander appeared more calm and at peace with himself than Dax could remember seeing him since . . . well, ever. He gave her a tight-lipped smile, then pointed his chin at the seat beside his own, obviously pleased to have her there.

At either end of the table, two to each side, sat four Klingons Ezri had never met, three men and a woman, clearly the captains of the other Klingon ships. None of them said or did anything as Ezri and Worf entered, but in their stillness she sensed a vague foreboding. *How could they not be anxious,* she thought, *considering their leader's anxiety?* Observing pinched weariness in every pair of eyes she met, Ezri wondered if this whole group might benefit from a hearty meal, several kegs of bloodwine, and a long nap. What was it about Klingons that made them think they were above the needs of their bodies, redundant systems or not?

Her eyes flickered over the last character in the unfolding drama, trying to ascertain his identity. The broad-shouldered, snowy-haired Klingon was the only one who was not looking at her, but instead stood at parade rest beside the room's only window, watching the tumbling asteroids. And though he seemed utterly absorbed by the dance of gravity and inertia before him, Ezri knew he was equally aware of everything that was happening in the room behind him. It was, she decided, as if he were a chess master who was thinking not only about the play of stone bodies and space outside, but also about the pieces behind him. Nothing would happen, nothing would begin to move until he turned around and gave them all his attention, and then, perhaps, the pieces outside would cease to wheel and collide.

As she and Worf stopped in the center of the tiny open space, the figure turned, and Ezri saw that it was the clone emperor himself, Kahless. Older-looking than the last image she'd seen of him, but a formidable presence just the same. "Excellent," he said. "Then we are all assembled. Please sit down, Ezri Dax. You, too, Worf. We have much to discuss here today and while there is much you two already know, there is much more you do not."

"I believe that," Ezri said.

The sound of her voice seemed to rouse Martok and he looked up at her. A look of pleased surprise softened the grim lines on his face, and he stood. "Dax," he murmured, and extended his arms in a gesture of almost paternal greeting. "House Martok is honored by your presence. Your sense of familial responsibility does you credit, my comrade-in-arms and sister of my heart."

Ezri walked around the side of the table and, feeling awkward both because of the tight quarters and her uncertainty about what she could possibly contribute under the circumstances, stepped into the ring of Martok's arms, and they embraced. "I wasn't motivated only by responsibility," she explained, "but by my concern for you and your family."

"You are not wearing your Federation uniform," Sirella observed with an edge in her voice.

Ezri turned to her. "No," she said. "I'm not here as a Starfleet officer. I'm here as a member of this House, to offer what help I can in this time of crisis."

"What do *you* know of this House?" Sirella demanded, stepping forward. "You are no Klingon, Ezri Dax. You cannot pretend to be what you are not."

The room seemed to hold its collective breath, waiting.

Ezri understood that she was being challenged, and despite the rational voice in her head screaming at her not to say the words that came to her lips, some willful past part of her escaped and met Sirella's disapproving glare head-on. "I don't need to pretend *anything,* My Lady Sirella. I'm *Dax.* Among Klingons, that still counts for something. And as Dax, and the adopted daughter of this House, I pledge to be true to who I am, and to honor what I owe. But I'll have what is due me as well: *respect.*"

All eyes turned to Sirella, whose stern countenance never wavered, and Ezri suddenly found herself wondering what sort of blade would be sticking out of her chest in the next few moments. Then, ever so slowly it seemed, a smile spread across Sirella's face, and she reached out to embrace Ezri as Martok had. "Then you shall have what is due you. Be welcome among us, Ezri Dax, daughter of the House of Martok. Your presence honors us. Truly."

Huh? What just happened?

There came grunts of approval from around the room as Sirella released her.

Martok gestured her toward the empty chair next to Alexander, and said, "Sit, then. I will introduce you to the others, and then we will begin."

The first part of the tale, told by Martok, mirrored what Ezri already knew up to a point. Morjod was a member of the Klingon High Council who worked covertly to form alliances with many of the old, well-established families. After warning his allies to stay away from the Great Hall for Martok's return and welcoming ceremony, he crushed the Hall and those who had gathered with a diabolical weapon deployed from a cloaked robot craft in the upper atmosphere, now popularly referred to as Morjod's Hammer. The Great Hall had been obliterated and everyone within it and the surrounding square had been killed, but the collateral damage to adjoining property was minor. Civilian casualties from flying shrapnel, toxic-smoke inhalation, and other causes related to the attack had yet to be numbered.

"When Morjod revealed himself on a public broadcast," Martok continued, his tone dry and almost academic, "he was not, as I would have expected, vilified. We now believe this is partly attributable to a subsonic neural carrier wave that was carried under the transmission. *Partly* attributable," he repeated, his voice growing icy. "But it must also be noted that Morjod has seemingly tapped into a deep current of frustration and anger. The Klingon people—those whom I once called *my* people— are displeased with the path the empire seems to be on. Our alliances with the Federation and the Romulans during the Dominion War have made them feel weak. Worf, my brother, in particular seemed to be a focus point for Morjod's rhetoric, because of his direct influence in shaping the empire's political landscape over the last decade. Apparently, I was being 'manipulated' by him . . ." Here Martok looked down the table at Worf and grinned. "As if such a thing were possible." This small joke at Worf's expense made the starship captains grin, and Ezri saw that Martok was once again taking on his role as leader. It was practically a reflex with the man, a knowledge ingrained so deeply in his bones that he could not stand before a group and not try to bind them together.

"Morjod attacked my ship," Martok continued. "And the *Negh'Var* was lost, along with much of her crew. He attacked my lands doing I know not what damage, then took my wife and made her a captive." Now Martok paused, placed his fists on the table, and lowered his head. His voice dropped low and his tone grew darker as he said, "He tried to kill my son, but Drex, by warrior's skill and warrior's luck, was able to escape. He *did* kill my two daughters, Shen and Lazhna, and, for this alone, among all his other crimes, *I will kill him.* I vow it here with every warrior in this room as my witness." Martok ceased speaking for several seconds, struggling with barely contained rage. When he'd taken control of his emotions, he stood erect and began pacing the length of the table.

"And there is more, much more. When he learned that I escaped the destruction of the *Negh'Var*, he burned the Ketha lowlands down to the bedrock, slaughtering who knows how many. He took control of the Federation embassy and—for all we know—other diplomatic delegations. While none of our neighbors has yet retaliated, how long will Morjod's lies and apologies prevent them from taking up arms against the empire? And, worst of all, he has, by some trickery, resurrected the scourge of our people, our ancient conquerors, the Hur'q."

As Martok continued explaining the role the Hur'q had played in Morjod's coup, Ezri watched as his words sent shudders through the room. For her, it brought back memories of Jadzia and Worf's adventure with Kor during which the three of them had traveled to a planet in the Gamma Quadrant that had been home to a Hur'q base. There they had found the legendary Sword of Kahless, purportedly looted from Qo'noS when the Hur'q plundered the Klingon homeworld over a thousand years ago. Subsequently, Jadzia had studied the few archaeological surveys the Klingons had either performed or allowed others to perform about the Hur'q, but the entire occupation period still remained a huge question mark.

Recalling Jadzia's readings, Ezri had formed the opinion that the modern Klingon persona had emerged at least in part as a response to the trauma sustained during the Hur'q invasion. Very little was known about the people of Qo'noS before the Hur'q, but when they left—their sudden departure being another mystery—they left behind the fiercest, most aggressive warriors in the quadrant. An oft-discussed question in galactic sociological circles was "What would have happened to the people of Qo'noS if the Hur'q had never come?" Of course, the debate was irresolvable, but Ezri could not help but wonder which traits of the Klingon character were remnants of the people the original Kahless had inspired half a thousand years before the Hur'q, and which might be compensation for nearly pathological feelings of vulnerability. Whoever had pulled the Hur'q demon out of the Klingon closet of nightmares deserved commendation for such an effective strategy. But something still nagged at her. Something in Jadzia's memories about the Hur'q . . .

Martok was relating the details of Drex's and Darok's encounters with the Hur'q when Ezri found the memory snippet she'd been fishing for. She straightened up in her chair and raised a finger to catch Martok's eye.

He turned a questioning gaze on her.

Ezri shrugged. "Excuse me, but, well, I want to make sure I understand something."

Martok gestured for her to speak.

More pairs of Klingon eyes than she cared to count drilled on her. *Keep it short,* their expressions said.

She quirked a half smile, swallowed hard, and continued. "All the evidence Jadzia found regarding the Hur'q indicated that they'd vanished from the quadrant—perhaps even became extinct. Where have the Hur'q been for a thousand years?"

Martok began, "These Hur'q aren't like the original invaders. They're—"

"More like Morjod's pets," Alexander interjected. "They move where he points. They stop at his orders. They kill on his command." Noting Martok's perturbed expression, presumably from Alexander's interruption, he quickly added, "At least that's how it looked from what I saw. You probably know more than I do, Chancellor. I mean, you most definitely know more than I do." He winced at his own verbal clumsiness, dropping his eyes to the conference table.

Ezri squeezed Alexander's arm reassuringly. "So Morjod controls them. How?" she asked no one in particular. Ezri surveyed the others in the room, expecting that someone would be able to answer her question, but found only blank, but frustrated, expressions. "Doesn't it matter?"

Two of the Klingon captains fingered the blades on their belts, perhaps waiting for Martok to abandon this *meeting* in favor of a full-on assault of Morjod's position in the First City. One captain sat with arms crossed over his chest, teeth clenched. He glared at Ezri; she offered him a weak smile in return. Even Worf, sitting beside her, shifted a few times in his seat. *All the lurking, talking, and waiting must be taking a toll on him as well,* Ezri guessed.

"Do not assume that talk is wasted, warriors!" Martok growled. Shaking his head, he opened his arms expansively. "To know one's enemy is to know how to defeat him. Impulsiveness will only give victory to our foes. Listen." He pointed to his own ears. "Answers, not weapons, might better serve you in this battle."

Ezri looked around, expecting bared teeth or drawn *mek'leth*s, but saw none. If the captains and Drex smarted under Martok's reprimand, they didn't show it. *Maybe Worf was right,* Ezri thought, feeling a faint tinge of pleasure suffuse her. *Martok really could be the "leader of destiny" if this is how he chooses to govern.*

"Now to answer your questions, Ezri Dax. We have reached a place when such questions at last have answers, troubling as they are. Morjod may control the Hur'q, but another controls Morjod." Martok continued, "I must make this as plain as possible: *Morjod is not our primary enemy.* Though he may not know it himself, he is but a piece in another's game."

This was new information to Ezri, as apparently it was to the starship captains. Two of them began to converse in a stilted Klingon dialect too quickly for Ezri to follow, and the other two adjusted themselves in their chairs. *This revelation is more disturbing to them than anything they've heard so far,* Ezri realized. *But why?* And then she heard one of the two conversing captains say the Klingon word for "Federation" and she understood. They were worried that Morjod's handler was an outsider.

Martok, too, must have understood what they were

thinking and quickly corrected them. "No, my friends. Do not misunderstand. Our foe is not an alien. Perhaps if that were the case, the battle before us would be clearer. But our enemy, though every bit as monstrous as the Hur'q, wears a Klingon's face. Her name is Gothmara and though much of her story is not known, I believe we may anticipate her motivations and her goals from what we do know. But that part of the tale should be told by he who discovered it." Martok turned and indicated Kahless, who had been sitting silently throughout the chancellor's recitation. "Emperor," Martok said. "Tell us what you have learned."

Kahless rose then and, in his deep, sonorous voice, began his tale.

4

Kahless began, "I am known by many as 'the clone emperor,' 'the Ghost of Kahless,' and, my favorite, 'Kahless the Forgotten.'"

Every Klingon in the room stood, protesting his words, but Kahless waved them back into their seats.

"Stop, stop," he said. "I cast no aspersions. Neither do I disagree. My time as emperor has been . . . less than distinguished. When I returned and Gowron challenged my legitimacy, Worf forged a compromise. I decided to serve my people as an example of what Klingons—who had fallen from the true path laid down by the original Kahless—could once again be. This was a noble and glorious challenge to me and I took it into my heart, but it was not long before I realized that Gowron would never allow me to have any meaningful effect on my people."

Listening to the emperor's words, Martok recalled their few discussions before he became chancellor and the single one after. During much of Gowron's soul-crushing administration, Kahless had seemed exhausted and ready to abandon his mission. Then, several months before Gowron died, Kahless had called Martok to a brief, secret meeting. The emperor had been kindly, even solicitous, and had seemed interested only in Martok's health, his emotional well-being. This had confused the general, but he did his best to answer all the questions put to him. When he asked if there was anything Kahless wished to know about the war effort, the emperor had simply said, "I am not worried about the war."

"Then what *are* you worried about, Emperor?" Martok had asked with a touch of anger.

"Nothing now. I just wanted to see how you were doing." That had been, more or less, the end of the interview, and Martok had left shortly after. He hadn't thought about the meeting since that day, probably because he had attributed Kahless's seeming renewed good spirits to his feeling reassured that the alliance would be victorious.

Then, shortly after Gowron had died, Kahless had called him to another private interview—this one in a small tavern on a Klingon starbase—and Martok had been concerned to see his emperor dressed in the ragtag clothes of a beggar. Fearing that Kahless had lost his senses, Martok had spent several tense minutes trying to determine if there was any way to drag him back to his ship unnoticed. But then, after only a brief conversation, the chancellor had seen that Kahless's wits were, if possible, keener than ever.

When Martok had asked if he was glad Gowron was gone, Kahless had responded cryptically, "But is he?"

"I saw his body with my own eyes," Martok had said. "But can he truly have passed if his spirit still lingers?" Kahless had replied. "A poison has polluted the souls of our people; Gowron is only a symptom of its foulness. I have been on a quest for a cure and will not return until I have found it."

Further questioning did not produce any useful information, and the two had parted ways. In the succeeding months, Martok was so distracted by the escalating war that he was unable to devote any thought to the matter. Perhaps now, as he addressed this council, the meaning of Kahless's words would become clear.

"I left Qo'noS and took to traveling as a beggar. It was surprising how easy it was to become a faceless entity and this despite the fact that my likeness is carved into the edifices of many buildings and my image can be found on government documents, in newsfeeds, even on currency. But as your eyes now show you, my beard and mane have gone white since my return. And few will look into a beggar's eyes. Even those who will seem only to find a reflection of their own misery." Kahless shook his head sadly and Martok began to worry that they would be in for a lecture before the old man got to the point. Though he regretted his impatience and inwardly chastised himself, there was no ignoring the fact that Kahless enjoyed having an audience and could, at times, tire out even the most devout believer. Still, Worf, Alexander, and even old Darok were listening patiently, almost reverently. He did not bother to turn to see how Sirella was responding to all this, because he had heard her vent similar opinions in the past. It would give his wife some small satisfaction to hear that the emperor agreed with her on many issues, though Martok could not forget that she had been one of the most vocal protesters when the clone emperor had come into power.

"I turned my back on the joyless, savage brutes who called themselves Klingons and went in search of those who still remembered the essential teachings of the original Kahless. It was," the emperor said, "to be a long, frustrating search." Walking to a small refreshment table in the corner, Kahless poured himself a small cup of water and drank it off quickly. Martok had noticed since his return that Kahless no longer drank bloodwine or, indeed, anything stronger than the juice of the prune that Worf favored. "But my quest was not my only concern," he continued. "I made certain to keep a watchful eye on the empire's leadership. When the conflict with the Dominion began, Gowron was sucked into the maelstrom of war, then quickly became its seething eye. But I have seen enough wars to know that one should always carefully observe what happens around the ragged edges, where chaos reigns supreme. Studying intelligence reports passed on to me by allies I have made, I noted the movements of members of the High Council and, soon enough, found the opportunist I knew would be there."

Worf said, "Morjod."

Kahless nodded. "My contacts back on Qo'noS confirmed my suspicion: while the rest of the council was embroiled in fighting a war, Morjod was amassing power. The more I learned about this enigmatic, though admittedly charismatic, figure, the more I discovered that there were suspicious lapses in his background."

"Such as?" Sirella asked. This revelation had obviously piqued her curiosity. Martok's wife had always prided herself on her ability to uncover useful information about her House's allies and enemies. In addition to all the pain Morjod had caused her family, her failure to discover anomalies about his past injured her pride.

"There were several minor inconsistencies," Kahless explained. "Most of them were inconsequential on their own, but they added up to a picture of someone who was attempting to conceal his past. For example, his family was supposed to have gained its wealth through mining concerns in the Hromi Cluster."

Worf furrowed his brow at this. "There are no Klingon mining concerns in the Hromi Cluster. It is controlled by Ferengi and Orion concerns." He sneered. "Most of them illegal, I might add."

"Precisely," Kahless said. "Though I might point out that very few Klingons would know this since we consider it distasteful to discuss commerce."

"It is not a warrior's concern," said B'Tak, captain of the *Ya'Vang*. It was the first time he had spoken in the council room since their discussion had begun.

"It is precisely that attitude that allowed Morjod to hide his true dealings," the emperor explained. Turning to B'Tak, he asked, "Why isn't commerce a warrior's concern? Should a warrior not need to know where his house gets the materials and wealth he needs to fight his battles? And, more importantly, what is the point of battle if not to ensure his family's security so that they all might enjoy the fruits of his skills?"

B'Tak was confused, even flustered. He hadn't expected Kahless to explore this line of thought. "The point of battle," he said, practically sputtering, "is battle."

Sighing heavily, Kahless turned away from the captain and looked closely into the eyes of every other Klingon in the room. Apparently not finding what he sought, he turned to Ezri Dax and asked her, "Do you believe this?"

"I'm not a Klingon," Ezri said.

"That's not what I asked you," Kahless said. "I said, 'Do you believe this?'"

"Then, no, I don't."

"Why?"

"Because battle without a goal, an end in sight, is just . . ." She wavered, struggling to find the right word. Finally, she found it and, almost whispering, said, "Chaos."

"And what does chaos lead to?"

Without hesitation, Ezri said, "Death. Only death."

Kahless stared at her for several long, silent seconds, then turned to look at B'Tak. "Do you agree?"

"No," B'Tak said brusquely. "To do battle is a privilege. To die in battle is an honor."

"Ezri Dax," Kahless said without looking away from B'Tak. "How many times have you died?"

"Eight," she replied. "I am the ninth host of the Dax symbiont."

"And were any of those times in battle?"

"Yes," she said. "More than once. My last host, Jadzia, she died in a kind of battle."

"In the end," Kahless asked, "were any of your deaths more glorious than any other?"

Ezri snorted. "No," she said. "Death's only glory comes from a well-lived life. By itself, death is only death."

Kahless continued to stare into B'Tak's eyes, but as Ezri finished speaking, the emperor's mouth broke into a soft smile. "Thank you, child." He turned to look at Martok. "She is a worthy addition to your house."

Martok only nodded, but was more proud in that moment than he knew how to express.

Simultaneously anxious and elated, Worf listened intently to the debate between B'Tak and Ezri and marveled at his own serene viewpoint. Where once he might have felt compelled to insert himself between such polar extremes and try to reconcile them—especially since they so closely mirrored his own oft-divided soul— today he was content to let them argue. It might not last long, but today, at this hour, Worf, son of Mogh, knew who he was and what he must do. Kahless had shown him the way. In a way that he would have been hard-pressed to explain to anyone—except possibly Jadzia— Worf felt smugly pleased with himself. All those months ago, when he had called Martok "the leader of destiny," it had been mostly rhetoric meant to inspire the council. But, now, if what Kahless had revealed to him was true—and he had no doubt that it was—then his brother Martok was even more a man of destiny than Worf had suspected.

B'Tak surprised Worf by not pursuing the argument, but seemed content to let Kahless continue with his monologue. Worf resolved to watch the captain carefully. The suspected betrayal at Ketha by one of the crew of the *Negh'Var* still stung. Of course, Worf had no proof that any of them had revealed their location to Morjod and, if he did, he probably paid for his treachery with his life, but the former security officer of the *Enterprise* disliked being surprised. He had made it the point of his life to be prepared for every eventuality thrown at him.

But for the time being, Worf would sit, listen, and learn. There was still so much about their enemy he did not understand, and if he was to aid the emperor and his brother, then he would have to be prepared.

"Morjod's official record," Kahless continued, "lists his birthplace as a small town in the Chak'ok region of the Homeworld. I checked their archive and found a document, which I believe is a skillful forgery. It was so skillful in fact that I knew I could never prove anything with it. However, whoever had constructed the concealing tapestry of Morjod's history had not snipped every loose thread. My associates and I performed a careful search of records and found that a child matching Morjod's description had traveled several times back and forth between Chak'ok and Boreth."

Pausing to let this revelation settle in, Kahless poured himself another glass of water. Looking around at his audience, he said, "I see most of you understand the significance of this information."

Several pairs of eyes slid over to look at Ezri.

Observing that most eyes were on her, Ezri said, "I suppose this is the point where everyone is expecting me to raise my hand and say, 'I don't understand.' "

"Do you?" Kahless asked.

"Actually, I think I might" she said, brightening. "You were—for want of a better word—born on Boreth. Perhaps 'created' would be more correct—by clerics or monks of some kind?"

Kahless nodded. "The *r'tak* of Boreth created me from the original Kahless's genetic material. Our people have very little tolerance for experimentation with genetic science, so only those in the most remote, private places have the opportunity to carry out such experiments."

"And Morjod has ties there?" Ezri said.

Kahless exchanged glances with Martok, then nodded.

"I'm beginning to see what this might have to do with the Hur'q," she said, furrowing her brow.

He offered Ezri a sage smile before continuing. "I traveled back to Boreth in secret. My goal was to uncover anything I could about Morjod's past, and after a very short investigation, I learned much more than I had expected."

Ezri, who clearly enjoyed playing along with the emperor, asked, "What did you find?"

Kahless let the question hang for a moment, then said, "His mother—and my own."

"What are you saying?" Worf snarled as he leapt to his feet. "Morjod is another clone of Kahless?"

Ezri winced. All the Klingons began talking at once, most of them very loudly. The captains had abandoned their chairs to gather around Worf. Only Sirella, who remained stock-still in her chair, and Darok seemed unperturbed by the emperor's words. When Ezri met the old *gin'tak*'s gaze across the table, he shrugged and raised his mug in toast.

For several seconds, Kahless stared in bafflement at the crowd gathering around him before waving Worf and the others back to their chairs. "Worf—forgive me for lapsing into metaphor. No. Morjod is not a clone. All I am saying is that Morjod's mother, Gothmara, was the one who conceived of the idea of cloning me from the preserved blood of Kahless. Not only did she plan the procedure, but she was largely responsible for executing it, too. As learned as Koroth and his order are, they are scholars and priests, not scientists. It was Gothmara who facilitated my creation. She is an astonishingly adept scientist, possibly the greatest our race has produced in the past century."

"And the most insane and immoral," Martok added. He exchanged glances with the emperor and then waved

Kahless to a seat. "As much as it pains me to speak of this matter before my family and honored allies, I believe it again falls on me to take up the tale."

As Martok spoke, Ezri's trained eye caught a fleeting expression of cold fury—an expression no one else seemed to notice—flash in Sirella's face. Maybe now she'd find out what had come between Martok and Sirella. *Poor guy. If we were at Quark's I'd buy him a bottle.* As a gesture of support, she slid out of her chair, poured a mug of bloodwine, and passed it to Martok, who accepted it gratefully.

After draining half the cup, he wiped his mouth and said simply, "House Kultan." Looking around, he studied the faces of the others and noted their expressions. "What does that name mean to you? Worf? Anyone?"

Kultan . . . Kultan . . . Why does that name sound so familiar? Ezri puzzled. *Not a Jadzia memory, though. Too long ago. Must be Curzon. . . .*

Martok's wife stirred, but did not reply directly.

"You know, Sirella. Your father was active in the council." Finally, he looked at the emperor and murmured, "And of course you know. But probably no one else."

Draining the rest of the wine in a gulp, Martok stood. "How to explain?" he asked, and walked around the table to stand before the others. "It was a lifetime ago, a different era. We had finally made peace with the Federation, the Defense Force was at its strongest in decades, and the Romulans had yet to betray us. The empire was, in many ways, at its peak. The Praxis disaster was behind us. Trade was excellent. Many worlds still paid us tribute, but we no longer needed to crush every insurrection that dared raise its head." Sighing, Martok said,

43

"Many would say it was a golden age, brief though it was."

"With respect, my brother," Worf said. "What has this to do with Morjod?"

"My point is simply this: In an earlier, more desperate era, a scientist of Gothmara's character might have been embraced, even venerated for her skills. But in the time I speak of, because we were secure in our power, the empire did not accept what she and her father offered."

Worf said, "Bioweapons?"

Martok grunted in ascent. "Though other races in the quadrant were not so discriminating, the council repulsed such overtures . . . but I'm getting ahead of myself."

Martok's voice dropped and all strained to hear him. "When I met Gothmara, she was the science officer aboard her father's ship, *Gothspar,* named after his dead wife. I was a lieutenant, having just been elevated following the Battle of Tcha'voth. Kultan was, in his way, as seductive as his daughter. Everyone in the ranks knew that he invited only the best to join his crew, warriors of proven abilities, and he did not care about social rank or family status. Your value was measured in your worth to *him.* Nothing else mattered and we were the most fanatically loyal crew in the empire."

"I have known others who inspire that loyalty," Worf interjected.

"Your praise—if I am interpreting you correctly—is appreciated, my brother," Martok replied, "but my desire has always been only to be an able warrior and inspire the same in others. Kultan *expected* you to be the best. If you were anything less, you were sent away, broken and spent. He was ruthless, but there was a glory in his service that I have never felt anywhere since." Martok grinned and Ezri could see he was drifting back to simpler times when all he needed was a strong back, keen vision, and a willingness to serve. "And I was among his chosen elite," he continued. "Kultan made me his tactical officer and we were an unstoppable force."

Clearly savoring the memory, Martok continued. "Gothmara served as science officer and even then she must have been working on her genetic experiments. The moment her bridge shifts ended, she fled to her labs and labored through the night. She was tireless, as driven as her father. I admired her dedication greatly and found myself amazed and intrigued by such a woman.

"But I was ignorant of many things in those days," Martok said, more to himself than the others. "And made it a point to never listen to shipboard gossip, feeling it was beneath contempt." He glanced at Darok meaningfully. "Now I have others who do the listening for me, but only because I learned the value of knowing what rumors the lower decks were chewing like cud. Had I been wiser in those days, I would have discovered, long before I did, that many of the crew had concerns not only about Gothmara's research, but also about how Kultan financed his house."

"He was *selling* bioweapons?" B'Tak asked, his voice thick with disgust.

Martok nodded. "I did not learn this for many weeks and by that time I—" He paused. "My loyalties were conflicted."

As she listened to Martok diplomatically relating this tale from his past, Ezri believed she'd figured out why Martok told this story instead of Kahless, why Martok had a vested interest in Gothmara's treachery. *No wonder Sirella is angry,* she thought, recalling some of Worf's more irrational outbursts of jealousy. *How humiliating to have to reveal this in public.*

"My rival on the ship, the second-degree tactical officer, Manx, showed me records he had pulled out of the ship's database. It did not occur to me at the time that the only reason he told me was because he knew I would be fool enough to confront Kultan."

Clearly lost in the well of memory, he paused in front of the window, gazing out at the stars. "But I surprised Manx," he said softly. "I did something he could not have anticipated because, despite the evidence, I could not believe that Gothmara, the woman I'd come to love, was involved."

A tense silence filled the room as the council absorbed Martok's last revelation. Even her anticipation of this truth didn't shield Ezri from the shock of hearing Martok confess that he had ever loved anyone other than Sirella. *Martok and Gothmara lovers? And that could mean Morjod . . .* She contemplated the ramifications. *Morjod as Martok's—? Whoa. . . .* None—including Ezri—dared look in Sirella's direction. Ezri imagined that Sirella's pride must be stinging with angry humiliation, since she so despised discussing even the smallest personal detail outside the family.

For a moment longer, Martok maintained his position in front of the window. He then turned to face the council, his head held square on his shoulders. One by one, he looked deeply into the eyes of each individual seated at the table, whether to offer reassurance or penance, Ezri couldn't guess. When he reached Ezri, she offered a sympathetic smile that he acknowledged with a wink of his single eye. All politely averted their gazes when Martok faced Sirella.

Indicating the time for reflection had passed, Martok tossed his hair imperiously and threaded his hands behind his back as if he were assuming command of the bridge. "Instead of confronting Kultan with *bat'leth* and disruptor in hand," he continued, "I tracked my lover to her lab, hoping that together, we could liberate the *Gothspar* from her father's treachery."

5

Stalking down the corridors of the *Gothspar,* Lieutenant Martok felt the red curtain of rage threaten to cloud his vision. *It cannot be true,* he thought. *But if it is, Kultan must pay.* But first, he knew, he must inform Gothmara of his plan and find a safe haven for her. When the rest of the senior crew learned of Kultan's infamy, there would be bloodshed.

"Bloodshed! *Ha!*" he said aloud, and swung his *bat'leth* in a bright arc. *They will tear Kultan limb from limb.* Though imperial law had banned bioweapons, Klingon pride had spoken long before the legal ruling. A warrior should face a foe looking him in the eyes while he slew him. Even when space was the battleground and the weapons were starships, each side squared off against the other as an equal combatant. Bioweapons were cringing and cowardly. Anyone who would make them, let alone use them, was beneath contempt, as cowardly as a Terran and as conniving as a Romulan. *Sniveling* petaQ *Kultan!*

But for his captain to have committed such perfidy right under Martok's nose? How could he have been so blind? What if he and Gothmara had wed? Then *his* name would be linked to the scandal when it was uncovered, as surely it must be. In the name of honor, his own and Gothmara's, he must expose Kultan's treachery.

Crew members stepped to the side and pressed themselves against the bulkheads as Martok strode past. Though he knew the ship's schematics as well as the curve of Gothmara's back, he rarely visited this part of it, mostly because his lover had asked him to stay away. "I cannot work when you are near," she had said, stroking the ridge above his eyes. Martok had smiled when she had said that and pulled her closer, their warm, slick bodies sliding together. The memory made him miss a step and he felt his resolve waver. What if Gothmara tried to persuade him to spare her father? Her love for Kultan was, in its way, as intense and palpable as her love for Martok. An admiration for their familial closeness was one of the characteristics that had brought him into Kultan's service in the first place. Such a strong House! But Gothmara was not her father. Surely she would not condone such dishonorable conduct . . . would she?

"No!" he shouted, and a maintenance engineer who was rounding a corner jumped back in surprise and stared at him wide-eyed as Martok swept past. Gothmara would be as revolted as he was when he showed her the data spike Manx had given him. The recording clearly showed Kultan delivering a bioshielded case to an Orion trader in exchange for a credit chip—who knew how much?—and the accompanying scan data revealed that the case held virulently mutagenic organisms unknown in the current taxonomies. There could be no doubt. Kultan was a traitor to the Empire.

Coming to the doors to Gothmara's labs, he pressed the entry-request key, and when there was not an immediate response, he banged the butt of his disruptor against the metal frame. "Gothmara!" he shouted, then again, and was preparing to fire his weapon at the lock when the doors parted.

Standing there, annoyed and unkempt, she looked like a storybook warrior-princess who had been roused from a much-deserved rest after a battle with the hideous *jybok*. Martok knew her well enough to know that she hadn't been sleeping at all, but had, in fact, been wrestling with a foe of sorts. Gothmara was already famous—or infamous—on the ship for her multishift lab sessions, sometimes working for two or three days in a row if she could arrange to have her bridge work covered by others. Even as he stood looking at her, disheveled but oh so desirable, the first worm of doubt began to creep into his soul: *How does she always manage to find someone to do her work? What currency does she trade with?*

"What is it, Martok?" she hissed. "I asked you to never disturb me . . ." Then she noticed that he was holding weapons. "Are we in battle? My father did not alert me . . ."

"No battle," Martok snapped. "None from the outside." He grabbed her arm and tugged her into the lab. "Perhaps in our midst, however. But first, you answer my questions."

She tried to prevent him from moving past the antechamber and into the main lab. He noticed that the small room had been transformed into a makeshift airlock, that it was even pressurized so that no atmosphere could escape the inner lab. Martok also noted that Gothmara was wearing an airy semitransparent gown instead of her uniform—but, incongruously, that she had a biofilter mask dangling around her neck.

"What *are* you doing down here?" he asked, unable to hide the suspicion in his voice.

Removing the filter mask, Gothmara placed the heel of her hand against the center of his chest and pushed back as hard as she could against his advance. "None of your *damned* business, *Lieutenant*. You are off limits here. *Go!*" Martok's head snapped back as if she had struck him. Her voice . . . her voice had a curious tone and he felt confused yet compliant. Why was he here anyway, surely he had work to do? His reason for coming . . . he mused. And it struck him. *My reason for coming*. He wrested his anger from the muddle in his mind and clung to it.

Tugging the data spike from his belt and holding it aloft, he said, "Here is something you must see. Your father has dishonored your house and threatens to bring ruin to the empire. He . . ."

Gothmara flicked her hand against Martok's and sent the data spike spinning out of his hand to crash against a wall. "My father," she snarled, "has done nothing of the sort. My father is *a visionary*." When the word emerged from her lips, a thrill ran down Martok's spine and he momentarily found his respect and, yes, even affection for Kultan rising up within him. "He alone understands what we must do to make the empire great again."

"Again?" Martok asked angrily. "What do you mean again? When have we ever enjoyed a greater period of prosperity and prestige? The Klingon Defense Force is unrivaled throughout the quadrant. Our warriors are respected and the other races have even begun to see the value of our arts and culture. *Kahless and Lukara* was performed last month before the entire Federation Council . . ."

"Opera!" Gothmara shouted. "Before the Federation Council! What unfettered delight! And did our ambassador go down on his hands and knees so that the Federation president could use him for a footstool? Fifty years ago, if a company of a hundred Klingons had stood before the Federation Council it would have been because they were about to slay them! But no, not now, not today. *Now* we *sing* before them!"

Momentarily struck dumb by the depth of Gothmara's rebuke, Martok tried to recapture some of his rage. "But your father . . . Bioweapons are dishonorable. . . ."

"Bioweapons are *weapons,* just as proffered aid and cultural exchange and 'combined scientific research' are weapons. Are the lessons of history lost? What about our alliance with the Romulans? What happened there?"

"The Romulans were untrustworthy. . . ."

"But the Federation is not?"

"There are, among them, warriors of honor. . . ."

"Such as *who?* Or are you referring to the legend of the *petaQ* Kirk? My father told me of him. Yes, he was a man of 'honor' when it suited him. After killing thousands of Klingon warriors, in his dotage he decided it might be time to make peace and have a few less ghosts spitting on him."

Shocked, Martok reeled back. "This is lunacy!" he shouted. "What kind of crazed ravings has your father been . . . ?"

Gothmara slapped him. This was not an angry, peevish smack to the cheek, but a body-twisting crack to the jaw. Martok almost fell to the ground, and it was only the cold stream of air from one of the pressurized blowers that kept him conscious. Rising up to his full height, he towered over her and felt hot blood pour down his cheek and jawline. She had scratched him, too, and the cut throbbed and pulsed. Looking down at her hands, he saw his blood on her nails; the sight made his pulse pound even harder.

"*My father,*" Gothmara said, her voice unexpectedly low and seductive, "*is a hero.*" Then she lifted her bloody hand to her lips. She tasted the blood; then, moving her hand slowly and seductively, Gothmara drew her fingers down over her throat, painting a line of crimson that trickled between her breasts. Without warning, Martok suddenly felt light-headed, as if the pressure pumps were drawing atmosphere away from his head; he stumbled forward only to find that he held Gothmara in his arms. He breathed deeply, inhaling her scent.

"Your father . . ." he began, struggling to find his words, but then her mouth was on his, her tongue probing between his lips. Breaking the kiss, she playfully bit his lower lip, licked along the edge of his jaw until her tongue was in his ear. He found that he cupped the curve of her hip with one hand, stroked the swelling curve of her breast with the other. When she bit his jaw, Martok groaned and his knees weakened. Clutching a handful of her hair, he yanked back her head, exposing her throat to his teeth. . . .

When his blood had cooled, Martok found himself lying in a heap of discarded clothes, his head cushioned with her gown, Gothmara astride his hips. He felt a strange buzzing sensation behind his eyes, as if she had removed a portion of his brain and replaced it with tiny whirling insects. "What . . . what . . . happened?" he stammered.

Gothmara leaned down over him, her breasts brushing against his chest. "We were just discussing my father," she murmured. "And your place in our future plans."

"*Our* future plans?" Martok muttered. He knew there was something he had to do, someplace he had to be, but he couldn't dredge up the memory. His jaw ached and his tongue tingled and Gothmara had just moved her hips in *that* way. Martok wanted to rest, wanted to close his eyes and let the darkness descend, oblivion. . . .

"We have a campaign mapped out," Gothmara said into his ear. "But I can only imagine it would be improved by your review. My father has told me he has never met a warrior with your gift for tactical planning."

This provoked a smile. He reached up to caress her, but his hand missed her face and flopped against the floor. "Ow!" he yelled. Something had stabbed him. He grasped the offending object and held it up so he could see what it was.

The data spike.

Gothmara snarled when she saw it and tried to wrest

the spike from Martok's grip, but he refused to release it. She sank her teeth into his hand, but that only made him grasp it tighter so that the spike's tip sank into his palm. The pain . . . the pain was a good thing. It helped him focus, to clear his mind. Blood ran down over his wrist and dripped into the cleft of his elbow. Gothmara's rage grew and the growl in her throat became higher and louder with every passing second. Before his eyes, the red curtain fell.

Martok snapped his arm forward and she tumbled off him, a piece of his flesh between her teeth. He grabbed for his weapons among the wreckage on the floor, found the disruptor, and pointed it at his lover's head. There was blood on her mouth, her chin, and tiny spots on her breasts. The streak of blood she had painted earlier was gone now, erased with sweat and friction. "Don't move," he said. "I *will* kill you now if I must, but I'd rather turn you over to the council alive."

Gothmara spit and some inner voice warned Martok to avoid letting it hit him. With his head clearing, he began to wonder how much of their affair was chemistry and how much was simply *bio*chemisty.

Moving lightly on bare feet, Martok crept sideways to the inner door to the lab and waited anxiously until the sensor registered his presence. The doors slid open and he took a step backward, not taking his eyes off Gothmara. "In here," he said, pointing with the disruptor's barrel. "Now."

She complied. Her long hair had come undone and now was tumbling down around her shoulders. With blood on her mouth and nails, Gothmara looked like a crazed beast. "Down," he said. "Sit down."

"Martok," she said as she crouched on her haunches. "We can talk about this. . . ."

"No," he said evenly. "No talking. Stay there."

Moving quickly, only risking taking his eyes off her for a few seconds at a time, Martok completed a quick tour of the lab and found worse than he could have imagined. It was, he thought, as if she wanted to wallow in her twisted experiments, covering her floor and worktables with specimens and odd, tortuous equipment. There, under a counter, Martok spied a rack of the very same bioshielded cases he had seen in the video. On her computer screen he saw detailed notes for a study on an engineered virus designed to affect only humans and Alpha Centaurians. Most repulsive were the stasis tubes along the wall. Each contained dissected slabs of meat that could only have been specimens and experiments. Some of them, mercifully few, Martok saw, had *faces,* each wearing a death mask of agony.

Pointing at an apparatus sitting on a counter under a ventilation hood, he asked, "And what's this?"

"A new idea," she said. "Something I would use on Klingons."

"The brew you used on me? Did you dip your claws in it just before you answered the door? What would you have done if it was someone else?"

"It depends," Gothmara said, all pretense of affection gone. "On whether or not I wanted something from them."

"*Ha'DIbaH,*" Martok hissed.

"Fool," she replied with equanimity, reaching around behind her head.

Suspicious of her movement, Martok hesitated until he heard a sharp snapping sound. Though his aim was off, he fired without thinking.

The disruptor bolt grazed Gothmara's left arm, spinning her around and jerking her head to the side just as she was opening her mouth as wide as she could, jaws locked in a serpentlike grimace. A high-pitched whine whizzed past Martok's ear and he saw a tiny, white puff of smoke hiss out from between Gothmara's lips. *A skull gun,* he thought. *Kahless! She's even madder than I had thought!* He gaped, staggered by the revelation that Gothmara would use surgically implanted weapons. Such weapons were even less honorable—if possible—than bioweapons.

And, apparently, they were very painful too. Gothmara collapsed into a groaning heap, grasping the sides of her head. Martok had read enough about skull guns to know that if the shooter didn't hold his head in exactly the right position, he could snap his own neck with the recoil.

Stepping carefully around and behind her, Martok grasped both of Gothmara's wrists in one of his large hands and pulled her to her feet. Her head lolled to the side, but he could see that she was at least semiconscious and . . . hissing?

He cocked his head and listened carefully. No, the sound was not coming from Gothmara. Martok scanned the lab quickly, then saw it: a canister on the worktable near where he had been standing when she shot at him. A thin stream of gas was spewing from a crack. "Gothmara," Martok said, releasing her arms and jerking her head up. "What is that?"

Her eyes focused, then widened in fear. She tried to say something, possibly to scream, but Martok did not wait to hear what it was. As he leapt backward, his grip must have loosened, because Gothmara slithered out from between his arms and skittered across the floor and under a table. Not hesitating for a moment, not looking back, Martok charged through the pressure door, scooped up his uniform as he ran through the anteroom, and, hardly pausing to let it open, charged through the outer door. As it snapped shut, Martok heard an abbreviated crash from the lab, which was cut short by a clanging alarm.

Crew members appeared seemingly out of thin air and clustered around Martok, less curious about the alarm than about why he was standing there nearly naked with a disruptor in his hand. Someone even made a crude remark about getting into a fight with Gothmara before Martok collected his wits and tried to shove them all away from the doors. "Get back, you fools! The alarm!"

"What is it?" someone asked. "I've never heard that one before. Not a hull breach . . ."

We should only be so lucky, Martok thought, but didn't have time to reply because suddenly Kultan arrived, crewmen standing aside as the captain plowed through the crowd. "What in the name of Kahless is going on here!" he shouted. "Martok! What are you doing . . . ?"

Without hesitation, Martok lifted his disruptor and pointed it at Kultan's chest. Just as quickly, Kultan swiped one gigantic arm and the weapon crashed into the wall. Kultan drew his *mek'leth* and grabbed Martok by his throat. "Explain yourself," he said, "and if I like it, I'll kill you quickly."

"Gothmara," Martok choked. "Bioweapons . . ."

The light of understanding flickered in Kultan's eyes and he released Martok, who fell to the deck retching.

Above him, voices murmuring questions mixed with stunned silence. Only Kultan moved.

"Daughter!" he shouted. Martok saw his feet disappear from his line of vision and knew the lab's outer door had opened, because the volume of the alarm suddenly rose, then muted.

Under his hands and knees, Martok felt an explosion rock the deck, this one killing the alarm. All around him, crewmen collapsed; arms and heads cracked against the bulkheads. Lights flickered red. Above him, Martok heard a crewman say, "The primary power junction for this deck just went. What was she storing in there?"

Struggling to his feet, Martok said in a cracked voice, "Death." He tried to clear his throat and said, "Run! Get away from here! If we can seal the deck . . ."

But it was too late for that. Even as he staggered up to the deck's main pressure doors, another explosion ripped through Gothmara's lab, blowing the outer door out of its frame. Shrapnel and fire instantly killed anyone who was standing within five meters of it. The pressure doors began to drop and Martok saw in an instant how it would all play out. The captain was dead—good riddance—but he had to try to save as many of the others as he could.

The deck bucked under his feet again as another power junction farther up the hall blew out. Green plasma fire crept up the walls ten meters behind him. Suddenly, it was hard to breathe, and a part of Martok's brain was glad of it. *Fire might kill it, whatever it was in the canister.* But they had to get away. Staggering to the intercom, he slapped the All Decks switch and shouted, "Abandon ship! All hands! Abandon ship!" Instantly, a Klaxon screamed above his head. Yellow lights flashed and pointed the way to escape pods. Martok was surprised to see that there was a pod door directly across the corridor from him. *How odd,* he thought. *I had no intention of surviving this.* Destiny, it seemed, had other plans for him.

The green flames crept closer and the air grew thinner. A hatch door opened and Martok fell inside. Recorded voices spoke, counting down numbers, and then there was the sensation of thrust, thrust, thrust, then blackness and nothing more.

Strangely, as he slept, he dreamt of Gothmara as he would for many, many months thereafter.

6

They were all so afraid of how she would react that Sirella could practically smell their fear. She wanted to laugh, but she did not dare. Several captains would probably flee from the room if she did. Her laugh had that effect on some people, especially the weak-willed.

Moving only her eyes, Sirella studied the others in the room. Both Worf and Dax waited patiently for Martok to signal them as to what they were to do. Worf, she knew, could wait forever without impatience if he thought the cause was worthy. This new Dax, though—Sirella was not sure what to make of her. In many ways, this Ezri could not be much less like the infuriating and much-missed Jadzia: she was at once more somber and flightier, if that made any sense. But then, Sirella had looked into the girl's eyes when she stood up to Sirella's challenge, and again when she and Kahless and B'Tak had discussed the soul of their people. Sirella had seen something of Jadzia's blue steel in those eyes.

If Sirella could ever be said to worry, she might be said to have some small anxiety about how the four captains, their only allies, were reacting to this situation. The emperor had as much as admitted that he had abdicated his office and now her husband was telling them all that he had once had an affair with a madwoman and fathered her son. Yet, there they sat, still attentive and respectful. Martok had that ability, she reflected. Men tolerated his vices because they recognized that his virtues eclipsed them. If only he could recognize that about himself.

Then there was Drex, her only son and now her only child. She knew him well enough to know he was about to leap out of his chair—his armor, his very skin—for want of action. All this talk, talk, talk! It must be driving him mad, yet he had *not* jumped up onto the table and sworn to slay his half brother and avenge his sisters. Sirella had to wonder about that. Could these events actually be having an impact on what she had always assumed to be her son's impenetrably dense skull? If so, this was unexpected; Sirella had credited Shen and Lazhna as being the ones with the brains, the ones she could shape and refine. Drex was, had always been, his father's, though her husband had too often seemed oblivious to this fact.

Last, there was Darok, the old reprobate. She had been unaccountably pleased when she had learned he had survived the taking of House Martok. Of course, he had probably slipped out a long-hidden secret entrance as soon as Sirella had been captured, but she could not begrudge him his survival. Sirella could not have escaped; she had known that when the Hur'q came for her, but her sacrifice had made it possible for others to flee. The house had not escaped destruction, but Darok reported that he had seen several of the servants make it successfully into the scrub forest at the edge of the main compound. After that, he said, there was no way to know where they'd gone, or what had become of them.

When she had seen him again, Darok had actually gone down on one knee when he had returned her *DiHnaq* to her. The memory was sweeter than she dared allow herself to dwell on at this moment, though she wished she might. Circumstances required she stay focused on this abhorrent council, where the humiliations and mistakes of the past were being aired like a commoner's dirty bed linens. *Men can be such simpletons,* she thought as she considered Martok's disastrous affair with Gothmara. She refused to meet her husband's eyes as he concluded speaking, saving any emotional display for when they had privacy.

When Martok finished his tale and resumed his seat beside Sirella, Darok rose as quietly as his old bones would allow and made for the relief facility, a tiny airless cubicle in the corner of the conference room. *Too much* raktajino *this morning,* he decided, but it had been too long since he'd been on board a ship, the only place you can get really good *rakt.* The stuff they brewed planetside was just too . . . fresh. And flavorful. Not nearly enough grit in it. He'd almost made it across the room when Kahless *(the Longwinded,* Darok thought, grimacing as he returned to his chair) began speaking again.

"As you all know," Kahless said, "Gothmara did not perish in the destruction of the *Gothspar.* I've uncovered much about her past, but some things remain obscure, such as where she escaped to and why. While there is no way to know precisely what her next destination was, I believe her motives from that day forward were clear: to amass enough power to utterly destroy the man who destroyed her family."

Dax observed, "She waited a long time."

"Yes," Kahless agreed. "But I think there we can divine some insight into Gothmara's character. She is extraordinarily patient and does not mind waiting—"

Abruptly, the door slid open and the loathsome Ferengi, Pharh, clutching a glass to one ear, rolled onto the floor. He grinned nervously, sliding backward along the floor until he'd flattened himself against the wall.

"—as clearly our Ferengi friend cannot," Kahless finished.

"Don't mind me. I was just passing by," Pharh said.

Worf growled. "The Ferengi was eavesdropping."

"Pharh," Martok muttered. "Your interruption is inopportune. These are important matters."

B'Tak, who Darok had noticed had been chafing since his dressing down by Kahless, took the opportunity to speak up. "This is a council for warriors. As your servant does not seem to understand his place, he should respect this gathering and leave us, or I will cut off his ears. He will not eavesdrop again."

"Servant?" Pharh squeaked, clutching his lobes. "Hey, hold on there! I'm not anybody's *servant,* especially when there haven't been any negotiations for salary, benefits, medical coverage. . . . I'd need some paid holidays and sick days, maybe some kind of a retirement plan. . . ."

"PHARH," Martok shouted. "Restrain yourself. And, B'Tak, he *isn't* my servant. His efforts to rescue the Lady Sirella and me have earned him a place at this council if he chooses. Over the past several days, his ac-

tions have been more honorable than those of many so-called warriors. . . ."

B'Tak rose to his feet and looked like he was about draw a weapon. "As honorable as abandoning your own warriors in the lowlands in favor of taking a Ferengi into your enemy's lair?"

Darok felt his legs lose much of their rigidity, which was precisely the thing he required if he was going to successfully slide under the table when the fighting started. Sometimes, old age had its advantages. He exchanged glances with Dax, who appeared ready to join him.

Martok was on his feet now and Worf was pushing his chair back away from the table, ready to jump in between B'Tak and the general when the moment came. The other three captains were looking at each other, all of them obviously wondering what they were supposed to do next. Darok's neck and shoulders disappeared below table level.

But once again, the Lady Sirella did not fail them. She shoved back her chair and stood, the *DiHnaq* on her wrist clanking against the table.

Everyone froze into a tableau.

"Enough," she said softly, but with a whip-snapping razor's edge in her voice. "Can the source of the empire's current struggles be in doubt when I see behavior such as this? You are leaders of the empire. Act like it."

Martok instantly backed away. B'Tak swallowed loudly. Darok pushed himself back up into his chair. Everything was going to be all right.

"Of course, my wife," the general said. "You speak wisdom." He nodded at B'Tak, the closest he would come to an apology, then turned to Kahless. "As you were saying, Emperor?"

Kahless gestured for Pharh to take a seat. Once the Ferengi had taken his place—far away from B'Tak—Kahless picked up his thread of thought as if Pharh's interruption hadn't happened. "Gothmara conceives her campaigns in terms of years or decades, not weeks or months. Also, she develops multiple, independent battle plans should one of her plots fail."

"You have proof of this?" Worf asked.

"Worf, I *am* proof of this," Kahless replied. "As I implied earlier, my creation—my birth, if you will—was a complex scheme designed to undermine the empire. She traveled to Boreth disguised as a pilgrim and, after insinuating herself into the monastery, immersed herself in the disciplines of the order and delved deep into the ancient archives. She conceived my rebirth with the idea that it would begin a civil war, which, indeed, it might had you not interceded with Gowron."

"But there was no clue of this at the time," Worf protested. "I never met any woman named Gothmara when I stayed on Boreth. How could she devise such a complex conspiracy without my learning of it?"

"How does Gothmara accomplish anything, my brother?" Martok asked. "In addition to her cunning and her scientific knowledge, she has at her disposal every manner of manipulation. Pheromones, perhaps, or some other kind of hormonal tricks to deceive the senses. She did it to me. She may well have used her wiles on everyone at the monastery. Did you ever meet any women there at all?"

Worf reflected, then answered, "A few. Not many, and none in senior roles."

"Then perhaps there never were any women among the clerics, or perhaps she had them sent away. Another unanswered question I have been pondering," Martok said. "She may not be able to influence women at all. I have seen no evidence of it, not then, and not now. If so, we may be able to turn this to our advantage."

"No," Sirella said, her voice low. "She can. At least to some degree."

Martok appeared surprised, but his reaction was as nothing compared to Darok's. His belief that the lady could be affected by, well, by *anyone* or *anything* had swiftly become one of the bedrock tenets of his universe. Stronger than electromagnetism, more relentless than gravity, there was Sirella. "She spoke to you," the general said.

Sirella looked at him, but then addressed the rest of the room, her head held high. "When I was her prisoner, as they carried me out to be executed, that woman whispered something to me. I do not remember her words, but I know it made me feel . . ." She struggled to find the correct word. "Resigned," she concluded. "I decided it would be best to let it all happen however it would. There was no longer any reason to go on."

Her words trailed off and the silence hung heavily in the room. Darok felt a desperate need to escape then, to flee the room and find a very large barrel of blood-wine.

Kahless's gruff and powerful voice pulled Darok back. "Do not despair, Lady Sirella, and, more, do not doubt your own worth. Our foe's powers are formidable and she has had many years to prepare for this battle while we have had little time. I doubt not that the next time you are challenged, you will triumph. Does any warrior here doubt that?"

Martok shouted first, but a chorus of cries soon joined his voice and Darok bellowed as long as any of them. Even Dax beat the table with her fists and cried out, "Kai, *the Lady Sirella!*"

They finished on their feet, but the lady curtly waved them back into their chairs. "We have work to do," she said, but Darok could see the white tips of her sharp teeth glint under her lips. *Such a woman,* he thought. *If only I were a younger man . . . and the general a little less formidable.*

"Gothmara's initial plan to disrupt the empire by creating you failed," Martok said to Kahless. "When did she begin working on her current stratagem?"

"I would guess," Kahless said, "almost as soon as she learned she was pregnant, but she must have known she would need many years to bring her plans for Morjod to fruition. Even she must have understood that it was the longest of long odds."

"But she succeeded," Worf observed, then realized what he was saying and added, "to a point."

"A very sharp point," Martok concluded. "One she has driven through the heart of the empire. But Emperor, you have still not addressed one of the most puzzling questions: How did she tame the Hur'q?"

"And that is my last tale," Kahless said as he pulled a padd from an inner pocket. "In my adventures on Boreth, I was able to make a copy of some files I recovered from their archives, the forgotten backups of encrypted journal entries left by Gothmara that explain much of this. The short answer to your question is: she did not tame them, she *made* them. But the real and final answer is even more terrifying than that."

And with that, Kahless began to read.

The entries were numbered, though how often she'd made them was unclear. Using other references he found in the files, he estimated that the events described in the journal took place in the third year of Gowron's chancellorship, or roughly six years ago.

In the first entry he read, number 1015, Gothmara began by cursing Worf and every member of his family for his part in the negotiations that resulted in Kahless being installed as emperor. *"If my father were still alive,"* she had written, *"he would track down this traitor and slay him like the parasite he is this very day. Picard—this is Picard's influence. How could anyone so steeped in Federation rhetoric gain enough influence that he could manipulate a chancellor? There must be a way to devise an appropriate fate for this son of Mogh while my other plans come to fruition."*

Then, in entry 1047, Gothmara wrote: *"Work with Morjod goes well. His monthly visits for treatments have become routine. I do not believe he is even aware of the modifications I have made.*

"But much more important news to report. I have been given a great gift and I must meditate upon its meaning. I urgently desire to return to my discovery, to set all my energies to unearthing it and bring it back to the labs, but I sense that this would lead to disaster. There are times, moments like these, when I feel as if my father is guiding me, his hand on my shoulder, turning my head and pointing me in the proper direction. Today was one of those days. I must be patient. I must be worthy of his trust. . . ."

* * *

. . . Gothmara had come to enjoy the icy wastelands, to appreciate their purity and serenity. Most days, the wild winds tore at her like a great beast's claws, but they could not harm her. The flesh of the daughter of Kultan could not be so easily rent. This day, though, the winds were calm, even gentle, more like a child's clumsy and playful tickle than a lover's caress. The thin crust of snow that always dusted the surface of the ice like sugar crystals crunched beneath her boots, and she marveled at the sound.

How many days can there be like this on Boreth? Gothmara wondered, and knew the answer: Not many. Though not prepared for a long hike, she resolved to walk as far as she could and leave enough time to return before sunset. If the worst occurred and the weather turned savage, Gothmara knew she could call the monastery and arrange a pickup. The level of risk was acceptable.

Her goal, she decided, would be a narrow valley near a frozen lake Gothmara had noted on her charts several months earlier. Traveling to the spot by ship would have been simple enough, but the monastery owned only a few and the old man who maintained them had proven resistant to her charms. Hiking would suffice.

The walk was long, but not unpleasant. Gothmara could see the ice cliffs for many hours before she reached them, the walls glittering like jewels in the bright sunlight even through her glare-resistant eye protectors. Once, briefly, she even lowered her hood, uncoiled her hair from its knot, and let the breeze stir it. Many, *many* years had passed since she had allowed the reins to slip, to take a moment like this for herself. Morjod was permitted—briefly—to travel to other worlds, to walk under warm suns, but Gothmara was as much a prisoner of Boreth as she was its secret ruler. Her name, her face, were anathema in the empire and who knew how far outside?

"Fools," she whispered to the wind. "Ignorant, blind commoners." The face of one particular commoner shimmered to the surface of her mind and Gothmara clenched her teeth. *Harden your heart, woman,* she thought. *His betrayal was great, but your revenge shall be all the greater.*

The valley, alas, turned out to be little more than a narrow cleft, probably the remains of a streambed back in the day before Boreth's climate had cooled. When Gothmara finished exploring the place, she was glad she had not expended any resources to acquire a ship. She had almost turned around to begin her return journey, disappointed with herself that she had misunderstood her father's guidance, when she stopped to study the cliff face more carefully.

Mist rising off the lake's frozen surface obscured detail, but from where she stood near a low slope, Gothmara thought she saw a shadow where there should have been none. Her timepiece pinged, alerting her that she should begin her return journey, but again she felt the pressure of a firm hand on the back of her neck. *This is the place,* she thought. *Here, now, this is what my father wanted me to see.*

Approaching, Gothmara saw that the shadow was in fact a crack in the ice. The opening was much too narrow to be called a cave mouth. Stretching her arm, she tried to reach the back of the cave, but she could neither find it nor determine if the cleft narrowed or widened to any significant degree. The light from the small lamp she carried on her equipment belt proved insufficient. Sighing in resignation, Gothmara unbuckled her bulky thermal parka and let it slip to the ground. Without the coat and its heating coils, inside the cave, away from the wind, she could survive for five, possibly ten minutes before hypothermia set in.

A small voice in the back of her mind told her she was being foolish, risking everything with little hope of reward, but Gothmara recognized the voice as the one her mother used to employ when she had attempted to interfere with her daughter's plans. The thought of her mother made Gothmara smile with pleasure even as her teeth began to chatter with the cold. *I showed you who ruled our House, didn't I?*

Still, she had to admit that she was gambling, and that thought, too, made her smile. Her father had been famed far and wide across the empire as a strategist. His meticulous plans had been the ruin of many a Federation and Romulan general, but only Gothmara had known his true character. At heart, Kultan had been a gambler. In every one of his great victories, there had been a moment when fate, destiny, could take a hand and turn all to ruin.

And finally fate had betrayed him.

As she made her way deeper and deeper into the cave, past the broken, craggy floor near the mouth, the way became easier. She even fancied that it was growing warmer, but though this at first seemed like foolishness, a figment of her imagination, the farther back she traveled, the harder it became to contradict the sensation. Soon, Gothmara saw that there was even a haze in the air, condensed water—steam—released from sliver-wide cracks in the ice. *A surfacing underground hot spring,* she decided, which would account for the crack.

Stepping into a wide chamber, she swept her lamp in a quick arc over the ice wall, quickly catching a fleeting glimpse of *something*. Even before she flicked her wrist back, before her mind could even process what she saw, Gothmara felt the breath squeezed out of her lungs. An ancient fear ran down her spine and into her pelvis. Without knowing how or why, she shifted her feet, bent her knees, and tried to run. She tripped then, fell down face-first, and tore open the fabric over her hands and knees. The lamp flew from her hand and skittered across the cracked floor.

Sobbing with pain, Gothmara tried to rise, but all strength had fled. She hunched her shoulders, waiting for the blow to fall, for the giant hand to press her down to the floor, for the claw to rend her flesh. Her heartbeat thudded in her ears, and, distantly, she heard the sound of water dripping against rock. Her heartbeat slowed, the rush of air in her lungs slowed, and then . . . and then . . .

The blow never came.

Gathering her courage, Gothmara rose to her knees, then stood and walked slowly across the cracked ice to where her lamp lay shining against the wall. The cone of illumination it cast half revealed and half hid a large, gray, lumpish shape in the ice, but she resisted the temptation to look directly at it until she had the lamp in her hand.

Light is the thing, she decided. *Light will reveal all— tooth and claw.*

She held the lamp up and saw it there before her, frozen as if in midleap, the bane of Klingon nightmares, the stalker in the shadows for every Klingon boy and girl since any of her people could remember.

Frozen, it hung before her as if it had been here waiting for Gothmara—a chunk of destiny locked in time— the Beast, the Monster, and hers forevermore: a Hur'q of her own.

* * *

Here Kahless paused in his reading.

No one spoke for several seconds, each of them absorbing the visions transmitted by Gothmara's words and Kahless's voice. It was impossible, Darok decided, not to be impressed by the immensity of the discovery and even the discoverer's bravery. Still, there were questions that needed to be asked—he knew that—but he was glad to have someone else ask them.

"Did you know they were there, Kahless?" Worf asked.

The emperor shook his head. "The monks never mentioned anything about it to me. And why would they? It is possible that none of the brothers and sisters even knew the reason the valley was forbidden. Such things sometimes get lost with time."

"Did she find others or only one?"

"No whole bodies. She went back several times with scanners, but found only bits and pieces. The first—it might have been left for dead or have been a sentry or manning the outpost—who knows? Documents or recording devices, of these she found none, but knowing Gothmara as I feel I do now, she may never have looked. I do not think she cared."

Martok asked, "So Boreth was the site of a Hur'q outpost like the one Worf, Kor, and Jadzia discovered during the war?" This was new information to Darok, who was just about to ask what they were talking about, but the Ferengi spoke up first.

"Hellooo," Pharh called. "Not following you."

"Almost four years ago," Worf explained, "my wife, Jadzia Dax, Kor the Dahar master, and I discovered a planet in the Gamma Quadrant which must have been a base for the Hur'q long ago. He looked meaningfully at Ezri, but avoided Martok's eye.

Predictably, the Ferengi missed or, more likely, ignored the more important point in favor of the lesser, but more salacious detail. "I thought *she* was Dax," he said, nodding at Ezri.

"I am," the Trill acknowledged. "Ezri Dax. Jadzia was my symbiont's previous host."

"But you two aren't married," Pharh said.

"No."

"But you served together? In Starfleet?"

"Yes, on Deep Space 9."

"The station where the Grand Nagus used to be a maintenance worker." The Ferengi's voice was devoid of any note of surprise or incredulity. He was just trying, Darok decided, to keep the facts straight.

"Rom. Yes."

"Okay," Pharh said, shaking his head slowly, putting it all together. "But you're still part of Martok's House."

"That's right." Dax was obviously fighting the urge to laugh. The general rolled his eyes heavenward.

Pharh hunkered back down against the wall and muttered, "You people lead *very* complicated lives. No wonder you all look so tired."

Martok grunted his approval. Even Worf and the other male Klingons chuckled or guffawed, each according to his nature. Lady Sirella merely appeared annoyed, and Darok decided it would be best to struggle for neutrality, though inwardly he agreed: their lives *were* extraordinarily complicated sometimes.

Kahless laughed, but when he resumed his tale, Darok saw that the lines around his eyes suddenly were deeper and his voice grew as cold as he imagined the caverns of Boreth were. Answering Martok's question, he said, "From Gothmara's notes, it seems that the Hur'q base on Boreth is much more extensive than the one where they found . . . the one Worf and Dax visited. Fortunately for us, Gothmara found no functioning machinery, or our troubles might be even worse than they are. But she had what she needed to create an army for her son, who was by that time already accumulating power in the council."

"That's not at all what I expected you to say," Dax said, shaking her head. "I thought you were going to tell me she found some kind of wondrous machine that allowed her to clone Hur'q from thousand-year-old DNA. But that's not the case, is it?"

"No," Kahless said, and Darok knew that this was the reason for the shadows gathering around his head. "Something much worse. Unlike the techniques she employed to create me from centuries-old blood, what remained of the Hur'q could not be recreated the same way. She needed to find a compromise, and so she combined the long dead with the living to bring into being these abominations we now face."

Even before Dax or Worf, Sirella seemed to grasp the meaning of the emperor's words, and by some strange osmosis, so did Darok. Then, despite his best intentions and finely honed instincts, he said, "You mean . . . she combined the Hur'q DNA with living tissue?"

"Yes," Kahless said. "Using a mutagenic virus that she had already perfected, she . . ."

But Darok interrupted the emperor. "Combined it with what?"

Kahless paused and let a stony silence descend, not because he was angry, but because the question distressed him. Finally, he said, "She was on a planet covered in ice and snow. Devoid of native life. Gothmara used what she had at hand." Kahless looked at Martok, who had clearly already leapt ahead, then at Worf and the captains, Dax, and last at the Ferengi. Finally, he answered the question. "Klingon DNA," he said. "She made the Hur'q out of Klingons."

7

Ezri mentally retreated from the discussion as soon as she understood what Gothmara had done on Boreth. The others, the Klingons, all reacted more or less the same way—with various shades of anger and disgust—but it was obvious that the perversion *motivated* them, while Ezri felt enervated. *What am I doing here?* she asked herself. *What can I possibly have to offer these people? They're preparing themselves to fight monsters out of mythology and an evil sorceress and all I can think about is how out of place I am. . . . No! Back on Sappora VII in my room with my books and my music and my holos . . .* The thought of her room made her see the irony of it all. What were all those books, music, and holos about? They were tales of heroism and adventure, both historical and fictitious. She had stacks of Trill mythology, tales of the *Qieltau* and accounts of the travels of Evu, supposedly the longest-lived symbiont on the planet (though there was some doubt about the veracity of Evu's claims).

As a girl, she had read and reread biographies of Surak of Vulcan, the logs of the first *Enterprise,* the great mythological fiction of other worlds. How many times had she longed to accompany Ch'Vras, Thruzen, and Zheffra on their quest to hide the Rings of *Narath-anazhe?* The stories, in part, had inspired her to join Starfleet, to become like those heroes she dreamt about.

And now here she was in the presence of truly larger-than-life adventurers and all she could think about was how little she offered. If Gothmara needed therapy (and Ezri imagined she could use *years* of counseling, if not a lifetime of it), she was their woman. But dueling with resurrected demons wasn't exactly Ezri's forte. She wasn't afraid of physical danger—she had faced more than her share of that in the past couple of years—but it was difficult to accept the idea that she had a vested interest here. But then she chided herself; of course it wasn't *her* (Ezri's) problem. It was *Dax's* problem, and she *was* Dax. And whether or not Ezri believed she had the abilities to do right by House Martok, Dax *knew* she did. *I suppose this is one of the times when I'm just going to have to trust the slug.* She shook her head, as if the action would redirect her focus to the conversation at hand. It sounded like the outrage over Gothmara's experiments had receded and Kahless had again picked up the story of the time he spent on Boreth.

The clone was, she had to admit to herself, not exactly what she would have expected given Worf's descriptions of the emperor: less the warrior king and more like one of the monks he lived among on Boreth. There was something almost mystical about him, as though he did not live on the same plane as everyone else. He reminded her of someone, but it required several more moments of distracted thought before she put the pieces together. *Of course,* she realized, and almost snapped her fingers. *Benjamin, on one of those days when he was he was feeling especially "Emissary."*

". . . When I learned that Gothmara had succeeded in creating her pseudo-Hur'q and was planning to give them to Morjod to use as an army, I left Boreth as quickly and quietly as I could. As you may guess, it was not a simple matter for me to travel anywhere—least of all the planet of my birth—without being noticed, but I have learned a few tricks." He grinned in a most unimperial manner, like a little boy pleased with some small cleverness. Then, sobering, he continued: "But I was too slow. Gothmara was better organized than I had anticipated and by the time I reached the home system, Morjod had struck." Turning to Martok, he confessed, "I sat in a departure lounge at Ja'Gokor and watched the *Negh'Var* enter orbit over Qo'noS. When the news feeds said you were going to meet with me in the Great Hall, I knew what was about to happen. . . ." Kahless hung his head sadly. "I am sorry, Chancellor, for what has befallen you and your house. If I had moved more quickly or unraveled these secrets sooner, none of this might have come to pass."

Fascinated, Ezri watched Martok's reaction to Kahless's apology. "Emperor," he said, struggling for the right words, "Kahless, what else could you have done? You found my son and my brother, then rescued both my wife and myself. It is I who should be paying tribute to you." He paused, listened, clearly hoping nothing else would be required. When Kahless did not respond, he asked, "How *did* you make it to Qo'noS then? Alexander said you found him within hours of Morjod's attack."

Holding up his hands to indicate the hull of the ship, Kahless said, "Shortly after the attack, I found that the crew of the *Rotarran* was on the station awaiting their captain. They had just completed repairs and were chafing to be under way, disappointed that they could not meet the *Negh'Var* in orbit. I took command and told them to head for Qo'noS at best possible speed under cloak, which they did." Smiling fondly, the emperor concluded, "She is a good ship, Chancellor. I can see why you favored her."

"But you were not the only one in this room, Emperor, who was away from Qo'noS when Morjod attacked." Martok gestured at Ezri and asked, "How has the Federation responded to the crisis on Qo'noS?"

Considering her response carefully, Ezri replied, "I'm not privy to the inner circles of diplomatic activity, but I can tell you what has happened on the station. Colonel Kira is concerned. Admiral Ross contacted her shortly after he received word that something had happened in the First City and, I think, inquired whether I had heard from Worf. At that time, I hadn't and told her so."

"And since they learned that Morjod's forces took over their embassy?"

"Morjod claims they were safeguarding the embassy during a period of civil unrest. The Federation has not accused him of anything, only asking to speak with their people, which he has allowed," Ezri said. "Everyone is treading very carefully. No one wants another breakdown in relations, especially since neither the Federation nor the empire is in a position to wage another war."

"And the Romulans? Are they aware of this situation?" Sirella asked.

"They would have to be fools or blind not to be aware of it. Never underestimate the Romulans' ability to collect intelligence. But the Romulans won't attack anyone until they know they can win; that's their way."

"So for now Morjod is safe from outside interference?" B'Tak asked, every word clipped and angry.

Before Ezri could answer, Worf came to the rescue.

"The Federation will not act against him," Worf explained. "Not unless he expressly withdraws from the Khitomer Accords. He may publicly accuse the Federation and me of every crime imaginable, but unless he violates the treaty with some overt action, Starfleet will only listen and wait." He looked around the room at the sullen faces and finished grimly: "Which is why we must strike *now*."

"Explain," Martok ordered.

"This is a critical time for Morjod," Worf said, and held up one finger. "He has publicly stated that Federation influence is responsible for the decay of the empire, yet he has not withdrawn from the Khitomer Accords. Why? Because he has not consolidated his power. Every reasonable citizen will give him time to plot war against the Federation, but how long will they wait before the Defense Force takes matters into its own hands?"

Martok laughed heartily. "Ah, my brother, you are more of a political creature than you would ever willingly admit."

"I credit it to your influence," Worf retorted. Continuing, he said, "As he senses his time growing short, he will accelerate his plans. He has his generals and council members in key positions, all of them spreading propaganda, but they cannot stall indefinitely and neither will everyone believe them. Morjod will resort to repression and force if he has not already. Does anyone know if he again penned his pet Hur'q after we left Qo'noS?"

No one spoke up until Darok said, "I will check with the bridge," then rose, walked to a small monitor near the refreshment stand, and began to speak in low tones.

"In any case," Worf continued, "the more time passes, the more desperate he will become."

"But what of Gothmara?" Sirella asked. "She does not seem the sort to me to do something either desperate or foolhardy. She will restrain her son."

"I agree," Martok said. "But she could be distracted or goaded into an imprudent act if we choose our target carefully."

"And a great victory will rally your supporters throughout the empire!" Drex shouted as he rose to his feet. "We must retake Ty'Gokor! Surely many of the warriors at the command center are still loyal to you! No matter what tricks his mother wields, by now all the true warriors will have recognized that Morjod is nothing but another *politician.*" He spit the word out as if it left a bitter tang in his mouth.

"Be careful, my son," Martok said sardonically. "*I* am as much a politician as Morjod."

"Never, Father. You are a *warrior,* the general who led Klingons to victory. . . ."

"Stop," Martok said holding up his hand. "Let me consider your idea, because I believe it has both merits and flaws."

"Consider, my brother," Worf said cautiously. "Who controls Ty'Gokor?"

"Yes, my very thoughts: the *Yan'Isleth,* Gowron's former elite guard. Do we know where their allegiance has fallen?"

"I don't think that requires much thought," Kahless

remarked. "The *Yan'Isleth* has little love for either you or me. They were Gowron's. I undermined them and you, Martok, almost disbanded them."

"I wish now that I *had.*"

Kahless shook his head. "The people would have interpreted it as petty vindictiveness. Your offer to allow them to continue to control Ty'Gokor was a wise compromise."

"So that now they will fight us," Martok said.

"Undoubtedly," Worf observed. "But if we won, it would be counted a great victory, the kind of victory that would draw many to your banner."

"Yes," Kahless agreed, "but only a *military* victory. Some Klingons might see it as a sign to rise, but probably only those who are already prepared to do so. And then the empire would be divided and we would fight on for years and years."

"Or until the Federation or the Romulans invade," B'Tak added.

Kahless nodded. "Exactly. We need another kind of victory, one that will not only give us a military advantage, but will expose the depths of Gothmara and Morjod's infamy."

All eyes swiveled to Martok, who was staring hard into his mug. *At what?* Ezri found herself wondering. *At his reflection? At the bloody color of the wine?* Sensing their gazes, Martok looked up and stared back at each of them in turn.

Finally, he said, "Boreth. We keep coming back to Boreth. Gothmara flees there. Morjod is born there. You were created there, Emperor, as were the Hur'q. It is the knotty center of this puzzle."

"Yes," Kahless agreed. "And neither Gothmara nor

Morjod know how much we've learned. They will not expect a strike there because Boreth is not a military target. If we take the planet and expose their atrocities, it will send shock waves through the empire. The people will rise up to follow your banner and the forces of the coup will crumble."

Martok exchanged glances with Worf and Alexander, then nodded almost imperceptibly. The four captains talked among themselves, shifted in their seats, each of them grinning and making sounds of assent. Even the Ferengi smiled, though Ezri noted that Sirella's expression remained curiously neutral, her eyes never leaving Martok. Finally, the chancellor rose and slammed the table with the flat of his hand. "Yes!" he shouted. "We will take Boreth! And when we do, then shall Morjod and all his allies tremble!"

The Klingons drew their weapons, lifted them high, and bellowed in response: "MARTOK! *Kai* the Chancellor!"

To Ezri, it was precisely the sort of Klingon hubbub and bluster she would have expected. Then, unexpectedly, in the middle of it all and without her willing it, she felt Jadzia's judgment brought to bear and those more experienced ears found the cries to be strangely perfunctory, even subdued, as if each of them might have secret doubts.

Even as the cheers and shouts died down, Martok continued feeling satisfaction. At last—finally!—he had found a path that might lead them all toward victory, or, failing that, to some sort of conclusion. He was too experienced a military leader not to see that they would have only this one chance. If their attack failed or even if the battle ended in a stalemate, his small force would collapse. His core group would remain loyal—the *Ro-*

tarran, the *Ch'Tang,* possibly the *Orantho*—but all the others would slip away, not because they were cowards, but because they no longer saw any chance of victory.

For now, they must establish forward motion and momentum. In unity, his warriors had to set their hands to the task before them. Distraction must be avoided or they would be vulnerable to Gothmara's wiles. Never again would he underestimate what that woman was capable of.

On all sides, the exulting continued, enabling Darok to slip back into the room, virtually unnoticed, no doubt armed with information about Hur'q. Martok did not wish to dwell on the creatures, seeing them as causing a paralyzing—not motivating—fear in his warriors, so he cut off the old man before he could speak. "How long before we meet with General Ngane and his fleet?" He already knew the answer to this question, but he wished to have the others hear the response.

"Ngane!" B'Tak shouted, surprised. "He lives?!"

Martok knew full well that Ngane had once been B'Tak's much-revered commanding officer. He had intentionally withheld the information that the general would be joining their attack force, hoarding it as a gambler keeps his last credit in his boot, just in case he needed to tip a delicate balance.

"Lives?" Martok asked. "Of course he lives! No one in *Sto-Vo-Kor* wishes to see his grizzled, ugly, old face. He contacted the *Rotarran* as soon as he heard of our escape from Qo'noS and is meeting us with his fleet in . . . how long, Darok?"

"Two hours," Darok said. The true answer might be much more or much less, but Martok didn't care. He and the old man had survived enough campaigns by playing the odds that Martok trusted Darok to know when to keep his mouth shut and when to tell an easy lie.

"*Kai*, Ngane!" B'Tak bellowed and rushed from the room, the other three captains at his heels. As they receded down the hall, Martok heard him say, "We cannot fail now!" Grinning wolfishly, he saluted to Darok, who nodded wearily.

"How long really?" Martok inquired.

"I have no idea, my chancellor. Perhaps in the future you should inform me ahead of time that I will be performing in a play so I will have time to prepare my part better."

"You've never needed time before, you old fool."

"I grow older every day and my mind begins to fail."

"Good. You'll be less trouble that way. Quickly— which of these five ships is the fastest and in best repair?" One of the many reasons he kept Darok as an aide was that he possessed an unrivaled fund of information about the specifications, records, and status of every ship in the fleet.

"Without question the *Rotarran*."

"Agreed. Worf, she's yours. I may not completely agree with the wisdom of this mission you've proposed, but I trust you to do it quickly and well. Bring *Rotarran* back to me, brother, for I will have need of her."

"Fear not, my chancellor." And, without another word, he beckoned to Ezri and Alexander, and the three of them left the room.

"Darok, when we are done here, go to the captain of the *Ch'Tang* and inform him that I am taking command of her." Martok caught a glimmer of annoyance in Sirella's eyes. Clearly, she did not approve of his choice of cruisers, but this wasn't hers to negotiate. "I know that look, Sirella. Fear not. I've had my flag on *Ch'Tang* before. I know it as well as I know *Rotarran*."

His wife glared, but said nothing.

"Very good. My lady, you will board the *Orantho*, and Drex, go to B'Tak on *Ya'Vang*. Do *not* interfere with him, my son. He is the best captain in our fleet."

"Except for you," Darok offered sardonically.

Drex appeared on the verge of agreeing with Darok when Martok cut him off. "And you, my son, are neither my equal, nor B'Tak's. Conduct yourself accordingly."

Offering his father a curt bow, Drex turned away, scowling, and turned to bid his mother farewell. What happened between mother and son was not Martok's concern, however, so he turned his back, granting them a modicum of privacy.

Scanning the room, he asked, "Where did Kahless go? He and I have other things to discuss." Martok very much wanted to understand some of the more obscure points from their discussion. Kahless seemed at once both much more and much less than the man he had known before he became chancellor. He wanted to avoid any unpredictability from the emperor as they headed for what might be his last battle. Suddenly realizing he had forgotten something, he looked to his left and found Pharh standing there staring up at him.

"What do you want me to do, Martok?"

Martok considered the question. Unfortunately, there were no neutral worlds or starbases between their present location and Boreth, or he would simply drop the Ferengi off and bid him farewell. Somehow, though, he knew it would not be so simple. While he did not share any of Kahless's faith in forces that shaped his destiny, he *did* have the feeling that his fate and Pharh's were bound, at least for a time. However, Pharh deserved to have a choice in the matter.

"What do you *want* to do?"

"What I *want* is to go to this little bistro on Ferenginar and have one of the massage therapists stroke my lobes while I watch a show. How does that sound to you?"

Martok snorted. "I would enjoy that, my friend, but my wife wouldn't approve."

"Yeah, I can tell from the look on her face."

"What?" Martok spun around and saw that, indeed, Sirella had not left with the others and, no, she did not approve of the idea of him having his lobes stroked. She had *that* look on her face, the one that meant it was time to *discuss* something. "I see," Martok said. "Join Darok on the *Ch'Tang*. Have him assign you to quarters and stay there. Circumstances are bad enough without you stirring up the crew."

"Sounds good to me," Pharh said. "I can see I'm going to be spending a lot of time with Klingons for at least a while longer."

"If they don't slit your throat, yes," Darok said dryly, and gestured for Pharh to follow him.

Remembering that he wasn't yet alone, Martok repressed the urge to follow after the Ferengi and the *gin'tak* as they slipped out of the conference room. He had no desire to wrestle down this last, most precious of foes.

"We need to talk, my husband." Her tone did not promise romantic overtures, but Martok had already figured that out from her expression.

"Sirella," he replied wearily. "I have survived countless battles, both in space and on alien worlds. I was held prisoner by the Dominion for two years and forced to fight Jem'Hadar in order that they could learn how to kill Klingons. And now I am facing vicious attacks from my mad son and his mad mother. Despite all these things, nothing in the universe inspires as much dread in me as the words 'We need to talk, my husband.' " Sighing, Martok sat down opposite his wife. "You wield an extraordinary power, my wife. Never abuse it."

"I will not, my husband, if you promise to never again abandon your own."

Suddenly weary, Martok dropped his head and rubbed his right eye and then the patch of scar tissue where his left once was. "What nonsense do you speak, Sirella?" he asked irritably.

"I know the truth," she began icily, "of what happened after Morjod destroyed the *Negh'Var*. None of them, least of all your brother, speaks of it directly, but it has become clear to me that you abandoned your warriors to come search for me."

"Not for you alone. For the children as well," Martok added. "Do not forget about them."

"I *never* forget about them, husband," she said, her voice sharp as a needle. "You can be sure of that. I do not forget them because I know that sometimes you *must*. You are the chancellor and as such your first responsibility is always to the empire. And yet, when the first obstacle appeared, what did you do?"

"I *rescued* you," Martok said, his face a mask of betrayal.

"You *tried* to rescue me," Sirella countered. "You were caught and we were both almost executed. *Kahless* rescued us both, and even when we both could have left, you *still* insisted on fighting those creatures and risked yourself foolishly. First you put your family before the empire and then you put your own pride before it." She slapped the table with the flat of her hand, much as Martok had only a short time earlier. *"What is wrong with you?!"*

Feeling his face growing hot and the blood singing in his ears, Martok rose as slowly as he could and stepped away from the table. Breathing heavily, he struggled with himself, fighting down competing urges to drop down before Sirella to beg for forgiveness and to slap her in the mouth. Tiny white flashes sparked before his eyes, only slowly clearing with each deep breath. When he could clearly see her frowning face again, he pointed at the door and growled, "Leave me. Go to your ship. See that it is prepared. Your brother is still the helmsman aboard *Orantho?"*

She nodded.

"Good. I am pleased you will have *some* family with you, seeing the tattered thing that ours has become." He thought the blow would strike her heart, but Sirella did not flinch.

As she rose, she said only, "This discussion is not finished, my husband."

"Yes it is, Sirella. I am the chancellor and I say it is."

This comment seemed to give her some small amount of satisfaction, so Sirella said only, "See that you continue to act like one." Then, she left, her long cloak swirling imperiously behind her.

Watching her leave, all Martok could think to say was "That woman . . ."

"She is extraordinary, isn't she?"

Caught off guard, Martok spun around to face the speaker, only to see Kahless stepping out of a corner. Flustered, too many questions coming to his lips at once, he asked, "How did I miss . . . ? How dare you . . . ? What did you hear?"

"Don't worry about what I heard. I've been married, too, you recall. In many ways, your Sirella reminds me of Lukara."

"*You* were never married," Martok snarled. "Kahless was married. *You* are a copy of Kahless and you do not have the right to listen in to my private discourse with the lady of my house!"

Shrugging, Kahless said, "I am the emperor, so I have the right to do as I choose. But do not concern yourself. I am not one to gossip. I stayed only because I require a private conversation."

"You *require!?*" Martok shouted, and, his anger still seething, drew his *d'k tahg* from his belt and leapt at the emperor, forcing him back against the wall. "You *require?* What about what *I* require? What of *my* wishes? Here I am, supposedly the leader of the greatest empire under the naked stars, and what in my life have I truly ruled? First, my father drove me to seek a commission I never truly desired and then when I got it, Kor tore it from my grasp. I was a plaything of the Dominion for two seeming endless years, but when I returned it was only so that Gowron could take advantage of my loyalty. Then, Worf manipulates me into becoming the damned chancellor only to have my office stolen by a woman I haven't seen in decades—who forced me to sire a son who now wants to murder me and destroy everything I hold dear." Gritting his teeth, his face so close that the whiskers on Kahless's face prickled his skin, Martok snarled, "So, tell me, Emperor. What exactly do you *require?*"

To his credit, Kahless did not flinch. Not a muscle in

his face twitched and his eyes bore into Martok. He let the silence hang between them for one, two, three seconds, then breathed in once deeply and released it. Martok was surprised by how sweet the emperor's breath was. "Sometimes, Chancellor," he said, "we have no control over our lives simply because we have not yet chosen to take it."

Fixing his attention on a tiny drop of blood where the point of his blade touched the emperor's neck, Martok felt the slow fury that had been building up begin to ebb. It was not that Kahless's words relieved the pressure or even gave him insight into his situation, but the effort of untangling his pseudo-mystical nonsense had finally exhausted him. He no longer had the will to fight, no desires at all. Releasing his grip on the emperor, he said only, "I'm tired. . . ."

"Of course you are, my friend," Kahless said, straightening his tunic as if Martok had just helped him recover from an almost nasty fall. "We all are. And you should rest, but while we had a moment's privacy, I wanted to tell you something that I didn't think the others needed to hear."

Despite himself, Martok felt dully curious. What else could there be? What kind of deviousness yet lurked before him? Morjod's evil twin? An incurable plague brewed in Gothmara's labs? A planet-killer weapon? What?

"In the archives of Boreth, I found information concerning your father that I did not understand, and I wondered if you could help me."

"My father?" Martok looked up. He had not expected this.

Consulting his padd, Kahless said, "There was a document written in an obscure dialect where I found reference to a *'Katai* Urthog.' That was his name, wasn't it?"

Martok nodded.

"In the context used, *'Katai'* sounds like an honorific, like *'Dahar* master,' but none I've ever heard before. Do you have any idea what a *'katai'* might be?"

"None whatsoever," said Martok, who realized that Kahless had actually succeeded in discovering something worse than an evil twin, a plague, or a planet killer: he had found a mystery.

8

Ezri and Alexander followed Worf down the long, narrow hall that led to the bridge of the *Rotarran,* but they walked slowly, much too slowly. From Alexander, Worf was used to this sort of behavior. He had been slow since he was a boy. Whenever they had gone on a class trip or a tour, his son had always been the last one in the line, the lingerer, the ... What was the word one of his teachers on the *Enterprise* had used? Ah, yes: the lollygagger. Alexander had always been a lollygagger. Always, always, *always* there had been something that Alexander would find so interesting that he could not tear himself away, and the group would move along, leaving him behind, bewildered, lost, confused.

His laggardly ways had been enough to make a father despair.

And now he had to deal with Ezri *too.* Worf had explained the plan, told her what they must do, even attempted to impress upon her the need for haste, but still she hesitated. Though he hated to find himself thinking such a thing, there was no escaping the truth of it: Jadzia would never have lingered so long. His wife had understood the necessity for swift, decisive action, but this one, Ezri, she was too much like Alexander.

"Ezri," he pleaded. "Pick up the pace, please. Martok needs us back as soon as possible. If battle is joined on Boreth, it may not succeed without the *Rotarran*."

"I'm sure that's true," Ezri responded. "But what makes you think we can accomplish this task in the time we have? For that matter, what makes you think we can finish it before Qo'noS's orbit decays and the planet tumbles into the sun? Or—"

"Because I have faith in you," Worf interjected, though he wondered if she could sense the lack of sincerity in his words. Again, he knew Jadzia would have. "If anyone can do this, you can."

"I'm touched," she said, her tone revealing that in fact she *could* sense his sincerity.

"And our succeeding could spell the difference between Martok solidifying his leadership . . ."

". . . Or not," she finished for him. "So, no pressure then. Great." She glanced at Alexander, who was, naturally, bringing up the rear.

"Kahless thinks this is a good idea. He wouldn't have sent us if he didn't."

"The emperor did not send us," Worf said, correcting his son. "This was my idea."

"Oh," Alexander said distractedly. "Well, whatever. It's still a good idea."

Ezri studied the boy carefully. "He made quite an impression on you, didn't he?" she asked.

Smiling shyly, Alexander shrugged. "There's something about him. When I talk to him, I don't feel stupid or useless."

"Do you often feel stupid and useless?" Ezri asked in her counselor's voice, and Worf felt his eyes rolling up in his head. This was *not* the time to be having this conversation.

"A lot of the time," Alexander replied. "Depends on who I'm talking to. If I'm talking to a Klingon, then the answer is usually yes." He smiled. "But I know something else."

"What's that?"

"This discussion is making my father crazy."

"Thank you," Worf said emphatically. "We must get to the bridge."

As they passed a narrow porthole, Ezri paused to watch one of the other cruisers navigate into position behind the *Ch'Tang.* "It would be nice to have some backup," she said. "But we're going to be on our own, aren't we?"

"Yes," Worf said, trying to hide his exasperation.

"Should we consider contacting Deep Space 9?" Alexander asked.

Ezri shook her head. "No, they can't know what we're doing. If we told them, they would be obliged to tell the Klingon government."

"But Martok is the Klingon chancellor."

"It doesn't work like that. Whoever is in control of Qo'noS—and, by extension, the Defense Force and the client worlds—is the government. Even if the Federation knew the whole story of everything that's happened, I doubt they would attempt to tell Morjod that he isn't the legitimate ruler of the empire."

"I agree," Worf said.

"So then, Father, how will your involvement sit with

the Federation? I mean, you're an ambassador. What you have planned doesn't feel very ambassadorial."

"I am aware of my tenuous status, my son," Worf said. "And will deal with the consequences when the time comes. I have sworn oaths both to House Martok and to the Federation and I am attempting to live up to both of them. Where the oaths are in conflict . . ."

". . . May never really become an issue," Alexander finished. "I see your point."

Ezri looked at the two of them, first son, then father. "Maybe you two should switch jobs," she said to Worf. "I think he'd make the better ambassador."

Worf said, "I suspect you may be correct." Alexander grinned proudly, so Worf did not try to explain how he did not necessarily consider what he had said to be a compliment. "I must do this," he continued, "but you do not, Ezri. If you would like to back out, we can put you back in your shuttle."

Dax hesitated, but before she could reply, they were walking through the doors to the *Rotarran*'s bridge. Worf had been up here once already during the gamma shift and hadn't recognized anyone, but that crew had just gone off duty. Looking around, he now saw several familiar faces and felt himself relax just an iota. He knew these men and women, had served with them during the war, trusted them. If nothing else, he knew they would make it to their destination, because nothing could stand in the way of the *Rotarran* when this crew flew it.

Unfortunately, not all of the crew felt the same way about the trio walking onto the bridge. Several lips curled upon sighting Dax and there came muttered curses and Worf heard at least one man utter the Klingon word for "parasite." This last came from Ortakin, the very same officer who had challenged Jadzia when first she stepped onto the *Rotarran's* bridge. Then Worf experienced a strange and unexpected bout of déjà vu as Ezri levered Ortankin out of his seat, threw him over her hip, and leapt onto his chest with both knees, effectively crushing the air out of his lungs.

When Ortakin's head cleared, he must have felt the prick of his *d'k tahg* at his throat, but he didn't seem to mind. Looking up into Ezri's eyes, his mouth suddenly split into a delighted grin and he shouted, "Dax!"

Ezri grinned back, climbed off the man's chest, then helped him to his feet. By the time they were both standing, the rest of the bridge crew had gathered around the Trill and were patting her on the shoulders and back, many of them telling her tales about their experiences with her former incarnation. Looking down from his perch on the rear deck, Worf could only barely see Ezri's head among the hulking, shaggy figures clustered around her, but when the crowd momentarily broke apart, he saw her beaming up at him.

"I guess this means she'll be coming," Alexander said from beside his father.

"Yes," Worf said. "I believe it does."

Fifteen minutes later, after Martok and Kahless had beamed aboard *Ch'Tang,* the *Rotarran* went into warp for a destination known to only three of her crew.

After his sonic shower, a change of clothes and a hot meal, Martok felt better than he had at any time since the *Negh'Var* had returned to Qo'noS—how long ago now? Mere days? Could that be all the time that had passed? It didn't seem possible that so much could change so quickly.

His leg still throbbed where the Hur'q had fallen on him and broken it, Klingon bone regenerators not being quite as effective as their Federation counterparts. If he should become the chancellor again, Martok decided, he would address that problem. The Defense Force's teeth-gritting reliance on antique medical technology was ridiculous.

Despite his physical condition, now, seated in the captain's chair on the bridge of the *Ch'Tang,* he felt more comfortable than he had at any time since the end of the Dominion War. All around him his highly trained, efficient crew murmured and barked at each other, stations all over the ship preparing to get under way. Even K'mtec, the ship's former captain, had willingly accepted his new role as second-in-command and was currently down in the engine room helping to resolve a problem with the antimatter manifold.

Darok had assumed his usual position on the bridge near the ops station and had begun hectoring the officer about how they had done things in the old days, his dry, sharp tone a pleasant counterpoint to the low hum of the computer displays. Martok had heard whispered conversations that the emperor—usually trailed by a Ferengi prince (Martok's mind reeled when he tried to figure out how *that* rumor got started)—were walking the corridors of the ship offering encouragement and willing hands wherever needed. All in all, the crew was in good spirits. And why not? The prospect of a glorious death in an honorable struggle? It was the fulfillment of every Klingon's dream, warrior or not—to ascend into legend.

"A good day to die, indeed," Martok murmured, and

was surprised to find he spoke loud enough for someone to hear.

"Is it, Chancellor?" Darok asked. "Really? Perhaps I should have gone with the lady."

"Perhaps you should have, old man. In the past, I have found that nothing so improves my lady's opinion of me than to have you before her for comparison." Several on the bridge laughed at the weak jape, but Martok knew from much previous experience that a crew enjoyed knowing there was at least one person with whom their captain would and could trade barbs. He and Darok had perfected this routine over the course of many campaigns.

The problem was—the problem had always been— that there was always someone who didn't understand that the routine was a two-man show. Someone always wanted to get into the act. The weapons officer, a young warrior named Kurs, made the mistake of saying, "If you think the lady will be lonely, maybe I should beam over to the *Orantho.*" His good-humored grin fell as soon as he saw both Darok and Martok turn their frowning faces toward him.

Martok started to rise from his chair, but Darok waved him back. "I will handle this, Chancellor." And he did, too. Most efficiently.

When Kurs regained consciousness and staggered to the turbolift clutching his broken jaw, Darok chided him, not unkindly, "Think twice before you say the lady's name again, boy. The next time it might be she that hears you and she is nowhere near as merciful." This time, no one laughed, but an important lesson had been learned.

Flexing the fingers of his right hand, Darok moved to the side of Martok's chair and remarked casually, "It is always a good thing to learn where the limits are."

"Yes," Martok agreed. "And you are a fine teacher. I never truly understood how fond you are of my wife."

"She is a remarkable woman, Chancellor. In recent days, I have found that she makes me think of my mother. . . ."

"Really? I have heard you speak of your mother on more than one occasion, Darok, and I cannot remember it ever being complimentary."

"I did not say she *reminded* me of my mother. The Lady Sirella makes me aware of just how deficient my mother was . . ."

"Ah."

". . . And in so many areas . . ."

"Yes."

"Did I ever tell you about the time my mother chased me across the *graq* fields in an antigrav skimmer . . . ?"

"Yes, I believe you have."

"Shooting at me with the stun gun she always wore to catch vermin . . . ?"

"*Yes.*"

Mercifully, Darok abandoned the tale, and turned to watch the men and women around him completing their final checks. Then, bending down so that only Martok could hear him, he asked casually, "Did you two part amicably?"

"Such things aren't your concern, Darok."

"Naturally, Chancellor." He flexed his fingers again, then studied the glove leather at the spot where he had struck Kurs. "Still, he continued, "there are times I wished I talked to my mother one last time before she went off to fight the Romulans."

"Truly?" Martok said politely.

"Unresolved business, you know? Words left unsaid.

It's always a sad thing when a warrior goes off to battle with unfinished business back home. Things left undone . . ."

"Trouble me no more, old man."

"Yes, Chancellor." He rubbed a knuckle. "I believe I may have broken something," he said. "Old, fragile bones, you know?"

Martok inhaled deeply and let the breath out slowly. "Go to sickbay, Darok."

"I believe I will. Is there anything you need to do before we get under way?"

"Nothing that concerns you," Martok said. But before Darok was aboard the turbolift, Martok said, loud enough for the *gin'tak* to hear, "Hail the *Orantho*. Patch the signal into the captain's strategy room." Glancing over his shoulder at the closing doors, he saw a brief glimmer of bared teeth.

As he strode into the strategy room, the main monitor's speaker crackled to life, though there was no picture. Good. The comm officers were observing his orders to minimize wideband transmission, instead restricting themselves to the more easily disguised and encoded narrow-beam audio-only channels. "This is *Orantho*," came a voice from the speaker. "What are your orders, Chancellor?"

"I wish to speak to the lady Sirella. Monitor on."

"Yes, Chancellor. One moment."

Several seconds passed, and then the monitor flickered to life. Sirella looked down her well-tapered nose at him, proud and imperious. "What do you want, husband? You declared our discussion finished." She seemed steeled for a continuation of their earlier argument, but Martok's desire for combat had passed.

"Perhaps I was mistaken about that," Martok said. "Or perhaps I only wanted to see my wife's face again before I went into battle, and am willing to give up a little pride in order to make sure that happens."

Sirella's left eyebrow arched in suspicion, but when she did not detect any change in Martok's expression her features gradually softened. "I would be careful about how much pride I gave up, Martok," she said, her tone more playful. "We have precious little left to burn between us."

Martok grinned. "Were you here on my ship, Sirella, you would know what else still burns between us."

The corner of her mouth quirked up as if tugged by an invisible string. "You are a ridiculous old man who should have other things on his mind. You have an empire to win back."

"My wife, I have not forgotten this, nor will I ever, because the reason I must win the empire is to offer it to you as ransom for my heart, which is now and forever in your keeping."

An icon appeared in the corner of their screens, a signal sent by the tactical officers that a ship or ships were approaching. Both Sirella and Martok knew from its color and configuration that they had a few more minutes, but only that—a few. "Fight well, my wife. I will see you again on Boreth."

"Or in the halls of *Sto-Vo-Kor,* my husband." She saluted him. *"Qapla',* Martok, chancellor of the Klingon Empire."

Martok returned the salute. *"Qapla',* Lady Sirella, ruler of the House of Martok." For the space of a heartbeat, their gazes tangled, until Sirella cut the connection, leaving the chancellor of the empire to stare at a blank screen, lost in thought, for he knew not how long.

Returning to the captain's chair on the bridge, Martok felt, paradoxically, that he'd been freed of some burdens only to take on others. Perhaps they had settled something just then, he and his marvelous, frustrating, astonishing, and endlessly annoying wife. And perhaps they had not. It was always thus with them: whenever they had passed through and closed a door, they found themselves standing in a room with three more doors open before them. Whether Sirella shared his perception of their life journey would likely remain a mystery. Should he explain his thoughts to her, he expected she would categorically deny having any idea of what he was talking about and accuse him of speaking foolishness.

Smiling to himself, Martok shook his great head, laughing aloud. The bridge crew looked at him, he was sure, but no one offered any comment. Darok, back from sickbay with a bandage ostentatiously wrapped around his hand, would not meet his eyes, but smiled unrepentantly as if at some private joke.

9

"Signal resolving," the tactical officer announced. "It is General Ngane's flagship."

"How many ships are with him?" Martok asked.

The tactical officer read from his monitor. "Only two—small attack ships."

Martok grunted noncommittally. He had hoped for better. Ngane's flagship, the *Chak'ta,* usually patrolled with a full complement of four light cruisers, four attack craft, two supply ships, and a ground-assault carrier. Obviously, some of his captains had defected to Morjod or possibly—even more worrisome thought here—been destroyed in a battle. The chancellor was counting on Ngane's ships to be up to full strength. If they were not, he would have to amend the plan he had been formulating. While Boreth was not a military target, Gothmara would not leave it undefended, and Martok had to have resources available to hold the sacred planet after they claimed it.

One damned thing at a time, he decided.

"Hail the *Chak'ta*," Martok ordered. "Extend my compliments, then transmit coordinates for the rendezvous point."

"Sending," the com officer replied.

Tactical called, "General, they are not reducing speed."

"Are they being pursued?"

"Scanning." Pause. "Nothing sensors can detect."

"Scan for cloaked ships."

"I have, General. Nothing."

"Distance?" Something was wrong. Ngane should have braked and gone to one-quarter impulse. It was standard procedure unless he was experiencing some kind of emergency.

"One-point-five light-years; one-point-two . . ."

"Estimated time of arrival."

"Fifty-five seconds."

Behind him, Darok cursed. That was never a good sign.

"Shields up," Martok ordered. "Send warning to *Orantho, Ya'Vang,* and *B'Moth.*" Glancing back at his aide, he muttered, "Your mother would be grossly offended by that word."

"My mother," Darok countered, "would be firing all disruptors at this point."

Around them, the bridge crew mobilized. "Shields are up and at full power."

"Disruptors—hot. Torpedoes—loaded and armed," the weapons officer shouted.

"Sensors recalibrated for close . . ."

"Communication from the *Chak'ta.*"

Martok frowned. "On screen."

Though it troubled him to admit it even to himself, Martok had prepared for the possibility that Ngane might betray him. The reality that Morjod could manipulate or blackmail even his closest companions, whether by trickery or force, was all too apparent. Martok understood weakness. He understood how schemers like Gothmara could find the chink in anyone's armor. Clutching his armrests, he steeled himself for the worst.

Ngane's dismembered head loomed before them. His eyes were open, rolled up into his head, and his face was sunken and shrunk down over his bones. No one could say how long he had been dead, though it had not happened recently, because they could see a dry crust of blood on the ragged fringe of his beard.

Strong fingers were tangled in Ngane's hair and made the head bobble back and forth in a grotesque dance when the holder tightened and loosened his grip. Several of the bridge crew cried out for vengeance, but Martok quieted them all with a shout of "Silence!"

The head was withdrawn and another face replaced it. Morjod smiled and said, "Greetings, Father. Looking for your old friend Ngane? Like so many of your old friends seem to these days, he ran into a problem."

"You have no honor, Morjod," Martok said quietly. "And after today, you will have no life."

"I think not, old man." Morjod signaled to someone offscreen. "Good-bye."

The tactical officer almost leaped out of his chair. "Two light cruisers have decloaked off our stern and two Birds-of-Prey off the bow! All are charging disruptors!"

Dammit! Martok slammed the arm of his captain's chair. *Have I grown feeble?! The oldest trick in the book!* "Fire all disruptors at the *Chak'ta!*"

But Martok's order came too late. Morjod had prepared his attack well; disruptors and torpedoes barraged the *Ch'Tang* from four directions, almost tearing the ship apart. Bridge power was lost for several seconds and Martok felt the sickening lurch of the artificial gravity fluctuate beneath his feet.

"All power to the engines!" Martok shouted. "Get us out of here!"

No one responded to his command; he heard instead an agonized shout, then a sharp scream as the navigator's panel exploded into metal and plastic shards. Martok ducked as soon as he saw the blue-white light, and felt something graze his temple.

"Engineer—reroute the conn to me!" It was a long shot; he could run most of the bridge functions from the controls in his chair, but Martok could smell the fried insulation of overloaded power couplings and the sharp metal tang of coolant leaks. Morjod's first attack had been superbly aimed. He knew precisely where to hit a cruiser like the *Ch'Tang* to destroy bridge functions.

Someone scrambled up off the deck behind Martok and clawed his way to the engineer's panel. A combination of familiar curse words and general verbal abuse indicated that Darok was still among the living. "Navigation routed to your chair," he shouted. "Impulse only! Warp core is offline for . . . three minutes!"

Three minutes? Martok brought up the nav system. *It might as well be three months!* There was no way the ship could survive another fusillade, let alone the four or five Morjod could offer up in three minutes. "Tactical! Where's the *Chak'ta?!*"

"Scanners are offline, Captain!"

Emergency lights flickered on, died, then came back on again. The gravity sputtered once more, but then Martok felt himself drawn down firmly into his chair.

"Visual?"

Darok remained silent for several seconds while Martok listened to the ship groan and strain around him. A quick check of the damage-control systems told him everything he needed to know. *Ch'Tang* was dying. It was only a matter of whether she would hold together long enough for Martok to take some measure of revenge.

Then the main monitor flickered to life, casting enough light to enable the captain to see what was left of the bridge and her crew. The conn and navigation stations were destroyed, their officers cut into ribbons when the panels exploded. The injured communication officer, her face smudged with blood oozing from a gash on her forehead, was gamely trying to raise any of the three other ships. Everyone else save Darok was either dead or so badly injured that manning a station was impossible.

It doesn't matter, Martok thought. *I only need to know which way to point her.* "A picture, Darok," he shouted. "Static does me no good."

"Look now," Darok bellowed, his voice growing hoarse from the smoke. "Dead ahead!"

The picture wavered, the static shuffled from side to side, then finally cleared until Martok saw her: the *Chak'ta,* her fore guns glowing brightly, prepared to release another volley. Two light cruisers flanked her just beneath her bow. It would be difficult, but Martok thought he could thread the needle, make it past the light cruisers and into the *Chak'ta's* bow before the guns tore him apart.

Martok fed the coordinates into the system, feeling a sense of *nIb'poH* as the collision course was locked. *Unfortunately,* he thought, *Worf isn't here to beam us all down to Ketha this time.* His finger hovered over the Engage button as he looked around the bridge one last time. Allowing himself one luxury, he glanced back at Darok, who was busy trying to find power somewhere in the great shivering hulk the *Ch'Tang* had become. "Get ready, old man," he shouted. "We're going to go see your mother!"

Darok gestured toward the viewer. "You first," he said.

Laughing, Martok leaned forward, his back and neck straining as if the ship needed his muscles to fly. He was ready, he decided sadly, ready to die in a bright white flash, the kind he had so often seen on the edge of a blade.

Over the comm, a familiar voice shouted, *"Long live the Klingon Empire!"* A fierce joy rose in Martok's heart . . . and then crashed and burned.

On the monitor, a ship surged into view, cutting a diagonal path across the course Martok had plotted, impulse engines blasting at full power, disruptors blazing, and torpedoes flying in every direction, and with a certainty, Martok knew whose voice had been shouting a benediction to the empire.

"SIRELLA!" he cried out as the *Orantho* rammed the light cruisers flanking the *Chak'ta.*

On impact, a fierce explosion ripped through *Orantho,* torpedoes exploding in their tubes, and her bow section tearing away at the joint where it met the main hull. Now inertia's toy, the bow section spun up against the *Chak'ta*'s shields and rebounded into space. Cut off from its brain, the remainder of the hull became nothing more than a careening hulk. Her engines flared, then died, and she began a slow, inexorable slide into the first cruiser's underbelly. No shield generators or repulsion devices could withstand the kilotons of pressure, and the cruiser's hull plating gave way in a spectacular shower of sparks and released atmosphere. A critical energy conduit was severed and the cruiser died on the spot.

The pilot of the second cruiser must have had enough warning or preternaturally sharp reflexes, because he was able to shift the bow of his craft away from the straining *Orantho*, but fate was not kind to him despite his skills. A stray torpedo from one of the ships—it was impossible to say which—detonated less than a ship's length from her bow. The force of the explosion ripped through the hull plating and surged down the superstructure into the engineering hull and out through the engine manifolds. Martok recognized the chain reaction from other battles and knew that even as he watched, the engineering section was being flooded with coolant that would race down the unshuttered ventilation system. Anyone still alive on the ship would be dead in minutes, its interior a contaminated ruin.

But luck was with the *Chak'ta* and her master that day. Possibly with intent, but more likely without knowing what they were doing, the shifting courses of both the cruisers blocked the force of the explosions. *Chak'ta*'s engines glowed brightly as she strained to pull away and Martok watched as the ship disappeared behind a cloud of glittering dust and debris.

Martok looked down at his hand and saw that his hand still hovered over the Engage button. If he pushed it now, he might find his way through the wreckage, might be able to pin *Chak'ta* on the spike of his bow like a boy spearing a fish.

You might, a voice taunted him, *but your vision isn't what it once was, husband. If you miss, what then?*

She was dead.

He kept waiting for something to die inside him, for

his heart to harden like stone and to crash down in his chest, to crush him from inside, but the damnable thing kept pounding. Sparks danced before his eyes, then the monitor darkened as the *Orantho*'s engines surrendered to the inevitable and consumed themselves.

He had always assumed, however foolishly romantic the notion, that when she died, he would know it, feel her loss within himself; his body would then die of its own volition, being severed from the very force that gave it life. But, here he stood, alive—though it was not possible that he live without her.

"General," the comm officer called. "The *Ya'Vang* hails us. Your son requests pursuit of the—"

Martok snapped his head around. *Drex, the fool. He'll want to attack.*

"Tell him to go to warp if he can," Martok shouted. "Darok? Has it been three minutes?"

"As of . . . now, yes."

Martok looked back down at the Engage button. Tempting, so tempting. *I can be with you this day, my lady,* he thought longingly. But she would berate him for cowardice, accuse him of abandoning his duty to the empire and leave him, a lone man at the gates. He would rather endure eternity in *Gre'thor* than roam *Sto-Vo-Kor* without Sirella.

He wiped out the command and plotted a new course. "Drex will follow us," he ordered. "Contact the *B'Moth* and feed them the rendezvous coordinates, but instruct them to take a different route." He touched the controls to engage the engines and felt the inertial compensators gasp as the engines ground up to warp nine.

Having escaped the overload from the exploding

ships, the monitor blinked on again and Martok found himself staring at a streaming tunnel of stars. "Is *Ya'Vang* behind us?"

"Yes."

"B'Moth?"

"As ordered," Darok said, "but following a different course."

"Anyone else?"

Darok paused long, long, too long, as if he was searching for something that wasn't, shouldn't, couldn't be there. Finally, he said, "No, Chancellor." Then more quietly, barely audible above the sparking, chiming, and clattering, "Nothing. Nothing is there."

Martok lowered his face into his hands and counted the beats of his pulse in his ears, waiting for his breath to stop, his heart to cease pumping, but it kept going on and on. *It shouldn't be true if she's gone,* he thought, and felt the merciless bite of hope. *The bridge section spun away. She might have found an EV suit before the atmosphere escaped. She could still be there.* "Alert the *Ya'Vang,*" he called to the com officer. "Tell them I'm turning back."

"Belay that order," a new voice called.

"WHAT?!" Martok leapt out of his chair and spun around in midair to face his challenger.

Kahless stood before him, half the hair on the right side of his head seared away and a bloody stain oozing down over his cheek. His tunic was torn and charred and he cradled his arm against his body. Behind him, Pharh stood hunched over against a bridge rail, pale and gasping for breath.

"You dare—?" Martok shouted, arms flung wide. "Get off my bridge, old man! You do not rule here!"

114

Shaking his head, then wincing in pain from the movement, Kahless said only, "No, I don't."

Deflated, Martok lowered his arms, saying, still angry, "We have to return to search for survivors."

Kahless shook his head. "There are no survivors, Martok. I watched—*everyone* watched—from the engine room."

"Sirella might have . . ."

"*No,*" Kahless said with finality, and suddenly Martok recognized why Worf still considered this vat-grown relic to be the emperor of the Klingon Empire. When he wanted it to, his voice had a depth, a quality that could not be denied. "*No one* could have survived it. Your lady died to save you. If you honor her memory, you must not throw away her sacrifice on a foolish hope."

"But . . ." Martok stammered. "But . . . I do not *feel* any different. If she was gone, I would know it. I would *know.* . . ."

Kahless reached out and touched Martok's hand, and he felt something like a father's gentle reassurance creep up his arm. "She isn't *gone,* Martok. She is a part of you and you cannot be separated any more than I can ever be separated from my Lukara. But you will see her no more in this life. Lady Sirella is *dead.* Mourn her when you can, but what you would now do does not honor her memory."

Flicking a glance over at the comm officer, the sole functioning member of the bridge crew, Martok hissed only, "Cancel the order." Then silence filled the bridge as Martok grappled with his seething emotions.

"Martok?" Pharh asked quietly. "Is there anything we can do here?"

"Check for life signs," Martok replied. "Take the living to sickbay. The dead . . ." He looked around the smoky, rubble-strewn bridge and grimaced. "The dead we will mourn . . . when we have time."

Hours later, when the bridge was cleared of casualties and the worst of the damage was addressed, Martok called his son.

"Captain B'Tak is dead," Drex explained. "I have assumed command."

Martok had already learned this from the casualty reports, but his son's composure surprised him. He had expected to find Drex frothing at the mouth, ready to pursue Morjod with every ounce of strength left in his body. Instead, here was a calm, determined, even dignified ship's captain. What had happened to Drex on Qo'noS after the *Negh'Var* had been destroyed? Martok realized he had not had the opportunity to ask and neither was he likely to anytime in the near future.

"Very well," Martok said. "And as captain, I have your first task ready for you." He clicked a control on the arm of his chair and transferred a data file to Drex's console. "Darok has tapped into one of the Defense Force networks and determined what happened to Ngane's fleet. The ships we faced were the only ones Morjod was able to find or persuade to join him. Possibly Ngane told the others to flee before he was taken."

"The general would do such a thing," Drex said. "I was assigned to his ship when I was an ensign. He was a great commander."

"Something else to avenge, then," Martok said coldly. "The data I transmitted indicates their last known coordinates. Once we find them, we will go to Boreth. Engage cloak and go to warp eight."

Drex studied the data, then nodded. "Very well,

Chancellor. A worthy plan. Will the *Rotarran* know where to find us?"

"We determined that whoever arrived first in the Boreth system would set a beacon and wait. Worf knows this."

"Then I will get under way," Drex said, turning away from the monitor.

"Wait! Drex!"

The captain of the *Ya'Vang* turned back to look at him. "Yes, Chancellor?"

Martok struggled to find the words. "Your mother . . . She died bravely. . . ."

A tiny crease appeared in a fold of muscle between Drex's eyes. "Of course she did, Father. She was incapable of less."

Again, Martok found himself at a loss for words and again he was surprised at his son's composure. *When did he become this man?* He gathered his resources and said, "She was very proud of you, my son. She would be even more proud of you now."

A flicker of emotion fled across Drex's features. He closed his eyes and touched his forehead lightly with the tip of one finger. "Thank you, Father. I will try to honor her pride in me."

"I know you will, Drex. *Qapla',* Captain."

"*Qapla',* Chancellor."

Martok turned away from the monitor, half expecting to see Kahless and Pharh there again, but they were not. Kahless's injuries, though not life-threatening, were severe enough to require rest. Pharh had wanted only to return his room to have, he said, "a quiet nervous breakdown." Good. Martok didn't want anyone following him around, least of all a Ferengi.

Darok still manned the tactical station. He hadn't left

the bridge since the battle, not even to procure a cup of bloodwine to soothe his nerves. "Find someone to take your station, old man. We both need rest, and I suspect you could use a drink."

"And not you?" Darok asked. "We could drink to her."

Martok shook his head. "I will not again drink wine until I am toasting Sirella over Gothmara's corpse." He sighed. "Besides, wine brings dreams. I do not wish to dream."

"Ever again?"

Looking around the bridge at all the unfamiliar faces, Martok reflected that this was *not* the conversation to be having under the circumstances. "Not right now, in any case."

Nodding wearily, Darok submitted the call for a relief officer as Martok strode heavily toward the elevator. "I will be in my quarters if I am needed," the chancellor said.

"Of course you will," Darok said, but it was obvious from his tone that he did not entirely believe this was true.

The shuttle did not have a name, because Klingons rarely named small craft. When he had been stationed on Deep Space 9, Martok had been surprised to learn that all the Federation runabouts were named and doubly surprised that they were named for anything as quixotic as rivers. Still, now that he was aboard the small ship and guiding it out the *Ch'Tang*'s hangar door, he found himself wishing to name it, so, in his heart, he named the shuttle after his daughter, Shen.

Ever since she had been young enough to walk, his middle child had wanted nothing except to fly. One of the lucky few for whom a passion was also a gift, Shen had been an outstanding pilot from her first day in a craft. Martok had pushed her to make a name for herself as a pilot of high-performance experimental ships, but she had decided she could best serve the empire behind the controls of a fighter. Sirella had once told her husband that their daughter had not wanted anyone to think she had been given a prestigious assignment because of her father's influence, which would have undoubtedly been the case if she had done as Martok wished. "She is happy if she is flying," Sirella had said. "That is all you need to know."

Bowing to his wife's superior knowledge, Martok had given in.

And now Shen was dead, her entire wing destroyed by Morjod in the purge of Martok's House. Then, unexpectedly, the image of a faceless young woman wearing a charred fighter pilot's uniform flitted through his mind. The vision came on Martok so suddenly that his hands shook on the panel and the hangar's guidance system momentarily took control of the shuttle and nudged him out the door.

What was that? he wondered. And why was he left thinking about the last time he had celebrated a birthday with Shen? She had been little more than a child. A cadet, he thought. He remembered the cadet's uniform.

Clear of the hangar, Martok engaged the cloak and sped away at top speed. Sighing with relief, he fed Boreth's coordinates into the autopilot controls and settled back into his seat. He was on his way. Come what may, once again he had no one to take care of except for himself. Drex would find Ngane's fleet and guide them to Boreth. In the meantime, he would investigate. Prowl around. Perform reconnaissance in preparation of their arrival. He had never considered himself in the role of a spy, but there was a first time for everything.

The door to the shuttle's rear compartment slid open and Martok spun around in his chair. Pharh nonchalantly stepped into the pilot's bay holding a bowl of some kind of steaming stew in one hand and a spoon in the other.

"Hey, guess what? I finally found something Klingon I like!" He showed the bowl to Martok.

"That's borscht," Martok said. "A human dish. Worf programmed it into the replicator database the last time he served on the *Ch'Tang*."

"Oh. I figured being this color it *had* to be Klingon."

"You're not the first to comment on that," Martok said, sighing. "Pharh, what are you doing here?"

"Where are we going?" Pharh asked, ignoring him.

"*I'm* going to Boreth. You are about to be jettisoned."

"I think not," Pharh said, picking at a beet. "You need me. I'm your lucky charm. And, besides, I wouldn't survive a day on that ship without you there. That's why I decided to hide here. Just in case."

"What about Kahless? He'd protect you."

Pharh shuddered. "Even for a Klingon, he's kind of crazy. That's why I like you. No matter what happens, I feel like I always know exactly what you're going to do."

"I cannot tell you how reassuring I find that."

"I know. See? I'm your good-luck charm."

Martok saw that there was no escaping this fate. Acquiescing, he lowered the seat back and shut his eye. "I'm going to take a nap now."

"Okay."

"And you are going to be quiet."

"Okay."

"And eat with your mouth shut."

"O . . . Um, I'll do my best."

The sounds of eating diminished slightly. Martok felt himself sinking into the chair, the pull of gravity on his tired muscles growing stronger with every passing second. Just as awareness faded, he heard Pharh say, "Martok?"

"Yes, Pharh?"

"Sorry about your wife. She was kind of scary, but . . . well, she wasn't crazy, either. You two made a good couple that way."

Breathing in slowly, then releasing it, Martok said, "Thank you, Pharh. Now shut up."

And that was all he remembered until they reached Boreth.

10

Five heads lay in a row on the floor under *Chak'ta*'s main bridge monitor. Morjod had put them there to give him something to look at other than the stars hurtling past. He knew that, as captain, he could have ordered the monitor turned off, but he had somewhere formed the idea that the bridge monitor should show stars, so stars it was.

Unfortunately, Morjod did not like stars, especially *moving* stars. Looking up at a still night sky was fine. Moving stars were *unnatural*. He was no fool: he recognized that the ship moved, not the starscape, but drew no comfort from that knowledge. His distress had begun in childhood when he had frequently traveled the spaceways with his mother. One night, Morjod had formed the fancy that the little white and gold blobs of light stared down at *him,* as though they had a destiny planned for him. When he had told his mother of this fancy, she had replied, "Of course they have plans for you. Magnificent plans." Morjod had not understood her meaning. Panicked, he had fled and hid in a small cupboard in their quarters for the better part of a day. Strangely enough, when his mother finally came to find him, she had seemed to know precisely where he was.

Ever since that night, stars had made him . . . *uneasy*.

Decapitated heads, on the other hand, made everyone else uneasy, and didn't bother Morjod at all. It hardly seemed fair that he suffer alone. If spaceflight made him irritable and anxious, his crew would also be irritable and anxious.

Morjod looked around the bridge at all the fearful little creatures and indulged in an idle mental game: if he *were* going to remove a head, whose would he take? Most of Ngane's command crew were dead. When he had taken the *Chak'ta*, he had brought a squad of warriors handpicked by his mother; those should not be touched. One or two were old Defense Force hands, men and women of negotiable loyalty. A few of them were possible candidates, though, again, Morjod resisted the impulse. Alas, he'd found it necessary to keep a few of the *Chak'ta*'s crew alive to maintain some critical ship's functions that none of his specially selected men understood or cared to learn. He had so longed to finish off the rest of Ngane's warriors, especially now as he watched them skulk around his bridge.

Martok's escape was all the more frustrating for just this reason. Capturing his father's ship would have given him more to choose from. Before he left to find Ngane, his mother had said he could take Sirella's head if he wanted and, oh, how he had wanted to. . . . Back in the cell, back on Qo'noS, Sirella had talked to his mother about Morjod like he was a boy, like she understood him, if such a thing were possible.

Never again.

The memory of her impunity, both back in her cell and then with her ship—what a *ridiculous* sacrifice that had been—made him want to break something. He slammed the arm of his chair and every head on the bridge jerked up, except, of course, the ones that *couldn't* jerk anymore.

His two pets, both chained to the chair, seemed to understand his frustration and growled sympathetically. These smaller-than-usual Hur'q were not nearly as smart. For example, Morjod knew he could not trust them with weapons, not even knives, or they would damage themselves or each other. Mother had said to treat them like they were children and she had certainly been right about that: the beasts whined and bawled like a couple of infants, but Morjod had to admit even their cries sounded impressive. Sadly, over the past day or two, the pair had started to become listless, which he attributed to the fact that they never ate. Mother would have to make new ones soon. Nothing motivated a crew like his pets!

Mother had been worried about the older ones. Morjod could sense that before he had left on his hunt. Martok should not have been able to hurt them, let alone kill that pair. The man's luck was extraordinary. Just the memory of how he had escaped, not once but *twice,* prompted Morjod to leap up out of his chair and stalk around the bridge. Slipping up behind every man and woman, he hovered over shoulders and in ears, snarling or breathing heavily at every opportunity. Some tried pretending he wasn't there, while others tried matching him growl for growl, but their weak attempts to stand up to him failed. Morjod had an unparalleled gift for inspiring dread.

Completing his circuit of the bridge, Morjod stood

behind the tactical officer and bored holes into the back of his neck with a stare. Despite the fact that Morjod kept the bridge cold—the Hur'q liked it—the man began to perspire freely and beads of sweat dripped down off his nose onto the sensor displays.

Then, unexpectedly, the tactical officer seemed to forget Morjod's presence and fixed his attention on a gravimetric blip.

"What is it?" Morjod asked, his voice low.

"Here, Emperor," the man said, and pointed. Morjod had made certain that everyone on board knew to address him as Emperor. Not Chancellor, nor Captain, but Emperor. His mother had told him it would be all right now. One of the heads under the main monitor had belonged to the first man who had forgotten.

"I see it," Morjod snapped. "But what does it mean?"

"A cloaked ship traveling at high warp recently left this area."

"Martok?"

"No," the man said, trying not to be too encouraging. "We know roughly the course the chan . . . I mean, Martok took and it was dissimilar to the one we're seeing here."

"If we know where Martok went, why can we not pursue him?"

The tactical officer took great and obvious pains not to react overtly. "Because Martok might have changed course after he went to warp, sire. This other ship left the area before Martok and went in an entirely different direction."

"How is it we found this mysterious ship, yet not Martok's?" Morjod was growing frustrated. He did not want to continue this conversation, but felt he would need to be able to explain the situation to his mother.

"Pure chance, sire. We were scanning on the right frequency and picked up the warp signature."

"Do you know which ship it is?"

"I am running a check." They waited uncomfortably together for several seconds until an answer flashed up on the officer's display. "It's *Rotarran*," he announced.

Rotarran? Martok's old ship. But why? "A defection?" Morjod asked, but not truly expecting an answer.

"Perhaps, sire. Or perhaps a mission. There is only one way to know which." The officer stared up at him in a conspiratorial manner from under shaggy brows. Morjod resolved to have the man killed later. Obviously, this one was too smart by half, but not nearly as smart as he thought he was.

Not today, though. *Keep him alive for now. He has his uses.*

But tomorrow, what would happen after they had found *Rotarran?*

There might be six heads under the bridge monitor. Maybe even more.

Martok asked, "I'm dreaming again, aren't I?"

"Yes," the woman said. "Or, more accurately, you're in a dream space. It's not exactly the same thing, but for the purposes of this experience, yes, you are dreaming."

Though obviously an adult, the woman seated cross-legged before him was probably the tiniest Klingon Martok had ever seen. She gently stirred a small metal pot suspended over a low open fire and, strangely, Martok felt his stomach rumble as he sniffed the rich aromas rising from it. "Sit down," she said. "You make me nervous hovering up there."

Doing as he was bade, Martok slipped down onto a

small cushion across from the stew pot. The firelight cast deep shadows on the woman's face. Though the wrinkles on her face and threads of gray in her hair indicated she was older, her features were strong and her eyes were brightly alert. "Are you hungry?" *she asked.*

"Yes. Which is strange. I don't remember ever being hungry in a dream before."

"Clearly you are not listening. Your lady told me to expect as much." *She inhaled sharply.* "This isn't a dream. Not exactly. Different rules apply. Hold out your hand."

Martok extended his hand, expecting she was going to give him a bowl, but instead she smacked his wrist with the wooden spoon.

"Ow!" *he yelped, and drew back the hand.* "That hurt!"

"And you'll have a welt there when you wake up, too," *she explained.* "Let that be a lesson to you."

"What lesson?" *Martok asked, sucking on the back of his hand. He tasted some of the broth that had been on the spoon, which was succulent.* "Mistrust the offerings of old women?"

The woman tilted her head back laughing and he found he enjoyed the sound of it. She laughed with her whole body, her chest swelling and heaving, loose white hairs dancing in the firelight. "Actually, that's a good lesson, but my intention was this: Anywhere you go that you can have pleasant sensations—like the smell of my stew—you can also be hurt."

"I will try to remember that," *Martok muttered darkly.* "Except, now that I think about it, I seldom recall my dreams."

"When the time is right, you will remember," *she said. Reaching around behind her into the shadows, she lifted a small hand-thrown ceramic bowl over the pot and filled it, careful not to let any drop into the fire. "Here, take this." She looked at him expectantly and for a moment Martok wondered if she wanted his opinion of the food.*

"It smells wonderful," Martok offered, though he sensed she wasn't waiting for compliments. Then, unbidden, he remembered something his mother used to say before meals when he was a very young boy. "For the strength of the beasts and the grace of the birds, we give thanks."

"For the strength of the tree and the grace of the grain," the old woman replied in a rote, singsong voice, "we give thanks." She nodded her head then, indicating Martok should start eating.

The food met Martok's expectations: rich, savory, and delicious. He ate the slivers of steaming meat and chunks of vegetables with his fingers, almost scalding himself, then drank the broth in two or three quick gulps. Feeling the heat in his belly, and a surge of new strength, Martok felt contentment slip down over his shoulders like a warm cloak. "Excellent," he said, handing the bowl back, hoping for more, but the woman only set the bowl aside.

When she did not speak, Martok took a moment to study his surroundings and, remembering his other encounters in this dream space, was pleased to find that he looked out over a nondescript plain. The glow from the firelight picked out foot-stomped grass, broken twigs, and even the shadow of a small, scrubby bush nearby. The air at his back was comfortably cool and the cook fire pleasantly warm. All in all, Martok felt as contented as he could remember feeling for many days.

The woman stared at him, not unkindly, for several moments, and then, stirring the pot again, asked, "Do you seek answers from me?"

"I'm not sure," Martok said. "Let me think." He pondered her question, settling upon something that bothered him. "In the other visions . . ."

". . . The ones you don't remember when you wake up . . ."

"Yes. . . . I usually knew those who I dreamed about." Remembering Kar-Tela on the ice plain, he corrected himself. "Or sensed who they were, in any case. But I don't know you. Who are you?"

The old woman rolled her eyes and laughed again. "How easily they forget," she said. "You know my legend, but not my true self. I am she who is called Lukara."

"Kahless's wife?"

"If that's how history remembers me, so be it, but we were never wed."

"But . . ."

She must have caught the glimmer of disbelief in Martok's eye, because she latched on to the "But" and drew it out of him. "But, what?" she asked.

"But . . . you're so . . ." He struggled for a way to say it.

"So . . . what? Small-boned? Minuscule? Diminutive? It's all right. You can say it."

"All right," Martok said, relieved. "All of those. In the opera, they always play you as being . . ."

"Bigger than life," Lukara finished for him. "Well, I am bigger than life. But I'm short, too. How tall are you?"

Martok told her and Lukara shrugged. "When they tell your story years from now—assuming you have a story—you'll be twice the size of normal men. And you'll have both your eyes back except for when you're blind, which you will be sometimes because it makes for a good tale. And Sirella, too. Sirella will be the stuff of epics and song."

Martok smiled. *"Sirella was bigger than life,"* he said, and was surprised to discover that speaking of his wife in the past tense did not provoke the dry ache of loneliness he had anticipated. *"Where is she now? Do you know?"*

"The afterlife is not your concern. You will explore that place when the time comes," Lukara said. *"When called on, I teach other lessons, but no one tells me what's happening over there. . . ."* She waved generally at the darkness behind her back.

"What is your role, lady?" Martok asked. *"The stew was hearty and filling. And I feel a sense of peace here that I have not felt . . . well, in my lifetime, but I do not see what value that has given my present circumstances. Is there not something of warriorcraft or strategy that you can teach me?"*

"You are going on to battle your mad paramour and her damaged son with no one beside you but an over-grown Ferengi, correct?"

"Yes."

"And you fail to see the value of a hot meal and a sense of peace?"

Martok decided that there was no arguing the point and said so.

"If you had to ask about such a thing, then the Klingons of your day are much different than those of mine," Lukara said.

"Perhaps," Martok said. *"I know very little about the Klingons of your day. Only songs and stories."*

"You are unfortunate, then. Songs and stories are hardly enough since they tend to exaggerate. Doesn't

anyone in your day attempt to learn the truth of the past?"

This provoked an ironic laugh from Martok. "Only one person that I know of: Gothmara. And she will not stop until she has torn down everything our people have built since your day."

"And this tearing down. Is it all such a bad thing?" Lukara shrugged and replaced the lid on the stew pot, then swung the hook it hung upon away from the fire. Martok sensed that their discussion was coming to an end and he must awaken soon. He hoped he would retain the warm feeling in his belly. *"If there's nothing else you wish to know,"* the old woman said, *"then I have a question for you."*

"Certainly."

"How is Kahless?"

Martok was taken aback. While he did not have a complex conception of the afterlife, he had assumed that, somehow, the spirit of Kahless would be with Lukara. "I don't understand," he said. "You mean he isn't here?"

"Do you see him?" she asked, spreading her arms. "He's in your realm, the world of the living. The last you saw him, anyway. Correct?"

"Well, yes, but he's not the real Kahless. He's a clone."

"He's Kahless," Lukara said. "As much as anyone is, he's Kahless. How is he?"

"He's . . . fine," Martok said. "I suppose. Different now than when I first met him, but fine."

"Different how?"

Reflecting back on his first impressions of the emperor, Martok considered carefully before replying, then answered, "When I first met him, he seemed a great example, a standard bearer for our people."

"He is," Lukara said.

"What I mean is, he seemed only to be a symbol, an ideal. But the more I see of him, the more he seems something else. He is . . ." He struggled for the right word. "I knew an alien, Benjamin Sisko . . . ?"

Lukara closed her eyes and squinted. "I see him in your mind, yes. Because you know him, I know him, too."

"More and more, Kahless reminds me of Sisko. One who leads, but not simply because of his warriorcraft or his example."

"A seer," Lukara said.

"Yes, but more than that, too."

"Ah," Lukara said. "I understand. A katai."

Excited by the discussion, Martok felt like his mouth had been about to race ahead of his mind, but had suddenly crashed into a stone wall. "A what?" he asked. "What does that word mean?"

"Katai?" Lukara asked. "You don't know what katai means?" Throwing her arms up theatrically, she said, "I mourn for my people. What have you all become if you don't know what a katai is."

"Apparently, my father was one," Martok said. "Or so Kahless told me, though he didn't know what it meant either."

"Then he has lost knowledge in your realm. He should understand this since he was one himself. Katai—it means 'firebringer' in the oldest tongue. In the days before the Hur'q, when we roamed the plains, the katai carried the last ember of the previous night's fire to the new camp. Over time, the meaning has changed, so now you might say 'teacher' or 'builder.' Your father was a katai?"

"So I have been told."

"Then he was a great man," Lukara said with finality.

"Yes," Martok said, feeling the veracity of her words in his bones. "He was. Though I may only now be seeing his true nature."

"Perhaps this is why you were brought here, then," the old woman said, then stood.

Martok rose also, both out of respect and a feeling that he was being dismissed. Though the top of her head barely came to the center of his chest, he felt great power emanating from her, even greater than Sirella's. "Thank you," he said, "for the meal. And the talk."

Smiling, she opened her arms to him and Martok stepped inside their circle. Patting his back, she said, "You're welcome, boy. Now go fight your battle. Do well. Make us proud."

" 'Us'?" Martok asked, stepping away from her. "Who else . . . ?" But he fell silent, because Lukara was gone. At his feet he found only the almost burnt-out embers of the cook fire and the small bowl from which he had eaten. When he picked up the cup, Martok realized that he had seen it before in another's hand. Kar-Tela had offered it to him once, not so long ago, in another dream. Had he taken it?

The last ember died and the world went dark.

The chancellor slept.

"You're going to wish you hadn't come," Martok said, tapping his finger on the sensor display. "Look here."

Leaning forward in the copilot's seat, Pharh tried to make sense of the blips and swirls on the monitor. "I *already* wish that," Pharh said, squirming in his seat. "Why don't Klingons believe in seat padding?"

"A warrior does not need comfort. Comfort dulls the senses."

"Slumping is the natural condition of Ferengi. It's our morphology. Besides, I think the real answer is that Klingons just naturally have more . . . uh, padding."

Martok didn't reply. Awakening only a couple of hours ago after a long nap, he looked more alert and rested than he had since . . . well, practically since the minute Pharh had met him. Neither had spoken much since that time, both choosing to preserve the quiet respite. Pharh believed Martok might be, in his own way, in mourning, though he had to admit to himself that he didn't know enough about Klingons to know what that would look like. Mostly, he seemed quiet, even contemplative, but neither angry nor bitter, provoking a mild uneasiness in Pharh. He wasn't accustomed to seeing Martok this way. Angry and bitter, he had thought, was the man's natural state.

"What am I looking at?" he asked, studying the display. "I can't read the tags."

"I'm not surprised—they're in Klingon battle language. I'd forgotten that you can't read it." Indicating three purple blotches, Martok explained that there were three large ships in a stationary orbit over the monastery on Boreth.

"Klingon?" Pharh asked. "Could Drex have beat us here?"

"Klingon, yes, but not Drex or Worf or any of the others. Different classes, bigger ships." His lips formed a thin, narrow line. "Gothmara and Morjod are staking their claim openly now, it seems." He considered the enemy force for a moment. "We can't land without their seeing us."

"We could just *leave*," Pharh explained. *"There's a* possibility I bet you haven't considered."

"No," Martok said as he worked the controls. "I haven't. Here, look here." He had shifted the scanners so they were now looking at the surface of the planet below them. "The monastery has been bombarded from orbit. Impact craters here, here, and here." He pointed at three dark blue circles, then many smaller purple ones. Pharh did not understand what the colors signified, but he had been in business long enough to grasp Martok's message: Someone had attempted to destroy their ledgers before the auditors arrived.

"So, it must be completely destroyed," Pharh said.

"Not completely," Martok murmured. "Not necessarily. The sensors on this ship aren't good enough to pick up faint life signs. There may be someone left alive down there. I have to find out."

" 'Have to'? You really think? Because from where I'm sitting, I think waiting somewhere for Worf or Drex sounds like a better idea. You know, safety in numbers?"

Martok looked up at Pharh and for a moment his contemplative manner dropped to be replaced by the more familiar Angry Martok. "You chose to come," he said.

"I didn't expect this to be a suicide mission," Pharh retorted, "though upon further reflection I'm not sure on what I based that assumption. I mean, so far, that's been more the norm than the exception."

Martok stared at him for a moment, his single eye narrowing into a glare, but then, unexpectedly, his face split into a satisfied grin. "Pharh, you speak with the voice of common sense."

Hope rose. "So you're going to do what I said?"

"No," Martok replied, standing. "But it's good to know what common sense would dictate. I will do precisely the opposite. Gothmara won't expect that."

Exasperated, Pharh said, "Or maybe she knows you pretty well and this is *exactly* what they'd expect you to do." He looked down at the scanner. "And, besides, if you've seen them, haven't they seen you by now?"

"Undoubtedly. Our cloak isn't sophisticated enough to defeat their sensors."

"Why aren't they coming after you, then? Or at least shooting?"

Martok opened an equipment locker and began inspecting the contents. Moving slowly and deliberately, he hefted a large, heavy weapon off a pair of magnetic hooks and checked it carefully. "Excellent," he said to himself, then addressed Pharh. "If they pursue, I'd only run. If that's truly Gothmara—and I'm growing convinced that it is—she doesn't want me to run. She would like a confrontation."

"And you're going to give it to her?" Pharh asked. "Why? Because you've decided it's time to do something stupid?"

The Klingon tossed a heavy sack onto the deck and pulled at drawstrings, deliberately unfolding a mottled white and gray coat and coverall that seemed to shift and shimmer in the light. "Again, excellent," he said, impressed. "I wonder who stocked this ship." Reaching down, he lifted out a pair of thick-soled boots and deposited them on the deck. "And to answer your question, I'm doing this because it's what *I* want to do. Not Kahless or Worf or Gowron or even Sirella, but me. If Gothmara or Morjod are here, then it's time I go see them. It's what's meant to be."

Pharh snorted derisively. "I thought you didn't believe in destiny."

Sitting down and lifting his foot so that his boot was practically in Pharh's lap, Martok replied, "I don't. I never have, but it would appear that destiny believes in me. Now help me with my boots."

Twenty minutes later, Martok was dressed in Klingon cold-weather gear, had a heavy pack full of survival equipment strapped to his back, and was carrying the large, nasty-looking weapon. "Do you think you could use this transporter if I called you?" he asked Pharh.

Pharh studied the interface. "Probably. I could study it while you're gone."

"Good. I may need a fast beam-out if things don't go well."

"Please explain to me a scenario where things *do* go well."

"Hmm," Martok considered. "I kill Gothmara, defeat her son's army of Hur'q, and restore order and sanity to the Klingon Empire. How does that sound?"

"Everything except 'order and sanity' in the Klingon Empire," Pharh replied. "I don't think that's possible as long as there are any Klingons living in it."

"You may be correct, Pharh." Stepping onto the transporter pad, he asked, "What about the ship? Assuming things go the way you seem to be figuring."

"You mean, can I fly it? Probably, but not cloaked, though."

"Don't worry. They won't chase you if you try to leave. There is no honor in killing an unarmed Ferengi."

"You see? That's what worries me about Gothmara and her guys. I don't think they subscribe to that whole honor idea. They would think it would be great fun to kill an unarmed Ferengi. Maybe even *more* fun."

"That," Martok said as flipped up his head and fastened a scarf over his mouth, "is the reason why I must go down to the planet. The galaxy could not tolerate Klingons without honor. It would have to exterminate us and I cannot allow that to happen. Press that white control. Please."

Pharh pressed the button. As the transporter beam began to scramble Martok's molecules, the Ferengi called, "That's the first sensible thing you've said today. . . ."

Martok had set the transporter to deposit him a hundred meters away from the edge of the monastery grounds in order to give him a chance to survey the area from a place of concealment. Had he conducted a meteorological scan, he would have known that there would be no problems with concealment. Situated on a mountaintop near the planet's only sizable ocean, the monastery was periodically pounded by fierce blizzards, and one of these was currently under way. Martok could barely see more than a meter in front of his face. If not for the survival suit and the tricorder to point the way, he would have died of exposure in minutes. As it was, half the devices in his pack began to beep before he had crossed more than fifty meters, all of them warning him that they would crack open and die if not soon treated with tender, loving care. Martok ignored the cacophony and plowed ahead through the knee-deep snow.

By the time he reached the front gates, half the electronics, including, unfortunately, the heavy disruptor, had died. Pausing only long enough to toss away the weapon and remove the cover from his *bat'leth,* Martok moved forward, carefully picking his way across the broken, snow-covered square.

Gothmara had been very thorough. Not a single building or section of wall remained whole. Though they were covered by six inches of new snow, Martok recognized that most of the irregular hard-angled shapes before him were chunks of stone, slabs of concrete, and spars of structural steel. From previous visits, he recalled that many of the buildings in the square between the gate and the mountainside caverns had stood four or five stories high; now none was higher than his shoulder.

Wasting precious breath, Martok cursed Gothmara and Morjod, moisture condensing inside his mask and freezing in his whiskers. Was no act too dishonorable? This sacred place had been the seat of the Klingon soul for centuries. Down through the ages, whatever conflicts there were within or outside the empire, always this place had been protected, honored, because legend had it that the original Kahless had vowed to return to his people from here. To destroy the temples of learning built around that promise was an unthinkable act of desecration.

During a momentary lull in the wind, Martok heard a sharp snap as he stepped gingerly over a chunk of ice-encrusted stone. He trod on graves, he knew. He wanted to dig beneath the snow, to announce each of Gothmara's victims before the gates of *Sto-Vo-Kor.* Standing erect, Martok swung the *bat'leth* before him, and the blade glowed dully in the fading sun. Snow-flakes danced and swirled in the wake of its passage.

"Revenge," he hissed. "For all of you."

The door to the caverns gaped wide. After scanning the area, Martok slipped between the doors and stepped quickly into the shadows within. Once he was indoors, low torches guttering in sconces and oil lamps hanging from the ceiling lit the way, but Martok knew that many of these were holographic effects. After all, what was the sense of depending on burning oil on a planet with no natural resources? Obviously the monks had wished to project an image to their visitors. Still, for Martok's purposes, a few real, oil-burning lamps might save him, should the monastery lose power.

Holding his breath, Martok listened intently, but heard only the wind whistling through the door and the rhythmic clinking of the lamp chains as they swung to and fro. Satisfied for the moment that he was unobserved, Martok slid along the wall from pool of shadow to pool of shadow until he came to the narrow stone staircase that led deeper down into the bowels of the mountain. A faint whiff of drier, warmer air greeted him as he began his descent, reminding him to remove his face mask and lower his hood. Half-melted snow slipped off his head and shoulders and plopped onto the stairs. Unbidden, memories of Sirella in the dungeon under the imperial palace and his vain attempt to rescue her slunk out to assail him, and he felt unequal to his task. *Why not just wait for Worf and the others?*

Then, remembering the pitiful sound of the bone cracking under his foot, Martok gripped his *bat'leth* and moved down the stairway, stopping on every third or fourth step to listen. Halfway down, he heard a soft, wet rasping, the sound of someone desperately trying to breathe, but afraid to inhale deeply. Martok doubled his pace, but continued to move cautiously. Ambush was very much on his mind. He had not forgotten how Morjod had concealed the Hur'q in a pocket of subspace, and though he doubted the equipment to do this again was easily transportable, he watched every shadow carefully.

At the bottom of the stairs, in a pool of shadow beneath a guttering lamp, a monk lay facedown, his back rising and falling rapidly. After scanning the area and finding nothing, Martok moved to the monk's side and pulled out a field medkit from his pack. He was not experienced enough with a medical scanner to do anything more than search for injuries, take vital signs and receive suggestions for treatment. Unfortunately, the wretched machine offered a prognosis without hope, but Martok tried to make him comfortable.

He was an older man, white-haired, but with a strong chin and a noble brow. Martok thought he recognized him as he helped the man into a half-seated position, and said so.

"I'm Korath," the old cleric said, his words coming between gasps. He wouldn't lower his arms from his gut, and Martok's quick scan told him it was because his arms were the only things keeping his internal organs inside him. The pain must have been indescribable and Martok was impressed that the man hadn't passed out from shock. "I was once a master of this place." He shook his head. "No more."

"Who did this? Was it Morjod? Gothmara? Did they have soldiers or Hur'q?"

Korath, alas, was too far gone. His eyes moved wildly from side to side, not focusing on anything, but saw only who knew what strange and terrible sights. "I welcome the end," he murmured. Blood coated his gums and teeth. "An empire that would turn on itself deserves to fall. It's an offense to Kahless. . . ."

"Kahless is coming," Martok said, hoping the monk would take some comfort from the idea.

Korath either didn't understand him or wasn't listening at all. "Why?" he asked. "Why return to rule over fools and madmen? What is the point?" He lifted his head and stared up at the oil lamp. "Better," he murmured, "to let it all burn. Let fire take it all."

Then, deep in Korath's chest, something wet tore loose or burst under unknown internal pressures. The cleric gasped, tried to inhale, and a viscous bubble of blood and bile burst out from between his lips. The scanner beeped furiously and the recommendation screen flickered and flipped through half a dozen unavailable resuscitation regimens before finally freezing on the "Stasis not an option" screen. Martok considered holding open the old man's eyes and screaming for him, but recognized it would certainly alert anyone nearby of his location. No, better to find the remaining monks, assuming there were any, and permit them to perform the death rites.

Putting away the medical scanner, Martok was unprepared for the oppressive silence. Following after the usual shipboard noise on the shuttle, then Pharh's chatter and the howling winds upstairs, the gloomy stillness felt ominous. The long, narrow hallway was to his back and, feeling a tingling at the base of his spine, Martok looked over his shoulder. Another lamp hung from the ceiling ten meters away, barely bright enough to light the circle of hallway directly beneath it. No one was there.

Turning back to the cleric, Martok considered searching him. Possibly he was carrying a useful key or passcard, something Martok could use to find his way deeper into the caverns.

Behind him, Martok heard the sound of a sharp click on stone and a throaty hiss. He closed his eye, almost sighed with resignation, but fought down the urge and turned around to look.

Gothmara stood just inside the small ring of light the oil lamp projected, casting a long shadow before her. Two Hur'q, both hunched over almost double in the low-ceilinged corridor, flanked her. "Hello, Martok," she said, her voice calmly casual.

Martok lifted his *bat'leth* with one hand into the first defense posture and loosened his sheathed knife with the other. "You killed my daughters," he said flatly. "You killed my wife. I will kill you now."

"I didn't kill your wife," she replied. "She killed herself. Too bad, really, because I rather liked her. Did she tell you we talked for quite a while when I had her? She seemed clever—cleverer than you at any rate. You're so predictable, Martok. Would that hunting you down were more challenging."

In the narrow, low hallway, Martok knew he had some advantages. The Hur'q were built for long, sweeping attacks, and the constricted quarters would be a liability to them. They probably had energy weapons, though Martok couldn't see them from where he stood. A disruptor would even the odds, and he once again began to internally curse the idiot who had built the battery pack on his abandoned weapon. He needed more time to consider his options and that meant making her talk more. "Sirella indeed was wise, though much too kind. She pitied you, the scorned woman, cast aside and unwanted." None of this was true, of course. Sirella would have judged Gothmara even more harshly than Martok did, but he wasn't going to mention that at the moment.

As she took a step forward, Gothmara's shadow became longer and more tenuous, less humanoid and more akin to the monsters she had bred. "Your *targ*-bitch's pity means nothing to me," she snarled.

"Of course not. The small offering of a noble lady's pity matters little when your son sits on the throne!"

Gothmara tilted her head to the side and touched her chin. Martok was shocked to realize he remembered this peculiar gesture as a sign of genuine confusion. "My son?" she asked. "My *son?*" Shaking her head back and forth in disbelief, Gothmara said, "You still don't see, do you? Morjod is a *tool,* an instrument, and a blunt one at that. He was never meant to *rule.* I created him so that he would lay *waste* to the empire. Without my restraining hand, he's out there right now . . ." She waved her hand generally toward the far horizon. ". . . randomly destroying whatever crosses his path." She laughed, then said conspiratorially, "Recently, I've been playing a game that I'd like to share with you. Games are never fun unless someone else plays, don't you think?"

"I don't play games," Martok muttered. She had stopped moving and her pets weren't showing any signs of initiative, so he knew he still had a few seconds to plan.

"You should. Games might make you less of an old grouch. Look at yourself, Martok. You're younger than I am, but you're weak, scarred, beaten down. Wouldn't death be a relief now? A little quiet time?"

"Have you forgotten your game?" He didn't like the direction the conversation was going.

"My game! Of course." She seemed to suddenly realize how far away from the Hur'q she had moved and crooked a finger at them. "Here," she said, and the pair moved up to flank her. When one of them moved, Martok saw a telltale glint of polished metal. *One of them at least has a disruptor.* "I've been trying," she continued, "to figure out who will kill Morjod. Will it be the Federation, the Romulans, or 'his people'? Sooner or later, one of the other powers will have to step in. Maybe Morjod will attack their ships. Maybe he'll even convince the Defense Force to attempt an invasion of Romulus or Earth. He can very persuasive if he wishes, you know?"

"You altered his voice the way you altered your own?"

Gothmara laughed delightedly, then said, "You figured that out? How clever of you." Her tone of voice for that sentence was different than for any previous and Martok felt a shiver run up his spine. He had been prepared for it, expected it, knew what it meant, yet *still* he felt a jolt of pride in having her tell him he was clever. Clutching her throat, Gothmara coughed. "Maintaining my voice can be difficult if I don't treat my vocal cords with the proper compounds."

"You expect him to fail?" Martok asked. "What foolishness! A strategy that anticipates failure? A Klingon battles to victory. You have no plan, Gothmara." He glanced up at the lamp above him and wished there were some way to know for sure whether it was real or holographic—and, if it was the latter, then whether it carried its own battery pack.

"*This* is my plan: To do to you what you did for me. For you to die, but before you die to strip everything away from you. To see you suffer. Is there anything left that I can do to you? Have you suffered enough yet?"

For the rest of his life, Martok never knew if he chose that second to attack because it was the right moment or because he could not face the thought of answering her question. He flipped the knife up into an overhand grip and threw it. Naturally, both the Hur'q leaped in front of Gothmara, as they no doubt had been programmed to do, precisely as Martok had expected. His throw was flawless, and the blade flew straight and true into the metal plate that held the oil lamp behind them to the ceiling. He had concluded that this was the plan least likely to fail. If the lamp was real, the plate would break and the lamp would fall to the ground. If it was a hologram, the plate was the likely power source and he might be able to short it out.

Not stopping to see which was the case, Martok swung his *bat'leth* over his head and struck at the lamp above him. It was, in fact, real, and his blow, in addition to smothering the flame, cracked open the basin, spilling the oil into the path of the oncoming Hur'q. The lamp behind the creatures was also extinguished, so suddenly the hallway was quite dark.

Martok flattened against the wall, waited for the predictable two or three shots up the hall, then ducked and ran as fast as he could up the stairs. The satisfying crash behind him followed by screeching and hissing could only be one or both of the creatures slipping in the spilled oil.

Tempted though he was to turn and take his chances with the monsters in the dark, Martok ran as fast as he could, taking two or three steps in a bound. Yes, the desire to stay, to have an end to it all, was almost overwhelming, but a strangely familiar voice—an old woman's voice—spoke silently into his ear. It said, *"Not here. If there is to be a last stand, make it under the naked stars."*

Martok gulped air and felt the thrill of battle sing through his veins. *Let them come,* he thought. *Maybe she has taken all that I held most dear, but as long as I live, I can still deal death.* Elated, he cleared the last three steps without touching them. The sharp bite of the wind from the open door burned his face, but he ran swiftly into the night, to battle beneath a canopy of stars.

Below, down the stairs, through the narrow door, in the dark hall, Gothmara struggled to her feet. Unfortunately, the only way she could manage was to grasp hold of her creature's powerful limbs, which were covered in short, spiky guard hairs that she loathed to touch, especially now that they were coated in oil. Letting go of the Hur'q's quivering leg, she gripped the rough wall, scraping her hands and arms. "Go," she ordered, her voice low and ominous. "Kill him."

The monsters growled their ascent and bounded up the stairs baying, their blades and other weapons jangling against the stones. And though no one remained behind to hear her words, she repeated them with the reverence of sacred text. "Kill him."

Night had fallen. Crossing the snow-covered square, Martok stepped in a crack between two stones and almost broke his ankle, but the heavy boots saved him by keeping his ankle stiff. He tumbled to the ground, cracked his shoulder on a rock, but then rolled to his feet and was off again, running in long, loping strides, running low, trying to weave in and out of the wreckage. His breath came hard—fighting was one thing but running something else again, and he was an old man, or so he kept telling himself. *Old man, old man, old man,* he repeated inside his head over and over, each word the beat of his heart.

Passing out through the arch, he heard the large double doors slam open behind him. *Two hundred, maybe two fifty meters behind me,* he thought. With their stride and speed over open ground, the Hur'q would close that distance in less than two minutes. He had to find a spot to make a stand, someplace where they wouldn't be able to attack him in tandem or, better yet, somewhere he could stop long enough to call Pharh. If he trusted the Ferengi's technical ability more, he would have considered stopping now, but it would be too close a thing.

Out in the open field, with no broken stones beneath him, Martok tried lengthening his stride, putting more power into every step, but the snow was too deep and before he had gone more than five meters, he did little more than hop from hole to hole. The drifts wouldn't slow the Hur'q down, he knew; he had to reconsider trying to call Pharh. Martok slid to a halt and patted his pockets, searching for the communicator. All the bulges felt the same to him through the thick cloth and so he began to randomly unzip pockets, yanking out whatever he found, then tossing it into the snow when it wasn't what he wanted. The swirling winds drowned out every other sound so he couldn't hear how close behind his pursuers were, but then there came a hideous, ululating shriek that was whipped and spun through the frosty air.

The sound was like an electrode applied to the base of his spine; Martok leaped forward, almost helpless before the impulse to run. *More biochemical tinkering,* his calm and rational core explained, but muscle and sinew and instinct shouted, *Run!*

Boreth's small moon was barely bright enough to cast a sliver of light through the thick cloud cover. Between the wind and the thick blanket of snow, Martok's world narrowed down to the two meters he could see in front of him and the soft explosions of every footfall sinking into the white powder. His heart slammed against his chest wall and his breath came in ragged gasps as sweat poured off his face, freezing as it trickled into his beard. *Three more steps and I turn,* he thought, rationality almost lost. *Two more steps and I lift my weapon.* He anticipated a claw slashing through the back of his coat, then his skin, then his spine. *A step more . . .*

One leg sank into the powder up to the hip and there came a lurching, stumbling sense of space beneath him. The bank crumbled away and only the thick sheet of older packed snow around his leg prevented Martok from tumbling over the cliff. Thrusting back with the leg that was still on solid ground, he rolled onto his back and stabbed the *bat'leth* into the ground. Snow slid down around him, slithered from under him, disappeared into white space and twirling night. Gasping, he dragged himself back from the precipice, looking back over his shoulder as he felt the ground rumble beneath him. The Hur'q pounded across the field toward him. Did they know about the cliff? Could they see him where he lay? Perhaps if he kept his head low, they would run right past him right off the cliff. . . .

Despite his gasping for air, despite his fear, Martok tilted his head back and laughed up into the pitiless black sky. *Of course they won't run off the cliff. . . .* Weary beyond his ability to express, weighed down with snow, the tips of his fingers numb, Martok rose, shook his wet hair out of his eyes, and found his stance. If they ran headlong at him at least he would take one with him.

He felt rather than saw the first one coming, a sudden increase in air pressure before him, and then two giant eyes, black as obsidian, emerged from the white curtain. Without thinking, Martok threw himself back, bracing the *bat'leth* with both arms, point against the ground, and kicked up just as the giant's body fell on him. The point of the blade slashed into the pelt just below the creature's throat and ripped a hole down the length of it as Martok tossed it over his head toward the cliff. The monster's viscous blood gushed down over his head, making him feel warm for what seemed the first time in months. It screamed as it tumbled away, not an animal cry, but a screech filled with anger and fear and frustration.

The momentum from the blow took Martok back to the edge of the cliff and it was only the point of the *bat'leth* stabbed into the ground that kept him from falling over. Slick with blood, pummeled by the Hur'q as it had run over him, Martok pushed himself into a sitting position, then realized he might not have the energy to do any more. His fingers and toes were numb and his knees wobbled when he tried to stand.

Somewhere in front of him, screened by the thickening curtain of snow, Martok heard a hiss, then something like a muttered curse. This Hur'q, it seemed, was not too anxious to get closer, almost as if they had met once before. Martok wondered if this was one of the band that had been in the First City for his aborted execution. He had killed two of its brothers that day and now a third. Hur'q, he suspected, were not accustomed to being daunted.

Holding the *bat'leth* like a cane, Martok pushed himself up, feeling ribs shift inside his chest. One of them must have pierced a lung, too, because he struggled in taking deep breaths. Last, and worst, the leg he had shattered the day he was forced to flee Qo'noS was fractured again. He could barely set any weight on it.

The Hur'q circled to his right, looking for an opening. Martok saw the steam of its breath rising in the frozen air and heard the crunch of snow beneath its feet. Martok lifted his blade and the beast growled. It prowled around to the left, suddenly feinted in at him, then swiftly withdrew when Martok did not swipe at its head.

"You're going to have to do better than that." He coughed, spitting black spots out onto the snow, though the lung puncture might be the least of his worries. With each passing second, strength drained out of him and he felt a strange, unaccountable pressure in his chest around his heart.

Off in the distance, another creature howled; more of Gothmara's pets on the prowl. Almost as if it could not control itself, the Hur'q before him threw back its head and howled in response, and Martok knew he had his chance.

When the distant voice echoed across the plain again and the beast before him lifted its head to respond, Martok struck. If not for the deep snow and his shattered leg, the blow would have been perfect, but as it was, all he did was slash the monster's jugular. Blood jetted out onto the snow, but life did not flee the Hur'q's body. Snapping its head forward, the beast launched itself at Martok, who was ready for it. He aimed to deflect its attack, to give its heart time to finish the job, flutter and fall silent, but the edge of the cliff was too close and his body too battered.

The pair of them, monster and warrior, scraped to a halt at the lip of the precipice and, for a brief, thrilling moment, Martok thought he might be able to keep the blade pressed against its nose, to hold it, just long enough. Its eyes grew dim and he could feel its breaths coming shorter and shorter. Death would come. Its head would drop onto the ground and Martok would climb up over the corpse, find his communicator, and Pharh would get him out of there before the other Hur'q found him.

And then the ice shelf crumbled from beneath them both.

Falling, tumbling backward, Martok curled himself into a ball and felt the monster's body close around him. It was dying, of course, or dead and its muscles were contracting, but there was still something so strange about it. When they found him—if they found him at all—it would look like the Hur'q had taken him into its arms. *What will they make of that?* he wondered, and then they hit the first outcropping of rock and he thought no more.

On the lip of the ragged ice shelf, Gothmara shone a light down into the dark vale and said to two of her creatures, "Find him. Bring back his body." One of the Hur'q made a questioning noise and she replied, "Don't be ridiculous. If you eat him, what will we have to show to his son?"

The monster made a contrite noise, then slowly, carefully began to creep headfirst down the steep, icy cliff wall.

Below, in the Hur'q's embrace, Martok felt life ebbing away. He was warm again and part of his mind knew that this was a bad thing, but he didn't care. Warmth felt delicious or, at least, not being cold was soothing. On his face, each snowflake's kiss felt like a tiny coal. As his heart began slowing, the seconds lengthened. He refused to die with his eyes closed and so he exerted all his will and gazed up into the night sky. Each flake of falling snow looked like a star. Searching for breath within his chest, he tried screaming, to let Sirella know he was coming, but the wind outside stole his last breath.

The night sky was unexpectedly eclipsed by a ragged shape, and then he felt two strong arms pull him up from the Hur'q's embrace.

"Is he alive?" a voice asked, and Martok found he was ever so slightly surprised that he could understand the language.

"Barely," another replied. "The monster's body protected him or he wouldn't be."

"We have to get him back. We have to keep him alive."

"I know that," the second one replied. "I'll have to move carefully, though. Two more of her beasts are coming down the cliff."

"Then you go. I'll stay and take care of them."

"Are you sure? Against two of them? I could send help."

"Don't be insulting," the first one said. "Go."

As the second speaker began his journey, Martok felt consciousness fade. He would die now, he knew, and that was fine. Death would be warmer than being alive. *Let the fire come,* he thought. *Let it all burn away.*

PART TWO

"I accept your lives into my hands."

12

"Is that it?" Worf asked, pointing at the sensor display. "Is it?"

"Could be," Ezri said distractedly, obviously tired of hearing the same question asked over and over again. Alexander was tired of hearing it and he had only been on the bridge for a couple of hours, which meant Ezri must be near the point of wanting to take a swing at his father. After a fashion, it was interesting watching them interact and even more interesting to watch Worf pace back and forth across the bridge, almost leaping out of his skin every time the sensors alerted them to a speck of approximately the right size, shape, and metallurgical composition.

In other, much more important ways, watching his father and Dax work was torturous, which was why Alexander didn't spend any more time on the bridge than was absolutely necessary. Unfortunately, now it was necessary; Worf had scheduled him for a shift as environmental officer. Not wanting to watch his father and Ezri snarl and spit at each other for eight hours wasn't an excuse to ask for a shift swap. Everyone else on the ship had been watching them for the past forty-eight hours too.

More than once, he had wanted to say, "This is what you get for dropping a priceless artifact into a remote region of Klingon space." One of the bridge crew had made a lame joke about looking for a *mln* in a *gagh* pit, but Alexander considered this an inadequate comparison. A *gagh* pit, no matter how large, was a finite thing. It had edges and could be searched in a sensible, logical manner. Space, on the other hand, well, space had no edges. Newtonian forces (or, on Qo'noS, Kl'Vokian forces) being what they were, you gave something a push and it kept going unless (Kl'Vok's second law) something smashed into it.

About twenty-four hours ago, the ongoing "discussion" between Worf and Ezri, without either of them knowing it, disintegrated to the level of one of Alexander's grandparents' semi-daily dialogues:

"Where are the codecards to the back shed?" Sergey would bellow up the stairs.

"Wherever you left them last!" Helena would holler back.

"I put them right here on the table!"

"Then they're on the table!"

"They're not on the table! I looked on the table and they aren't there so you must have moved them!"

"I haven't touched them! Who was the last one to use the thing? Not me—you! So you must still have them! Check your pockets!"

"I don't have to check my pockets! I know I don't have them . . . !"

And on and on and on. Alexander had learned, as a boy, to simply close the door to his room and turn up the audio on the holotank. On the bridge of the *Rotarran*, Alexander lacked both a door to close and a holotank to turn up.

Countless variations on the same conversation replayed over the hours.

"Where's the Sword of Kahless?"

"Wherever you left it!"

"*We* left it in this sector of space!"

"*You* were the one who programmed the transporter!"

"Then it's got to be here! You're just not looking in the right place! Check your coordinates!"

"I did check my coordinates! You check yours!"

And on and on and on.

The quarreling almost made him feel homesick for Qo'noS, the planet where everyone was trying to kill them, cut them up into chum, and feed them to the Hur'q.

The tale his father had told him during their voyage was almost unbelievable. On the very mission during which Worf, Jadzia, and Kor had located the abandoned Hur'q outpost in the Gamma Quadrant almost four years ago, they had also recovered the Sword of Kahless—probably the most revered and legendary icon of the Klingon Empire—lost when the original Hur'q had plundered Qo'noS a millennium ago.

And though going into detail about the events that immediately followed its discovery clearly made his father uncomfortable, whatever had happened led the three of them to decide together that the time for the sword's return had not yet come. It had to wait, as Worf had put it to Kor, until it was destined to be found.

Now, apparently, Worf had come to believe that the time had come. As a symbol of restoration and renewal that, according to legend, Kahless himself had forged in the heat of the Kri'stak volcano when he first united the Klingon people, Klingons everywhere would follow whosoever wielded it. That was its power. And at this pivotal moment in Klingon history, Worf had come to believe beyond any doubt that Martok, and he alone, was the rightful heir to that power.

But to ensure that it would be a *Klingon* who would one day find it, Worf and his companions had returned from the Gamma Quadrant and set the Sword adrift in a remote region of Klingon space, on the fringes of an Oort cloud. And while Worf had a general idea of the coordinates the *Mekong's* onboard computer had randomly selected when they'd beamed out the ancient *bat'leth,* he lacked the expertise necessary to pinpoint the exact present location of the sword . . . which presumably had been tumbling end over end through a comet-strewn region of space for the last four years.

It was for that very reason that Worf had felt compelled to call upon Ezri. Jadzia's specific memories of the details of that event, as well as her formidable skills as a scientist, would both be needed to give them the best hope of finding the Sword as quickly as possible.

Suddenly, Ezri, who had been slumped against the edge of the science console, jumped up out of her chair. "That's it!" she shouted. "I saw it!"

"Where?!" Worf asked, pointing at the communications officer. He wanted the image posted on the main viewer.

"Wait . . ." Some of the enthusiasm leaked out of Ezri's voice and she sagged back against the console. Alexander had to remind himself that while Trill were not as frail as humans, neither did they have the stamina of Klingons, particularly Klingons on a mission. Worf had been awake for four or five days without anything more than a nap or two and the worst he would experience was some stiff muscles and eyestrain. Physiological redundancies allowed Klingons to endure prolonged physical demands with few side effects: one of the many reasons why they were such formidable opponents.

But frayed nerves showed when Worf repeated himself: *"Where?"*

"Hold on a minute!" Ezri said. She wiped her eyes with her fingertips, then stared into the viewer. Several seconds of twiddling controls did not produce any results. "I can't lock on," she said, her voiced edged with frustration.

"Can't lock on?" Worf rumbled as he rose from his chair. "Why?"

Ezri beckoned at the viewer and glared at him. "I don't know," she growled. "Why don't *you* take a look?"

Worf did as she bade, then spent several minutes checking and rechecking her coordinates. Finally, he pounded the console with his fist and cursed. "I cannot get a lock on it."

"That's what *I* said!"

Everyone on the bridge ducked their heads nervously. Alexander had lived on enough Klingon ships to know that this was generally the point where officers drew weapons and eyed each other's jugulars. None of the others understood that Ezri and Worf wouldn't attack, though, certainly, they had other ways of inflicting misery on each other.

Instead of being a spectator, Alexander decided to help. He ran a full-spectrum analysis of the minerals in the comet's tail, reviewing the results while Worf and Ezri snarled at each other about the relative merits of

Klingon scanners. Alexander asked, "Father, do you know anything about kelbonite?"

"Of course I do."

"Well, this area is saturated with it. It must have been inside a comet that broke apart during the last four years.

Ezri groaned. "I thought it couldn't be any worse after we got word of Morjod's last attack. Now this."

"We will never be able to lock on to it," Worf said.

"But I can get us a picture of it," Ezri replied, the animosity gone from her voice now that she understood the nature of the problem. She pressed a set of controls and the image on the main monitor shimmered. "There," she said. "To the left. It's hard to keep the image centered, but look toward the right for a bright crescent. . . ." And sure enough, when the image resolved, there it was, tumbling in a lazy arc, endlessly slashing through the fabric of space-time, the legendary Sword of Kahless, glistening in the starlight.

Alexander looked around him and saw that the bridge crew, collectively, sat straighter in their chairs, each gaze locked on the monitor. Even without a clear view of the weapon, each of them *knew* that before them was the *bat'leth* that had once been held by the first Emperor Kahless. Many of them—probably *all* of them—had met the clone, but somehow seeing this almost mythological relic breathed new life into the legend. At least once in a lifetime, every Klingon had sworn, "By Kahless's sword," and now, there it was, spinning in space before them.

"Tractor beam won't work. Does this ship have a shuttle?" Ezri asked.

"Yes," Worf said, "but thrusters might disturb the area

around the sword and send it tumbling away. If we lose sight of it, we may never find it again."

"A grapple?"

Worf looked at her skeptically.

"Never mind," Ezri said irritably. "It was just a thought." She sighed. "Fine, then. Only one thing to do."

"Yes," Worf agreed.

"Someone is going to have to go out there and get it."

Martok floated in a wine-dark sea, his arms and legs dancing in the waves like inflatable buoys. There was neither sun nor moon, but a diffused, leaden light filled the air, coloring everything—sky, sea, Martok himself—a uniform shade of somber gray. Though Martok had never feared the ocean, he had never trusted it. With a wild diversity of creatures lurking just under the surface of the Klingon seas, he knew that floating around in a horizonless gulf should concern him. Yet he felt relaxed and at peace. His arms and legs felt simultaneously heavy and light and he was not in the slightest bit worried about swallowing seawater or drowning. Were it not for the nagging sense that he was supposed to be elsewhere, about important business, Martok felt sure he would be forever content to skip along the tips of the rolling waves.

Without warning, the sea beneath him churned and the waves rolled upward into a peak as if a mountain were growing up underneath him. Martok slid down the slope, his body rigid, slashed beneath the surface, bobbed up like a cork, then swirled in the churning surf. Blinking the water from his eye, he turned his head and saw there was a mountain floating beside him, a sinuous mountain covered with silver-gray scales and edged with razor-sharp fins. He was too close to take in the whole thing, but he knew he was looking at a leviathan, some kind of immense serpent from prehistoric depths. Martok saw its gaping maw and its tremulous gills and wondered how many seconds would tick past before the creature decided it was hungry. Strangely, this thought held no particular terror for him; he was simply impatient for whatever was going to happen next to happen.

Glaring down at him with one of its unblinking eyes, the creature asked, MARTOK? IS THAT YOU?

This was not precisely the question Martok had been expecting, but since it's never a good idea to be rude to a gigantic sea beast, he said, Yes. I'm Martok. Who are you?

The serpent's slitted eye rolled heavenward and it replied (rather testily, Martok thought), MY NAME HAS NO MEANING TO YOU.

Yes, I suppose. All right, then what are you?

The monster said, I AM YOUR TRANSPORTATION. *And, with that, it opened its mouth, allowing kiloliters of seawater—and Martok—to slide down into its gullet. Martok screamed as he tumbled down into the glistening pink maw, then screamed himself hoarse when the jaws snapped shut and the light disappeared.*

Martok's face was cut by the wind of his passage as he plunged through the black. Fearful that the walls of the serpent's gullet were lined with knives, he curled himself into a ball, his face pressed against his thighs, not even noticing that he could once again control his arms and legs. He knew not how many seconds or minutes or even hours passed then in that timeless, lightless place. The serpent's gullet might have led to the center of the world, but Martok allowed his mind to go blank. For a space of time, he was a nothing, a fleck of sea foam in a torrent.

But then, after an eternity of feeling nothing but the wind against his limbs, the fear ebbed away and a thought pricked Martok's warrior's heart: This is not how a man dies.

Uncurling from a ball, Martok straightened, flung his arms out before himself, and, spearlike, slashed into the wind. The speed of his passage increased geometrically with every second until, even though it was dark, he knew that he traveled at a rate no terrestrial object could achieve. The flesh of his arms fused together, became rigid and edged like steel, and he felt his spine stiffen. I am the line that divides, Martok thought, and then he willed a change of course: not down—no more down for him, but up and away.

The tips of his fingers cut through the first layer of the serpent's spongy gut. Deeper in—or, more accurately, on his way out—he slashed through gristle, bone, and suet.

Suddenly, it was light again and Martok stared up into a bright orange sun framed by puffy, luminous amber clouds. He was out in the fresh air, arcing upward into the sky, propelled by his own force of will, catching an added boost from the creature's thrashing body. Blinded, he closed his eye against the sudden glare, but enjoyed the gust of wind against his face.

The rush of air slowed as Martok reached apogee and then, once again taken by gravity, he tilted forward, arms still stiff before him, and began falling back toward the ground. Below him, he saw the arch of a lovely emerald, gold, and burnt umber landscape and two tiny *figures at the edge of a rectangular field of waving grain.*

He was falling now, streaking toward the ground, but once again he was unafraid. A voice inside him said, You're a spear now. This is what spears do.

Martok the spear pierced the ground near the edge of the field, vibrating with released kinetic energy. A wild joy sang through his length, the knowledge that he was doing precisely what he wanted to do at precisely the right moment.

A large, gnarled hand closed around him and began to tug.

Urthog, father of Martok, picked up the spear and twisted it around to examine its point. Studying the spear carefully, without judgment, the old man said, "Here you are. I thought I had lost you."

Without hesitation, Martok asked, How did you find me?

Urthog looked back over his shoulder and raised his free arm to take it all in: the fields, the trees, the darkening sky. "I lived here in Ketha as a boy," he said. "There's very little of it I did not know."

It has changed a great deal, *Martok said.*

"I know. It was already changing when I was still alive, and not for the better. I was saddened by it, but there was very little I could do."

I didn't think there was anything you couldn't do, *Martok said.* When you set your mind to it.

Then, Urthog did something Martok could never remember seeing him do. His lips parted and he broke out into a smile. "Then you had many misconceptions about me."

You never smiled, either.

"*That can't be true*," Urthog replied, an eyebrow raised. "*I was renowned for my sense of humor.*"

I do not think so. I would have heard about that.

"*I swear to you it is true.*"

Mother never laughed.

"*That is because your mother had no sense of humor,*" Urthog said, "*but that is forgivable in a wife. I loved her until my dying breath. You know that, don't you?*"

I knew that.

"*Good.*" Urthog hefted Martok in his hand, gauged his weight, then cocked his arm back. "*You have to go now. Be well, my son. I am proud of you.*"

I will bring you honor, Father.

"*Honor me by honoring yourself,*" Urthog said, then threw Martok with all his might. He arched upward into the twilight sky, moving faster and faster, and left the fields and flatlands around the river far below. The stars beckoned, first glittering, then turning into quivering balls of orange-gold light as he reached the edge of the atmosphere. Plummeting back to Qo'noS, he felt the urgent tug of gravity, but knew no fear. Wherever he fell next would be the place he was meant to be.*

Kilometers below him, Martok spied a luminous red dot, which quickly grew into a glowing circle, then a shimmering pool. Waves of superheated air and a sulfurous reek roiled up from the pool, buffeting and tumbling him, pushing him first this way, then that. Now fear rose up within him again. Martok knew what it was below him. He had seen it from space on more than one occasion, impossible to miss when approaching the First City from the north, the prescribed pattern for military traffic. This was the Kri'stak Volcano, the mightiest of the Twelve Sisters, the ring of active volcanoes that dominated the inhospitable Kra'ta plains.

Kri'stak and her sisters had been bubbling and roiling for millennia unknown, volcanoes that did not scab over and seal, a seismic anomaly studied by every geologist in the quadrant. Some said it was because a demon was trapped under each of the Twelve; others claimed it was because Kahless himself had commanded that they never die because he might have need of them someday. Here it was that he forged the first "sword of honor" by dropping a lock of hair into Kri'stak, then plunging it into nearby Lake Lursor, twisting it with his bare hands into the characteristic curve of the bat'leth.

As Martok fell, he screamed, but could not hear himself over the sound of magma geysers exploding into the sky. No one watching could have noticed his insignificant splash when he crashed into the magma. Swirling in liquid rock, he changed yet again, unfolding, lengthening and stretching his arms wide in an attempt to embrace all of reality.

Before he could reach so wide that he was pulled apart, something grasped him and pulled him from the pool of molten rock. Shocked by the cold air, his skin turned black and sloughed off in flakes of ash, but beneath the black burrs, his almost liquid flesh burbled and threatened to lose its shape. There came then the rush of air and he was a swirling arc through the sulfurous night sky; then a downward plunge and Martok was chilled to his marrow, flesh growing rigid around his sinews.

Someone lifted him, still dripping, into the sky and swept him in a circle, encompassing the world, the galaxy, all of creation. All around him, he heard the echo of the voice of his creator, Kahless the Unforget-table, as he chanted the names of his father and his fa-ther's father and his father's father's father and all who came before them. When he reached the last name, Kah-less brought Martok down in a blow so powerful that the tip of his point cracked a great boulder, sending it flying in two directions, one to the volcano and the other to the lake.

"This," Kahless shouted, holding his blade aloft, "is the place of the new beginning." Twirling the weapon so that starlight glinted on the edge, he finished, "And this is the line that divides the old from the new."

Martok woke up.

Hunkered down beside his narrow bed sat Pharh, who was reading aloud from a small, leather-bound book. Mar-tok tried to speak, but found that his lips and tongue were too dry to form words. "Oh, hey there," Pharh said when he saw the bright eye gleaming. "You're awake. Finally."

Martok raised his hand very slowly and pointed at his mouth. Pharh understood the gesture and lifted a simple wooden cup to his lips and helped him to sip water. When Martok could feel his tongue again, he said, "Thank you."

"You're welcome. We were pretty worried about you for a while there. I'm going to go get the other guys. They said I was supposed to do that when you woke up."

Martok nodded, then murmured. "How long?"

"Couple days," Pharh said, rising. "Surprised it wasn't longer. When they found you, you were in rough shape. How are you now?"

"Now?" Martok asked, and found that he was per-forming a quick audit in a sincere attempt to answer the question. Other than being tired, he decided he felt fine.

Rejuvenated, in fact. He attempted to explain this, but when he opened his mouth, what he said was "I am the line that divides."

Pharh cocked an eyebrow. "Ohhh-kay," he concluded. "You get some more sleep. I'll go get you some, uh, help."

"Good idea," Martok said, or tried to, but before he could get the words out he was asleep again. Pharh lingered for a moment or two and was surprised, most sincerely surprised, to see that the old Klingon appeared to be if not *happy* then calmer than he had ever before appeared.

Shaking his head, Pharh left him. As Martok drifted back into sleep, he heard, "There's just no way to ever know what to expect from Klingons."

When Martok awoke again, he was much more lucid (no more talk about lines and dividing) and, much more important from Pharh's point of view, ravenously hungry. Pharh watched in awed wonder as he slurped up bowl after bowl of *katch,* the thick gruel the *katai* subsisted on. Pharh had no idea where the gunk came from or what it was made from, but he loved it. *Katch* was bland, belly-filling goodness, and he was strangely pleased to see Martok enjoying it so much. He felt better for knowing they had something in common.

He had only been awake—really awake—for less than half a day, but the old man seemed different. Putting a finger on exactly what had changed—well, there was the puzzle. Was he acting any differently? No, not really. Martok was every bit as grumpy and irascible as before. Did he *look* any different? Again, not really. He had the same gray, rumpled mane, the same worn and haggard face, and the same slab of scar tissue where his left eye used to be. If anything, he looked even the worse for wear, compared with the last time Pharh had seen him on the shuttle. His battle with Gothmara's pets had been hard on him. If the *katai* were to be believed (and Pharh most definitely *did;* it was difficult to imagine any of them lying), there was no force in the universe that could have healed Martok. Kept him alive, maybe, but *heal?* No. According to Angwar, their chief medic, Martok's spinal cord had been broken in several places and he had received major trauma to his brain. Falling three hundred meters down a cliff—even if you're curled up inside a Hur'q's body—does a lot of damage. He didn't understand how Martok could be alive, yet, undeniably, here he was scraping at a morsel of food with his fingertips.

"Good, isn't it?" Pharh asked.

"Awful," Martok said, extending the bowl. "But I'm famished. More please."

"I'm going to get the recipe before I leave," Pharh replied, looking into the kettle. The stuff left in the bottom was so badly dried he could barely stir it, but Pharh managed to crack off a piece and ladle it into Martok's bowl. "On Ferenginar the franchise rights will make me absurdly wealthy, not to mention the offworld rights."

"I'm very happy for you," Martok said. Pharh sat and watched the Klingon eat for several minutes, uncharacteristically silent, enjoying the companionable moment.

"Angwar said you would be hungry for a while. The healing ceremony they used burns up a lot of resources."

Martok lowered the bowl, his beard dotted with specks of congealed gruel, and asked, "Were you here for any of it? Did you see what they did?"

Pharh shook his head. "Only the last bit. By then, the

katai had contacted me and talked me through the use of the transporter. By the way, the automation on your computer is useless."

"Pharh, the ceremony . . ."

"All right. Lots of smoke and drums and blankets. The *katai* chanted and you talked in your sleep a lot. Do you remember any of that?"

Martok set his bowl down on the floor beside his pallet and stared into the middle distance. This tiny cell—more like a recovery room than anything—was dimly lit but cozy, and Pharh was aware of the constant low hum of background music. All the elements combined to create a restful, even meditative space, which not only aided Martok's recovery, but also made it possible for him to reflect on his recent experiences. "I remember . . . *everything,*" he said. "All the visions, from the very first back on the *Negh'Var,* just before Morjod attacked."

"You've been having visions since then?" Pharh asked. "Why didn't you mention them to Kahless? He strikes me as the sort of fellow you'd want to tell. For one thing, he'd believe you. The rest of your friends, I'm not so sure."

Martok refocused his eye on Pharh. "Visions are not such an unusual thing for a Klingon to have," he explained. "Don't Ferengi ever receive sendings from the other world?"

"Yeah, but those who do typically are sedated for their own protection."

Martok laughed and took up his bowl again, but he appeared to have lost interest in eating. He just wanted something to hold. "How much of the rest of the temple have you seen?"

"Some," Pharh said. "There's a lot to see between here and my room and the kitchen. Mostly small rooms like this one and some larger ones where the *katai* gather to talk and exercise and eat."

"Have you spoken with any of them?"

"Not much. Even for Klingons, they're not much for chitchat."

"Anything more insightful you want to contribute?"

"Not really," Pharh said, then reconsidered. There was a lot to say about the *katai*, but he wasn't sure if he possessed the correct vocabulary to describe them. He wanted to say something general like, "They're very . . . ," but then he ran out of words. Very *what*? Calm? Reserved? Dyspeptic? Wait—was that even a word? Possibly not, and probably it didn't make any sense in the current set of circumstances. *Whatever* the *katai* were, Pharh concluded, they were not typical Klingons.

"Very . . . ?" Martok prompted.

"Very . . . good cooks."

Martok stared at the empty bowl in his hands and sighed. "Where are we precisely? How far from the other monastery?"

"Since I've never been to this other monastery, it's difficult for me to say, but I do know we're deep under a mountain. I had to beam down outside and then be led through kilometer after kilometer of corridors. Doubt if I could make it out again if I had to."

"I don't think that will be a problem," Martok said, and threw the light blanket off him. In spite of his nakedness underneath, Martok didn't attempt to conceal himself when he stood. Pharh, on the other hand, very definitely *was* modest and so almost fell off his chair in an effort to avert his eyes. In the milliseconds before he could do so, however, he was absolutely astonished by the quantity of scar tissue he saw. *How can one body sustain so much abuse in one lifetime?* he wondered. Martok padded around the small room, opening the few cabinets and the drawers on the single wardrobe, obviously looking for clothing, but finding nothing more than the simple garments that the *katai* wore.

"Do you know what they are, Martok? The *katai*, I mean. I've never heard of anything like them before, but maybe they're one of those Klingon things that outsiders never hear about."

"No," Martok said, slipping a shirt over his head. "I mean, 'No, they're not something Klingons keep from outsiders.' I only heard the word *'katai'* for the first time a few days ago. Kahless said that my father was one of them. I believe they've had a bigger influence on my people's history than is known, but they wanted their efforts to remain a secret. I'm not sure about this, but if my visions are correct, they've been guiding us all along. Either them or some being they serve. . . ."

"A god?"

Martok smiled. "Perhaps."

"I thought Klingons didn't believe in gods."

"We believe in them," Martok said, searching under the bed for footwear. "We just don't fear them and we'll never *serve* them."

"Not even the really scary ones?"

"Especially not the really scary ones."

Having finished dressing, Martok stood with his hands on his hips and regarded the door. "No one has been down to see me since they brought you here?"

"No one," Pharh explained. "They seemed to believe I was your—what was the word?—*cratact?"*

Laughing, Martok corrected the pronunciation: "*Kr'tach.* An ancient word. It means 'shieldman.'"

"Like a servant?" Pharh said, not feeling at all uncomfortable if that was the case. *There could be worse jobs,* he decided.

"More like 'companion,'" Martok explained. "The one who carries my shield into battle."

"Klingons don't *use* shields."

"Precisely. So the *kr'tach* would act *as* the shield."

"Ah," Pharh said, but did not make any other comment. Inwardly, he thought, *Worse job.* "Where to now?"

"Let us find our hosts."

"And?"

"How long did you say we were here?"

"Can't be exactly sure. More than two days," Pharh estimated. "But less than four."

"Then," Martok said, holding up one finger, "in order, we have to find out why Gothmara hasn't found us." Second finger: "What happened to Kahless?" Final finger: "And where is Worf?"

"This isn't an EVA suit," Ezri Dax complained. "This is a personal, armored biosphere." Despite warnings that she should not, Ezri kept pressing buttons and switches that activated various defensive or offensive systems. Worf and Alexander had deactivated the most destructive and unpredictable systems, but she continued to find knives, concealed disruptors, throwing weapons, grapples—the usual sort of things one might find in a potentially hostile environment. Was it the Klingon species' fault if they had routinely discovered more hostile environments than their Federation friends? Worf thought not, and he had always considered Starfleet suits to be woefully-equipped. Recalling the encounter with the Borg on the hull of the *Enterprise* during their jaunt back to the twenty-first century, Worf remembered how glad he was that he had made special modifications to his suit.

"Be glad you'll have the protection," Alexander said soothingly. "And don't touch that switch. Especially if you're going to point it at me."

"Why?"

"Just don't. You'll regret it. *I'll* regret it."

Worf was pleased to see that his son got along so well with Ezri. They seemed to enjoy the sort of loose, relaxed banter that Worf had seen many of his Federation colleagues share over the years, but which he had been comfortable with only on rare occasions. Briefly, during a moment of light banter, he even found himself wondering if there might be some romantic attraction between the pair (Worf still couldn't accept that Ezri was currently involved with a man who played with *toys*), but then came the insight that Ezri was, in a sense, Alexander's stepmother. Concluding that his family life was more complex than anything he could have ever possibly imagined, Worf decided to focus on saving the empire, a decidedly more straightforward task.

Fitting the admittedly massive helmet onto the suit's locking collar, Ezri's knees almost buckled. "Can we lower the gravity in here?" she asked.

"Unlike Federation craft, Klingon cruisers are built to be simple and resilient," Alexander explained. "A ship this size does not have area gravity controls." He said this without pride, but merely as one conveying information.

"That's right," Ezri said. "You spent several years aboard the *Enterprise*, didn't you?"

"The D, yes. It was my home for almost three years."

"Have you seen the latest incarnation, the E?"

Alex smiled. "Yes. She looks like a hawk, a predatory bird. My *Enterprise* was more like a big, friendly fish."

Ezri laughed, especially when she turned and saw what she had to assume was an appalled expression on Worf's face.

"A *fish?*" he asked.

Obviously embarrassed and worried that he had hurt his father's feelings, Alexander attempted to explain. "When I was a boy, I heard the human story of Pinocchio and the whale who swallowed the boy and his father and then they lived in his belly for many years. Is that how it goes?"

Ezri shook her head. "I have no idea. Worf?"

Worf had no idea either.

"In any case, whenever I saw pictures of *Enterprise*, I thought she looked like a big, happy whale, and my father and I lived inside its belly."

"Did you like it?" Ezri asked as she lifted the helmet off and handed it to Alexander.

"Very much. It was a fine place to live, though looking back I can hardly believe we were allowed."

" 'We'?" Ezri asked. "You mean you and your father?"

Alexander was puzzled. "What? Oh, wait, I understand. No, not 'we' my father and me, but the children. All my friends. It was a different time then, a different galaxy. Can you imagine having children on a starship *now*, even though the war is over?"

Ezri considered the question carefully, then replied, "No, not really, though there are plenty of families on

DS9. I see children every day. But on a starship? No." She turned to Worf and asked, "Airlock or transporter?"

"Beaming into an area impregnated with kelbonite makes transport risky. The beam could be deflected and the signal lost."

"Lovely. Then airlock. Where's the closest one?"

"This way," Worf said, and led them out of the prep room. Before he left, he picked up a device about the same size and shape as a walking stick with a bulbous top. "Take this with you. It's an isolinear transponder. Using it, even in the kelbonite field we will be able to beam you back to the *Rotarran*."

"Good," Ezri said. "Zero g was never one of my strong points at the Academy."

On the short walk to the airlock, Worf fell behind the pair as Ezri resumed her conversation with Alexander. "The *Enterprise* may visit the station someday," she said. "You should try to arrange to be there if that happens."

"If the opportunity ever arises," Alexander said. "Assuming we resolve our current difficulties. There are several people I would like to see again: Commander Data and Captain Picard, and Deanna Troi, of course."

Ezri appeared to search her memory. "That's right. You were all very . . . familial for a time, weren't you?"

Alexander looked away from Ezri and his voice lost some of its assurance. "Yes," he said finally. "For a time." He glanced over his shoulder back at Worf, then back at Ezri. "It's not my tale to tell."

"Whatever you think is best . . ." Ezri began, but Worf interrupted.

"Alexander," he said. "It was your life, too. Of course it is your tale to tell."

"I only meant that I did not wish to presume . . ."

"You have not," Worf said. "You have never been anything less than considerate and respectful."

Alexander stopped in midstride and regarded Worf carefully. He remained silent for several seconds, then said, "Thank you, Father."

"Thank *you.*"

Ezri looked up at both of them in wonder and said, "Are you sure you two are *Klingons?*"

"Would you prefer that we hit each other?" Worf asked. "Because we could if it would make you feel better."

"We would do that for you, Ezri," Alexander said, grinning. "If you'd like."

Shaking her head, Ezri continued down the hall toward the airlock. "I think I need to go outside. Everyone on this ship is losing their minds."

Alexander shrugged. "We're Klingons," he said, as if that was an explanation, which, in fact, it was.

"Do you see it?" Worf asked through the comlink in her helmet.

"I see the comet's tail," Ezri answered, wondering how many times she was going to have to answer the same question. "Which I'm heading toward. When I get close enough, no doubt I'll see the sword." Part of the problem with traveling in zero g was that it was difficult to know how fast you were going without a reference point. The ship had matched the comet's speed, about seventy-one meters per second, and had imparted that speed to her when she left the airlock, but Ezri needed to go faster still or she wouldn't be able to cross the gap between ship and comet. She touched the control stud on her wrist, and the thruster pack punched her in the back as the chemical jets flashed.

Flecks of ice and dirt clinked and splattered against the helmet's faceplate as she moved in behind the comet, and Ezri suddenly felt very grateful for the heavy EVA suit. Without a forcefield, a Federation EVA suit would have been cut to ribbons by the high-speed microscopic dust.

She steered herself toward the outer edge of the comet tail where the debris thinned out and checked her velocity. Shooting past the sword wouldn't do any good, especially since reducing speed depleted the chem jets as much as acceleration would—and the pack had a limited fuel supply. Sensors were useless this close to the comet's tail, so all she had to work with was her own two eyes. Sweeping the powerful wrist lamp back and forth, she looked for something shiny or glinting, but quickly discovered the problem with looking for a metal object in an ice field: *everything* was shiny and glinting. It was, she decided, like standing inside an avalanche that had been suspended in time; ice crystals and specks of dirt danced in formation around her, but did not tumble past. A silver-gray cloud of motion enveloped her, but nothing truly moved.

"Ezri?" Worf's voice boomed into her ears.

Ezri felt herself jolt awake. "What?" she said too loudly.

"Do you see it?"

The trance had crept up over her so insidiously she had barely felt it. Ezri squeezed her eyes shut, but still felt sparkling lights dancing behind them. "No," she said. "Everything is the same color and nothing has an edge. It's like looking at a fractal diagram." Her suit's sensors could not be tuned to scan for metal composition, but perhaps a different index of refraction? First touching three controls on her wrist, she then moved her arm in a regular pattern before, above, and below herself. The tiny HUD on the inside of her helmet flashed and she grinned. "Found it," she said.

"Where?" Worf asked, his voice tense with excitement.

"Below me about three hundred meters, very close to the main body."

"Good. That will help you maintain a fix."

"Which I'll need because I'm going to be blind." She fed the coordinates to the jet pack's computer and let it calculate the optimum burn rate. "This is a one-way trip, right?"

"We have a lock on the transponder," Alexander said.

"All right. I'm going in." The chem jets fired again and Ezri moved forward, though she had no sensation of movement. To her, it seemed like the cloud of ice crystals parted before her and swallowed her up. There was a word for this, she knew, an expression she had heard in one of her lives. What was it? And then she remembered: "whiteout."

Ezri sliced through the comet's tail toward the Sword of Kahless. Just as the silver curtain closed behind her, she heard Worf's voice simultaneously rise and fade. He was shouting something about a ship—*"Off the starboard bow . . ."*—but the kelbonite consumed the signal, leaving Ezri entirely alone.

"It's the *Chak'ta*," Alexander called. "And two birds-of-prey decloaking off our stern."

Worf shouted, "Full spread of torpedoes! Fire!" The weapons officer responded instantaneously and Alexander watched the sensor displays intently.

"Two hits!" he called. "One ship has been disabled. The other . . ." He watched the statistics crawl up the screen. "Damage to their secondary hull, but still functional."

"The *Chak'ta?*" Worf asked.

"Is powering up her main disruptor. Should be at full power in twenty-five seconds."

"Shields to full," Worf said. "Evasive action, but stay between *Chak'ta* and Ezri."

Leskit glanced over his shoulder at Worf in disbelief. "How can I . . . ?"

"Do it!" Worf snarled, and Leskit turned back to the nav console.

Gravitational forces too great for the inertial compensators to overcome pressed Alexander first to port, then starboard as Leskit took the *Rotarran* through a series of severe turns. They had less than twenty seconds to disable a heavy cruiser. The only reason any of them were still alive was that the *Chak'ta* could not have powered her weapons before decloaking. But how had Morjod found them? A question for later, Alexander decided as he checked the sensors, assuming they survived. *"Chak'ta* is attempting weapons lock," he reported.

"His escorts?"

"Neither is moving. The damage to the second ship must be more severe than I thought."

"Or perhaps the crew is taking the opportunity to stay out of the battle," Worf said, then turned to communications, the station manned by Ortakin. "Any sign of Ezri?"

"Nothing," Ortakin snapped.

"Disruptor lock!" Alexander shouted.

"Hard to port!" Worf ordered. Leskit obeyed instantly and the bolt only grazed their starboard port shield. "Excellent!" Worf shouted. "Bring us around for a pass."

"We cannot damage their shields, Father," Alexander said. "The *Chak'ta* is too large a prize for us."

"I know, but we have to give them a reason to stay away from the comet."

"Do you think they know Ezri's out there?"

"We cannot let them stop to think about it," Worf said, "one way or another."

Here, her sensors told her. *Right here in front of you.*

But Ezri couldn't see it. She couldn't see *anything,* let alone a *bat'leth.* Reaching out carefully into the silver-white field, she swept her hand back and forth in slow arcs, fearful that striking the blade would send it spinning off into a new, unknown trajectory. Worse, the suit's gauntlets had poor feedback receptors, so it was difficult to tell even when she *was* touching something.

She touched a control, the chem jets burped, and she moved forward half a meter. Swinging wide from the shoulder, Ezri moved more recklessly, worried about her fuel supply, worried about her air supply, worried about what was happening outside the corona of the comet. How long had she been inside?

The HUD flashed an emergency signal. Outside the corona a massive amount of energy had just been expended. The suit's computer analyzed the energy source, estimated its current location, and suggested several methods for eliminating it—dependable Klingon AI routines—then warned that a shock wave moved toward her. Before she could find the Klingon suit's emergency controls, a gigantic hand slapped her in the back of the head and she fell forward, tumbling through the icy mix.

Rotarran rolled to port and the weapons officer released a volley of torpedoes. All of them exploded harmlessly on the *Chak'ta*'s shields, but, as Worf had planned, they now had the cruiser's undivided attention. He tapped a set of coordinates into the navigational computer and instructed Leskit to make for them. Banking hard, *Rotarran* skipped over *Chak'ta*, leaving a trail of aquamarine energy emissions where their shields met. The larger ship opened fire with all of her flank guns, but Leskit maneuvered too fast and, besides, knew the cruiser's standard firing patterns. He could dance in and out of the fire for the rest of the afternoon if he wanted to. Besides that, Worf could not escape the feeling that *Chak'ta*'s crew was not trying as hard as they could. *Do they wish for us to escape so they can follow, or is this a subtle rebellion against Morjod?*

Worf glanced at Ortakin, who, despite being head down over the com board, seemed to sense the attention and shook his head. "Nothing," he said. "No signal."

"Transporter lock still good," Alexander reported without being asked. One of *Chak'ta*'s gunners got lucky and *Rotarran* shuddered. "Aft shields down twenty-five percent. And that was just a graze, Father."

Worf nodded and fed new coordinates to Leskit. *Should they pick up Ezri whether or not she signaled?*

What could she be doing? Sightseeing? *What was taking so long?*

Someone had punched her in the stomach very, very hard. Bright red lights flashed before her half-closed eyes and someone was shouting at her in Klingonese to wake up. One of Curzon's memories intruded: He was a young man and had gotten involved in a fistfight with a Klingon, a matter of honor over—typically—a young lady he had never met before. Curzon was down on hands and knees, his ears ringing, his nose smashed into pulp by a single punch, and Kor was shouting at him to get up, *get up!* A large shadow blocked out the light and Curzon sensed a large boot headed for his midsection, which would account for why his ribs already ached so badly, except, wait, no . . . He was Ezri now. Ezri's midsection hurt. Someone had kicked her. Someone shouted at her.

Ezri opened her eyes and said "Shut up" in Klingon. The angry voice stopped in midword. She was snowblind, so she shut her eyes and tried to make sense of what had happened. *Something hit me—a shock wave from an explosion.* She opened her eyes, checked the status indicators on her suit. Not optimal, but at least manageable.

Carefully, to avoid dislodging herself, Ezri waved her arms around slowly and found that she was wrapped around a long metallic object. The shock wave must have shoved her here. Then she realized what held it in place.

The comet.

Moving ever so slowly, fearful of slashing her suit open, Ezri traced the length of the sword. Three-quarters of the way down, she found the point embedded in the frozen surface of the comet body. Silently damning the Klingons for the lack of proper feedback circuitry in the gauntlets, she poked at the sides of the *bat'leth* until she found the grips. Slipping her bulky fingers inside them, Ezri twisted herself around until her feet were em-bedded in the frozen slush, then tugged.

"Anything?" Worf roared over the roar of frying electronics. *Chak'ta*'s gunners had clearly found some inspiration.

"Nothing," Ortakin said. A wound in his left arm bled profusely and he was applying pressure with his right arm, but he hadn't taken his eyes off the communications console.

"Lock is stable," Alexander called, "but we'll have to drop shields when it's time to beam her in."

Rotarran's deck bucked and swelled under Worf like a straw cottage in an earthquake. Ortakin leaped from his chair milliseconds before one of the panels on his console blew out. The circuit breakers kicked in before a fire could take hold.

"Not a problem anymore," Alexander yelled.

"No lock?" Worf shouted.

"No shields."

"This would probably be easier if my ribs didn't hurt so much," Ezri hissed between clenched teeth. Her left foot skidded out from under her, but she did not release her grip on the *bat'leth*. If she fell off the face of the comet, she would never be able to find her way back. Resetting her foot, she tried wiggling the blade back and forth in the frozen snow. *Frozen . . .* she thought.

"Ezri tapped her gauntlet and called up an inventory of her suit's equipment on her HUD. "Come on," she whispered. "I saw you here earlier . . . there you are!" Hitting the proper controls, a laser torch suddenly deployed from her forearm.

Ezri reset her feet so that her legs were spread as widely as she could manage inside the suit. "Well," she concluded as she took aim and activated the laser, "if I lose a foot, I'm sure Julian can get me a new one."

"Find her, Alexander," Worf said.

"I have her, Father," Alexander said. "I think."

"You *think?* For the past fifteen minutes, you had a lock, but now you *think?"*

"There's interference."

"From the kelbonite?"

"Something else," Alexander said. "High-energy source. Laser, I believe."

The comet body was right in front of the *Rotarran,* its trail of icy crystals and gray dust flowing behind. *Chak'ta* perched right behind them, its main gun powering up for the killing blow. *Now or never,* Alexander thought. *Come on, Ezri. Let's go. We have to go.*

"A laser?" Worf asked. "On a comet? If she hits a pocket of frozen oxygen . . ."

A brilliant purple spike blossomed on Alexander's sensor display. The transporter console beeped at the same second Ortakin called, "Here she comes!"

Just before he activated the transporter, Alexander glanced up at the main monitor and saw that the comet now moved in a corkscrew spiral where once it had been moving in a smooth, straight line. Above it arched Ezri Dax, trailing a cloud of dust and debris of her own. In her hand, she grasped a metallic arc that captured and released the glory of the stars.

Ezri Dax disappeared in the glitter of a transporter beam and *Rotarran* slid into a warp space like a diver into deep water.

Behind her, *Chak'ta* paused only a moment to trace her quarry's path, set her course, and followed.

14

Footprints.

If someone had reported that a ship had dropped down out of the sky, scooped up Martok, and carried him away into the clouds, she would be disturbed, but not as much as *this* disturbed her. If someone had witnessed Martok ascend bodily into the heavens with the aid of nothing more than tiny wings that had sprouted from his ankles, *that* would have disturbed her, but not as much as this.

Footprints.

For the better part of the past two days, her patrols had swept the area, checked every centimeter of the cliff face searching for Martok, but all they had found was a pair of dead Hur'q and then, ten hours ago, a new report: almost-filled footprints in the snow. If the storm had lasted for another hour, two at the most, there would have been nothing, no footprints, and she would—Goth-mara admitted it to herself if no one else—have felt some anxiety, some uneasiness, but would have only assumed that the body was buried. Sensors were, after all, almost useless on Boreth because of the cold.

But this—this was much worse.

Footprints.

Gothmara rose from behind her desk and walked around her lab inspecting the status of various experiments. She hadn't been here in several months and most of the projects had either gone to ruin or been put in stasis by the lab programs when interesting results started to show up. Pausing briefly to inspect each station, she glanced at the status reports without truly seeing any of them. She was glad to be back inside the Hur'q base she had found all those years ago, if only because no one knew its location. Her Klingon officers found it distressing. Too bad. She needed to be here, as did her pets.

Where did the footprints go? There was only one way to find out for sure and so she had sent out the first patrol—a squad of Klingon soldiers—almost ten hours ago to backtrack the trail, but they had never returned. Five hours ago, she sent out the second patrol—three Klingons and three well-behaved Hur'q—and they had not returned either.

So, a fourth patrol was dispatched: six Hur'q and twelve Klingons. Perhaps she was being overcautious, even paranoid, but these were dangerous times. After all, she was destroying an empire. Some people might be expected to resist.

The lab computer said, *"Request for access."*

"Who?"

"Commander Q'ratt and Hur'q number twenty-two."

"Together?" She had not been expecting this. The Klingons and the Hur'q would work together when she insisted, but there was no reason for number twenty-two to come up with Q'ratt.

"Number twenty-two," the computer explained flatly, *"is carrying Commander Q'ratt."*

"Ah," Gothmara said, comprehending. "Admit them."

The Hur'q carried the parts of Q'ratt that were still more or less contiguous into the lab's anteroom and allowed the bits to slide onto the floor.

"Report," Gothmara said. "Quickly."

"My lady," Q'ratt rasped. "We followed . . . the trail to a cavern . . ." He gasped and a drop of blood slid down out of his nose over his lips. "Side of the mountain."

"Which mountain?" Gothmara asked. She already knew the answer, but couldn't hold her tongue. There *was* no other mountain, after all.

Q'ratt knew it, too, and knew he had little time left to explain. "To the north," he said, breath rattling in his throat. "Ten *kellicams*. The beast knows where."

"Where are the others?"

"Dead. All of them."

"Even the Hur'q?" She tried to keep the astonishment from her voice, but then realized, *What's the point? He'll be dead soon and the beast doesn't care.* "Who did it? How many?"

"One," Q'ratt said, answering the only question that seemed to matter to him. "He was hiding under the snow. Came up when half had passed over him."

"One?" Gothmara shrieked. "One *what?*"

"One man," Q'ratt sighed with his final breaths. "One demon. One warrior. He was . . . glorious." Then he lowered his head to the floor and died. The Hur'q sniffed Q'ratt's remains curiously, then glanced at Gothmara.

"Do you know where the cave is?" she asked it.

In its fashion, it reassured her that it did. A warm meal, however, would be appreciated before it had to lead the way.

She waved at the body. "Take it outside," she muttered. "I don't need to listen to you eat. Then assemble the troops. All of them."

The Hur'q purred, picked up the remains of Q'ratt, and lurched out through the door.

One warrior, she mused. *Astonishing.*

Later, ever so briefly, Gothmara would recall that she had not asked whether this single warrior had been killed or if Q'ratt and number twenty-two had been permitted to escape.

"Martok," Kahless said, staring at the *Ch'Tang*'s long-distance sensor scan of Boreth. "I am here. Where are you?"

"Is that the shuttle there?" Darok asked softly.

"Yes."

"And I count—how many? Seven other ships?"

"Yes."

"They will fall before us like grain before the scythe."

"Yes." They had found Ngane's fleet; all seventeen ships were prepared to lay waste to the traitors who had so ignobly murdered their general.

"But you're not happy." It was a statement, not a question.

"It means nothing if Martok is dead."

Darok sighed. While he agreed that this was true, he did not wish to be confronted with the fact. "Whatever fate he has found, it was his own decision."

Kahless glanced at him. "Thank you for stating the obvious."

"You're welcome," Darok said with a tip of his head, "though I would add that nothing is ever obvious where the general is concerned."

"It fascinates me," Kahless responded, "that you speak to me, your emperor, in such a tone, while you continue to refer to Martok as 'the general,' despite the fact that he is, in fact, a chancellor."

Darok furrowed his brow. "I have served the general and his family for most of my life. Indeed, I would even go so far as to say that without the general, I would probably not be alive today."

"And I?" Kahless asked.

"You are someone whose picture I see on coin and whose face is frequently carved into statuary."

"Ah, well. There we have it." He looked around the bridge and seemed to Darok to be able to perceive the mood of every man and woman around them. "If they learn Martok is dead, will they still fight?"

Darok nodded. "To their last breath."

"And if he lives?"

"No force in the universe will stop us until we find him."

Kahless grinned. "Prepare for the attack."

Darok rose and signaled to the communications officer. "Alert the fleet," he said. "Assume battle formation. Prepare to drop cloaks in five minutes. We go to find Martok!"

The bridge crew roared its approval, then erupted into a frenzy of activity. *General,* Darok thought. *We are ready to die for you. But we would prefer to live for you.*

Padding down the hall in his bare feet, feeling the cool slap of every step against the soles of his feet, Martok marveled at how well he felt. What had they done to him while he was unconscious? Microsurgery? Perhaps a complete nanobiological refurbishment? He had heard that these kinds of procedures were available in some systems, but did not believe they were performed on any Klingon world, let alone by a group of monks in the bowels of a mountain under an ancient monastery. But if none of these things had been done to him, then what had happened? Feeling like a boy again, the pains from his most ancient injuries, poorly knitted bones, and badly healed muscles of decades past had dissolved—as if the injuries had never happened. After walking down the long, dimly lit corridor for what seemed an eternity, Martok began running, not because he was impatient, but because he enjoyed the pure sensation of blood pumping through his veins.

They emerged from the shadows so quickly that Martok hadn't seen any movement. Both of them were plain-enough-looking Klingons, no larger or taller than he himself, yet as soon as they stood before him Martok was aware of their power. Seeing them, he instinctively took a step backward, nearly crashing into Pharh. Most of the way, the Ferengi had been a half-dozen steps behind him, panting heavily from the effort of keeping up. He staggered to a halt beside Martok and gasped an epithet.

"Sorry," Pharh said when he caught his breath. "You scared me." Possessing a graciousness that surprised Martok, Pharh introduced the two Klingons as Starn and Angwar.

"I am forever in your debt," Martok said to the pair.

"There is no debt," Angwar said. "You are as a brother, father, and son to us."

"Does that mean you get three gifts for every holiday?" Pharh asked.

"Pharh, be quiet," Martok said, expecting a sour face from Angwar, but was surprised to see him smile.

"I apologize," Angwar said. "We do not mean to be cryptic. Much of what has occurred to you in recent days requires explanation. Starn and I were just coming to get you so that you could speak to Okado, our eldest brother."

"Then please take me to him," Martok said. "I have many questions."

"Will your *kr'tach* accompany us?"

"If he can correctly judge when to keep his mouth shut," Martok said with a withering sidelong glance, "then yes."

"I promise to be good," Pharh said meekly. "Especially if there's more food."

"We will see what we can do," Angwar said, then turned to lead the way.

"My lady?" One of her Klingon retainers stood at her lab door. He was an older man, one of the handful Gothmara had spared at the monastery, mostly because she liked the fact that he could enter and exit a room quietly.

"Yes?" she said distractedly. The search teams were sending in reports every ten minutes and she did not wish to take her eyes off the com screens. "Quickly—tell me."

"Yes, my lady," the old man said. "Ships are entering orbit. *Many* ships."

"Morjod?"

"No, my lady. Not your son. Enemies—attacking your ships."

"Klingon or . . . ?"

"Klingon."

Quickly and efficiently, Gothmara ran through the possibilities: Kahless, some ally of Ngane's seeking revenge, Worf, or an alliance of all three. Mentally tallying the options, she concluded that this was not the worst of all possible outcomes. The most they could have was a thousand warriors and likely many fewer. If she could tempt them with an offer of a swift victory, their ridiculous warrior pride would not permit them to refuse. She would instruct the captains of her ships to beam down the bulk of their troops and let the attackers destroy the nearly empty starships. Then they would land their men on the surface and she would have all her enemies in one place. If by that time she had Martok's head in her hand, she would break their spirits and Morjod would go unopposed. And then, oh, how the empire would burn.

A gamble, but an appealing one.

"My lady?" the retainer interrupted.

Irrationally, Gothmara slashed her nails across the little worm's throat. If she had been wearing her gloves, the blow would have probably crushed his larynx (she was much stronger than she looked), but since she was not, his throat opened along a thin red line. The worm's eyes opened wide and he clutched at his throat, but swiftly he became too weak to even raise his hands. Blood pumped out between his fingers in awkward, pirouetting sprays, and he lost consciousness, collapsing to the ground.

Gothmara managed to avoid the worst of the deluge, but the soles of her boots quickly became sticky as she carefully stepped around the body. *That was careless,* she decided. *I should have let him call the ships first.*

"This is too easy," Darok said.

Kahless studied the reports from the attack on Gothmara's ships and he was forced to agree. Four of the six ships were already flaming balls of plasma falling into

Boreth's atmosphere. One of the other two would be crushed soon enough and the sixth had surrendered as soon as her captain had realized who commanded their attackers. Kahless could scarcely countenance it. A Klingon *surrendered*.

And all of this was accomplished without a single lost ship on their side.

"She must have most of her men on the surface," Darok continued gloomily.

"I agree," Kahless said, looking at the scans of the surface near the monastery. He was not familiar with all of the conventions for the ship's scanners, but he recognized the shape of mountains, the concentric rings that indicated water, and the sweeping lines that meant open ground. "But where? The mountains in this area are cut through with tunnels and caves. We cannot scan deep enough from this distance and if we move in too close, we will be vulnerable to ground-to-air missiles."

"Do we know she has them?"

"Can we assume she does not?" Kahless asked. "Gothmara has had many years to prepare her defenses here."

"Hmmm." Darok seemed to be staring off into the middle distance, but Kahless had, in their short association, learned the value of waiting for Martok's advisor to process information. Despite the man's sometimes too-cavalier tone, Kahless enjoyed Darok's attitude. They were, he knew, two of a kind: two terrible old men who had survived to their respective ripe old ages through a combination of guile, ruthlessness, and endurance. In short, Kahless liked Darok because in a slightly different universe he might have become him. Pointing at a section of the mountain to the north of the monastery, Darok said, "If I were her, this is where I would be."

"Why there?" Kahless asked, looking at the spot where Darok was pointing midway between the open ground and the mountains. He noted also that many tiny red and green dots were beginning to appear seemingly out of thin air.

"First, because ships could land there, near the frozen lake, but still be screened from the monastery by this ridge of hills."

"I see . . ."

"And the supply of fresh water. Not too many other places on Boreth where that would be easily obtainable."

"Agreed," Kahless said. "And well reasoned."

"Thank you," Darok said. "Also, I noticed that, oh, approximately three hundred men and several dozen large creatures are exiting this particular mountain."

"Ah, yes," Kahless replied dryly. "The red and green dots."

"Life signs."

"And here?" Darok pointed at three large gray spots blooming on the side of the mountain. "Anti-ship guns."

"So no landing?"

"No. But if I recognize the configuration—and I do—then she cannot aim them at the ground."

"But she might have gun emplacements to cover the field."

"She might," Darok agreed. "But this doesn't look like an attack formation. These men . . ." He pointed at the dots fanning out from the mountainside, all of them headed north of the monastery. "They're searching for something."

"Martok?"

"Is there anything else on this ball of ice that's worth looking for?"

"Alert the fleet captains," Kahless ordered. "Prepare ground troops for an assault."

"Ngane's crews are all light. Each vessel has barely enough crew to maintain vital systems."

"I place great faith in your ability to inspire them, Darok. I am guessing you have a gift for such work."

The terrible old man smiled. "That would be correct, my emperor."

The round-shaped council room where Angwar and Starn had led him was located deep in the mountain; lit by torchlight, it felt neither stuffy nor was smoke-filled. Either hidden modern technology was at work or the *katai* stronghold was extraordinarily well designed or perhaps both. Regardless of what "magic," seen or unseen, created the environment, Martok felt as if he'd taken a journey outside time where an ancient era coexisted with the present. That he'd come home to a place he'd never been. The sensation simultaneously comforted him and made him uneasy. He had questions. Many questions. And the *katai* patiently answered each one.

"Why did we heal you?" Okado asked, repeating Martok's last question. "For many reasons." The *Katai* Master was, Martok thought, the most ancient-looking Klingon he had ever seen. Older than Kor he was, older than his father, older even than Darok (if such a thing was possible), though he did not *act* old. In fact, he reminded Martok of a young boy, though that might be attributable to the fact that Okado reminded him of, more than anything (and here was a puzzle for another day), Alexander Rozhenko. Okado sat placidly on a low stool in the center of a half circle of thirteen stools, each one to his left and right slightly higher, each person visibly younger. The two warriors on the extreme right and left (one a man, one a woman) were approximately Drex's age and sat on stools so tall that their legs did not reach the ground.

Martok affixed the label "warriors" to these men and women despite the fact that none of them wore armor or carried weapons. He knew they were warriors the same way a master carpenter would recognize good wood without even needing to rap on it with his knuckle. "Forgive me if I fail to understand your meaning, *Katai*," he asked. "The last I remember, I was dying. Yet, here I am, less than two . . ."

"Three."

". . . three days later and not only am I healed, but I feel better than I have in many years. And I remember my dreams now, if I can call them dreams."

"Do you?" Okado asked, eyebrows raised. He seemed inordinately pleased to hear this. "What dreams do you refer to?"

Martok shifted uneasily on his feet and behind him he heard Pharh struggle to stay silent. "*All* my dreams," Martok said. "But especially the dreams of Kar-Tela, my father, and Lukara."

"Your dreamworld is rich with complexity," Okado said, eyes flashing merrily.

"Pardon, but I don't believe that's the issue at hand."

"Then what *is?*"

"The issue . . ." Martok began, frustrated, but then his innate sense of self-preservation took control. Angering or threatening these warriors would be worse than foolish; it would probably be fatal. Calming himself, he began again. "I am troubled that I do not yet know who you are, what your interest in me is, and what you have to do with my father."

While none of the thirteen men and women stirred a centimeter, Martok sensed a shifting in the subtle spaces between them, as if each was looking into the eyes of all the others and smiling in affirmation. "Ah, ha," each was saying. "Here we are at last."

Rising from his low stool, Angwar spoke first. "As for your first question, we are the *katai*. If you have been paying attention to your dreams, you know the meaning of the word."

"Firebringers," Martok recalled. "Yes, I remember now."

"Correct. We are the last true disciples of Kahless, the father of our order. Though we are based here on Boreth, we have lived among our people for as long as we have called ourselves Klingons. Some of our artifacts suggest that we were here before the coming of the Hur'q. These caverns," he said, pointing over their heads, "were carved from this sacred mountain in a twilight time that has long been lost to memory."

Quickly absorbing Angwar's meaning, Martok responded, "Your brotherhood is older than recorded history. You must know of life on Qo'noS before the Hur'q."

Angwar shook his head. "No, you misunderstand. The Hur'q destroyed almost all that they found. While these catacombs survived, no records were preserved. Rather . . ."

"You *are* the records," Pharh inserted.

Martok felt he was almost accustomed to these interruptions, but he could not stop himself from saying, "*Pharh!*"

But Angwar laughed in a manner most un-Klingon, enjoying the Ferengi's impetuousness. "No, do not chastise your *kr'tach*. He is correct. The old tales speak of the Two Thousand who survived in the most inhospitable reaches of Qo'noS's arctic reaches, as far from the Hur'q as they could go and still survive."

"The Two Thousand?" Pharh asked. "Someone . . . ?"

"It's a legend, Pharh," Martok explained. "A group of warriors who carved out a fort in an icy cliff where they waited out the Hur'q invasion."

"That doesn't sound like a very Klingon thing to do," Pharh commented.

"It was in a time before the word 'Klingon' meant what it means now," Angwar said. "Martok is correct in every respect except one: these men and women were not warriors." As soon as he said this, he corrected himself: "Not *exclusively* warriors. They were, in fact, much more. They were wise men and learned women, teachers and scholars, priests and preservationists. And, yes, they knew how to fight." He grinned. "Very well. When the Hur'q departed, some of the Two Thousand left Qo'noS as well. Others emerged as some of the greatest men and women of their era. As our world began to heal, others joined our order, or so the stories say."

"And what happened to them?"

Angwar stepped back and a young woman near the edge of the group slipped down from her high stool. Martok felt himself deeply moved by the depth and clarity of her eyes and the nobility of her manner. *Here is a woman that Sirella would have been proud to call "sister."* Then, remembering his two murdered girls, he felt his heart swell in his chest: *Or daughter,* he finished. *If only Lahzna and Shen could have learned of this place. What might they have accomplished here?*

As if taking up her part in a play, the young woman bowed, then said, "Time passed and Qo'noS began to develop a new character. No more were we the hunters and gatherers, weavers and artists of the days before the Hur'q. A harder people grew up in their place. They were brave, true, and fearsome warriors, but they lacked discipline and rigor."

"They forgot what Kahless tried to teach them," Martok said.

"Yes. Kahless taught Klingons the value of honor and discipline, knowing it was the only way to harness the terrible energies our fear produced."

"*Fear?*" Martok asked, shocked. "The Klingons fear nothing."

The woman shook her head. "And this is the lost wisdom of Kahless," she said. "The greatest lesson that he taught was simply this: We Klingons should fear nothing except *ourselves.* No one could destroy us except *ourselves.*" She paused here and allowed Martok to inhale deeply and release his breath slowly. Continuing, she added, "This is a harsh lesson, one our people have forgotten. Why this is so, we cannot say, but we *katai* have made it our law. We do not forget."

"Only the Klingon can destroy the Klingon," Martok said softly. "Yes, I see it is so. Always with us it has been the battle without and never the one within." Nodding his head, he looked up and down the line of the thirteen men and women. "I have been fighting the wrong war," he said. "I believe my father tried to warn me of this."

"Urthog was a man of great wisdom," Okado said,

"but not, alas, a patient man. Sensing that you might have a great destiny, he tried to explain our teachings to you too soon, I think."

"Or perhaps I was too dull-witted to understand them," Martok said.

Okado shrugged. "Who can say? The point, as you might say, is that your destiny has brought you *here*. And unless I miss my guess, much about the fate of the Klingon people will be decided before the sun again sets over this mountain. Blood will stain the snow—most of it Klingon—but we will settle this *today* and you, the son of my old friend, are the pivot point, the edge of the *bat'leth,* upon which it all depends. What, Martok, would you now do?"

Martok hesitated, mindful of forces in play that would never let him forget whatever he said next. His mind was troubled because, on one hand, he knew in the pit of his being that the *katai* spoke truly. His people, the Klingons, were on the verge of self-destruction; their improperly channeled energies would ignite the galaxy, turning all against them. They possessed all the attributes they needed to become the great people they hungered to be, but they were out of balance. Though they paid lip service to the concepts of discipline and honor, their actions had become a sad pantomime, their hearts locked in the past.

My people need something to remind them of the old virtues, he decided, *but also they need to see how these virtues can fit into this new galaxy. They need . . .*

An example, my husband.

The words rang as clear as if she stood beside him and spoke into his ear. Martok did not turn his head. Slowly, he had acclimated to the idea of a spirit world that occasionally intruded on his own. So he closed his eyes and listened to Sirella's voice, trusting fully, as ever, in anything she said.

"What about Kahless?" Martok asked, and the *katai* seemed to think the question was directed at them.

"The monks were too literal," Starn said. "It was not the body of Kahless that our people required or even his mind, though both these things have value."

Our people need a leader like Kahless, Sirella whispered, *who will fight with his heart.*

Martok's eye, which had been closed, snapped open as he recalled the vision of the battle in the Jem'Hadar camp and his father reaching into his chest.

Then you had better use this, Urthog had said, showing Martok his beating heart.

"Long ago," Okado said, "Kahless promised to return to his people, on Boreth. The *Katai* have waited ever since. We believe that wait is over."

You must become the leader they need, Sirella whispered.

And though he never knew precisely to whom he was speaking, Martok answered, "Yes."

15

Even wrapped in furs, even with her personal force shield turned up to maximum, even with other enhancements fully engaged, Gothmara shivered. "By all the ghosts of Boreth," she said, her breath steaming, "I hate the cold." She didn't use to, she realized. Once, long ago, Gothmara had loved these windswept, icy wastelands; her heart had thrilled to the sight of sunlight glistening on the jagged, snow-packed peaks. But those days were gone. *Why?* she wondered. *Once, I possessed the capacity to admire things outside myself, to enjoy a vista simply for the spectacle it presented. . . .* But here, today, looking out at the gray-blue plains of the northern reaches, she thought only of being warm again and Martok's blood staining these lifeless reaches.

What has happened to me? Gothmara wondered sincerely and, for a moment, for a millisecond, caught a glimpse of herself as a child in her lab, looking into a microscope and trying to unlock one of the fundamental secrets of the universe. How old was she the first time she had found her way into Father's lab? Three? Four? Certainly no more than five, because by six years of age she had already committed to memory the fundamentals of microbiology, enzymology, and molecular genetics. He had been so proud of her, ready to believe she would change the fortunes of their House. How many times had Father said to her, "It's all up to you, 'Mara. With your genius as the weapon, our enemies will fall before us."

"And so they will," she said aloud again, though there was no one near to hear her speak. Gothmara sat alone in the soundproofed rear compartment of the snow vehicle, her private sanctuary cut off from the roar of the dozens of engines around her. Reports from the scouts trickled down the data screens arrayed around her, but she ignored them. Much of her attention was focused on the voices inside her head, but not all of it.

Before her was the cave.

How had Gothmara never seen this before? After her discovery of the Hur'q base, she had diligently scanned these hills for months looking for additional installations, but had never, *ever* seen this place. Her logs indicated that she had been here a dozen times, but none of the scans revealed a cave mouth. Someone had attempted to hide from her, and, most infuriatingly, succeeded. While she had long ago decided that she would kill whoever it was who had rescued Martok, now she resolved to make them *suffer.*

Behind her, arrayed in staggered rows, were her warriors, both Klingon and Hur'q. Neither group particularly liked working with the other, but they would do as she had instructed, the Hur'q because they had no choice and the Klingons for several reasons, the least among them fear of being torn limb from limb by the Hur'q. Additionally, the persuasive powers of her altered Voice had lulled them into compliance, but her hold lasted for only so long. *What, then?* she wondered. *Do they actually believe that Morjod will lead them to glory? That some new golden era lies before them?* Shaking her head in disbelief, Gothmara knew that she was not the only Klingon who hungered for destruction for destruction's sake. *At least my hatred is focused, has given me purpose,* she concluded, and thought no more about it.

Soon enough, behind her, they would come, the warriors from the attacking ships. Her scans, though feeble and fleeting, had told her enough. Currently, with the troops she had with her and those who had beamed down and were currently in hiding, she outnumbered the opposing force by almost three to one, but she reasoned that there was no way for them to know that. The invaders would fight fiercely, especially if they believed they were rescuing Martok. If she found him first and threw his mutilated corpse at their feet, Martok's forces would cower before her. Some might even decide to join her "cause." That would be delicious: the old retainers and the new all banded together in their delusion.

Her intercom bleeped, the pilot asking to speak with her. *"My lady,"* he said. *"Your warriors wait upon your wishes."*

Gothmara didn't like being interrupted, but she realized that she *had* been in her reverie for quite some time. Looking outside, she saw that some of the warriors struggled to remain standing in the cold. Tapping the control that would permit her to speak to all of her troops, Gothmara ordered, "Into the cave. Find Martok and bring him to me alive. Kill everyone else."

Almost gratefully, her force surged forward into the cave mouth. Well, most of them, anyway. A few black shapes remained where they were, apparently unable to move, but the Hur'q took care of them as they moved past. They required a great deal of protein, her pets, and none of the other Klingons seemed to mind. After all, shouldn't the weak fall and be fodder for the strong?

Settling back into her seat, Gothmara adjusted the heat again and wrapped her furs around her. *I am too old to be subjected to the indignities of the battlefield,* she decided. *How good it is that this soon will end.*

Pharh didn't understand what had just happened, which annoyed him more than it usually did when things he didn't understand happened. He was under the distinct impression that whatever he had just missed was important, not only for him, not only for Martok and his family, but for the entire empire and perhaps even many of its neighbors. Martok looked strange. *Which you would think I'd be used to by now,* Pharh thought. *Every time I turn around there's something going on with this guy.* On more than one occasion in the past several days he had wondered if perhaps his friend suffered from some sort of neurological ailment. *Stares into space a lot,* Pharh had noted. *Talks to thin air a lot. Doesn't sleep enough, either. Bet there's a pill you could take for whatever he's got.* But, no, Martok's problem wasn't a neurological disorder; Martok's problem was a surfeit of destiny. *Too much destiny is bad,* he concluded. *Too much destiny is how you find your-self too often in a disruptor's crosshairs.* Pharh was glad that destiny had more or less ignored him. *You're just an anonymous little Ferengi and that's a good thing to be.*

Characteristically, this line of thought did not address how "an anonymous Ferengi" could find himself in his current circumstances, but irony had never been Pharh's strong suit. While he might not be in destiny's cross-hairs, he was, undoubtedly, in the blast radius of des-tiny's hand grenade, though he did his level best not to think about that.

Without so much as an "Ahem!" or a scraped stool leg, as one, the thirteen warriors stood. "She's found us," Okado said.

"Who?" Pharh asked, but even as he asked he knew it was a foolish question and regretted it. "Oh, right," he said when Martok glanced askance at him. "Her. Never mind."

"What do we do?" Martok asked, clenching his fin-gers, clearly wishing he had a weapon in his hands. "Stand and fight?"

Starn turned to Angwar. "Down here, we could defeat many of them. We know these tunnels."

If Angwar considered the plan, he did not do it for long. "You are correct. We would defeat many, but not all." He closed his eyes and seemed to be listening. "Several hundred, including Hur'q."

"And how many of you are there?" Pharh asked.

Angwar turned to him, but, surprisingly, did not try to pin him to the ground with the annoyed look most Kling-ons specialized in. "Thirteen," he said.

"That's *it?*" Pharh asked, not able to stop himself. "Your great secret warrior society numbers *thirteen?*"

"How many did you think there would be?" Okado asked, cackling with a peculiar private glee. "Our order rarely leaves Boreth, so very few know we exist. Besides, few Klingons find our cold and relative quiet to their liking."

"Good food, though."

"Thank you, *kr'tach*. My honorable mother's recipe."

"Enough, Pharh," Martok said, his voice firm. Whatever had happened between Martok and the *katai,* the old, indecisive Martok was gone. "Find me a weapon and warmer clothes. We need protection against the elements."

"As you command," Angwar said, bowing, and all the other *katai* followed suit, even Okado, who, near as Pharh could determine, more or less ran the show. *Angwar puts a lot of feeling into his bow,* Pharh thought, *bowing like he means it.* For a moment, Pharh almost felt like bowing, too, until he remembered that this was Martok, the guy who had broken into his garage and stolen his Sporak *and hadn't even paid for it yet.* All right, sure, he was the chancellor of the Klingon Empire—such as it was, currently—and, somehow or another, the focal point of a lot of weird, pseudo-mystical craziness, and these guys seemed to think he was pretty important . . .

So Pharh bowed, too. Martok raised an eyebrow at this, but let it go without comment as they all filed out of the room and into the corridor.

"Where will we go?" Martok asked Angwar, who seemed to be the leader now that the talking was finished.

"Up to the surface," Angwar answered. "We'll split up when we get there and lead the main body away. You should attempt to kill Gothmara."

"She's here?!" Martok asked, surprised. "How do you know? And why would she come?"

"She's here because she knows you are. And as to how? Same answer. She has to be. Soon, Morjod will, too, as will all the other players. None of them has any choice."

"*Frinx* it all," Pharh said under his breath, winded from the fast pace through the dark halls. They came to a wide chamber with walls hung with weapons, armor, and clothing.

"You have a comment, little *kr'tach?*"

"Never mind," Pharh said.

"Go ahead, Pharh," Martok said as he lifted heavy leather armor off a hook. The well-oiled hide squeaked when he slipped it down over his head. "You've never hesitated to speak your mind before now." When Martok tugged on a pair of straps, the armor was pulled tight around his broad chest and then he twisted back and forth, feeling for the places where it gave. Dissatisfied, he swiftly undid the straps and threw the armor onto the dusty cavern floor.

"The way you talk, like all of this is all already written, like *everything* is already written," Pharh said as he began to inspect the thick furs hanging on the walls. When he had transported down, he had only been outside the caverns for a few moments, but it had been enough to tell him he would require some protective garments.

"Everything *has* been written," Angwar said, lifting a huge *bat'leth* from a stand. "Our role is to act our parts with conviction. Conviction is the key ingredient."

"I thought honor and discipline were the key ingredients."

"They are the method by which we reach the place where conviction can be brought into play," Angwar said, whipping the weapon back and forth in midair, testing its balance. "Once you understand that, everything else falls into its appointed role."

"What about me?" Pharh asked, pulling a large fur down from a shelf and wrapping it around his shoulders. "I don't think I have a role and I don't believe my part is already written." On the wall, previously covered by the fur, he found a small, round metal shield. An artisan had pounded a picture into the metal, a Klingon woman standing on one leg who held a sword in one hand and a cup in the other. Out of curiosity, Pharh took it down and slipped the shield onto his forearm. Surprisingly, it fit perfectly. *This must have belonged to a skinny Klingon.* "What do you say to that?" he asked Angwar.

"I would say, *kr'tach,* that your role is to play the skeptic and that you play it with conviction."

Pharh rolled his eyes. "With logic like that, there's no winning against you guys."

"Let us most devotedly hope so," Martok said.

Pharh turned to him and saw that a suit of armor had found his friend's approval. The jet black leather seemed to drink in the light and the glistening silver gauntlets and greaves reflected it back threefold. Reaching up onto a shelf, Martok pulled down a bundle, quickly tore away the front of the wrappings, then laughed. "It would seem you've been waiting for me," he said to the object, then finished unwrapping and lifted it onto his head. The helmet settled down over his head, fitting perfectly. In the low light, Pharh perceived there was something odd about the helm, but it wasn't until Martok turned toward Angwar, now fully armored and holding a torch, that the Ferengi understood what was wrong: The helmet had no left eyehole. Many centuries in the past, a smith had closed the hole with a rough patch and placed the helm on the shelf awaiting . . . what? A man not yet born?

Around him, the other *katai* were all outfitted, even old Okado, and arrayed in a loose formation around Martok.

"I suppose this means we're ready to go," Pharh said, finding his place behind his friend and slightly to the left. He was blind there and might need a shield.

"How close are they, Angwar?" Martok asked.

Angwar, on Martok's right, closed his eyes and concentrated for a moment. When his eyes opened, he said, "Close. Moving fast now. They were being careful for a while, looking for traps, but now they've grown bold."

"There are no traps?" Martok asked.

Angwar grinned. "What would be the value of putting traps where your opponents would look for them?"

To Martok, each stone hall looked the same as the last. But Angwar, running easily two paces ahead of him, never hesitated at any of the many junctures. First left at a T-intersection, then right at a split into two branches, then right, then left, then left again. Lamps flared into life as they neared, then dimmed as the group passed. All the while, Martok was aware that the ground sloped gently but inexorably upward. The *katai*, for whatever reason—or the people who had first carved these tunnels—did not much care for stairways, though there were places on their road where they passed shafts on either side which obviously led up toward the surface and delved deeper down into the complex.

To Martok's left, Pharh huffed and puffed as he ran, though Angwar was not setting a brutal pace. In fact, it seemed to Martok that the *katai* wanted their pursuers to make up some of the ground between them. At every fourth or fifth juncture, the guide would call for a stop and he would listen to Martok knew not what. He prided himself on having keen hearing, but even he could not clearly hear Gothmara's horde until they were quite near. Not surprisingly, considering the size of his ears, Pharh heard them at the same time. "There," the Ferengi said. "You hear that?" They had been running steadily for fifteen or twenty minutes and Pharh was gulping air, but he seemed to be able to catch sounds between gasps.

Martok nodded. There was an echo, a low, ominous thrum in the air, as if many feet were slapping against stone all at once. "How far to the surface?"

"Not far," Angwar answered.

The air suddenly seemed closer and Martok detected a heavy musky scent. *Hur'q,* he thought. *And enough that I can smell them.* "Then let's go," he said.

Moving so silently that not even his armor squeaked, Angwar turned and led them up the corridor. Fifty paces up the slope, Martok felt chill air on his face. Behind him, he heard a roar and a shout as the pursuing horde spotted their quarry. The sound gave Pharh's heels wings and he surged ahead of the rest. Ahead no more than thirty meters there were no more torches, but only the dim glow of natural light, and then, turning a corner, Martok was almost blinded by the glare. The howl of the wind across the plains swallowed the sounds of their footfalls, but not the roar of the Hur'q as they surged up behind them.

"Turn!" Martok shouted. "Turn and fight!" They would be cut down ignobly from behind if they did not, but Angwar only shook his head and pointed at the young woman who had sat at the end of the line of stools. She skidded to a halt and Martok tried to stop, too, but Okado, always the last in the group, grabbed him by the arm and with surprising strength dragged him on up the ramp to the surface.

Martok was a large, heavy man, however, and could not be moved easily. Okado forced him on by the strength of the grip on his arm, but there was just enough time to see the first line of Hur'q surge up out of the tunnel toward the woman. Drawing her *bat'leth,* she stood patiently, and as the Hur'q swung its great arms down at her head, she stepped to the side almost without moving a muscle and let it race past. The second monster closed on her. She dove for the ground, swinging her *bat'leth* down into the base of its neck as it ran past her. Howling, the monster crumbled, its head lolling to the side on a thread of gristle. Before it hit the ground, the woman rolled to the side, landing in a bent-knee stance, her weapon raised to ward off the blow from the first Klingon warrior up from the tunnel.

The warrior died less than two seconds later, his abdomen sliced open with a single stroke. The next wave—a Hur'q and two Klingons—were upon her in seconds, but the woman was more than prepared for the task.

Martok stood openmouthed, astonished by the grace, dexterity, and precision of her blows. "How long . . . ?" he asked.

". . . Can she keep doing that?" Okado asked. "I don't know. She was not one of my students. Long enough for us to escape."

"But what of her?"

"She serves," Okado said. "And she does it with conviction."

Behind them, another Hur'q bellowed its death.

"But if we are captured, it will be for naught," Okado said. Martok looked behind him and saw the others waiting at the top of the ramp framed against the blue sky. Grim-faced, he turned away from the *katai* warrior woman and ran toward the open air.

"What is it?" Gothmara shouted. "I can't hear you over all the shouting." One of her generals—she couldn't remember his name—yelled back at her, but his voice was drowned out by the screams in the background.

"We've found them!" he bellowed, struggling to be heard. *"They've exited to the northwest of your current position and are headed out into the plain!"* What sounded like several dozen simultaneous disruptor shots echoed in the narrow space where the general was standing. Someone nearby shouted, *"We got her!"* A ragged cheer erupted over the communicator.

"What's happening, General?" Gothmara asked. "Who did you bring down?"

Breathless, the general replied, "A warrior, my lady. We have defeated her."

"And Martok?"

"He is nearby, my lady, and will be ours soon."

"Excellent."

Over the communicator, Gothmara heard a deep groan, both from the General and many of the troops, including one of the Hur'q.

"What is it, General?"

"At the top of the slope, my lady. Another one. An old man, I think."

"An old man?" Gothmara asked. "Then shoot him!"

"We are trying, my lady. We are trying."

Gothmara checked her portable scanner to see how many warriors she still had arrayed around her and how many waited in hiding. Perhaps she needed to dispatch more experienced hands to help with the hunt. Perhaps, even, she needed to go herself. It wouldn't be the first time she had to take a hand in such matters. However, even as she activated her scans, Gothmara saw that she would need to reconsider her options. Energy signatures registered all around her as warriors beamed in. Hur'q who had been hunkered down against the cold suddenly stood and shook the snow out of their shaggy coats.

Martok's defenders had arrived.

Very well, Gothmara decided. *The moment has come.*

The cold struck Drex like a blow to his sternum, knocking him backward and leaving him breathless. Cursing his own arrogance, Drex tried to keep his head clear, to orient himself, but the wind and blowing snow made it almost impossible. Darok had tried to explain this to him—how the weather would be worse than any foe, more dangerous and debilitating—but Drex had ignored the old man's prattlings.

Where was he? The dusky predawn prevented him from identifying anything but snow and ice. When Drex tried removing a personal scanner from inside his tunic, his freezing fingers fumbled and dropped the device into the ankle-deep icy slush. He knelt down and patted the ground, but the snow's frozen kiss burned his fingers. *I'm going to have to call for a beam-out,* Drex thought, and though his violently chattering jaw ached, it was not half as bad as the pain of humiliation.

Even as he carefully reached up to his belt for his communicator, a huge, shaggy shape rushed at him from out of the snow, vaulted over him, and charged toward a faint, blue outline that Drex could barely make out in the middle distance. The searing sizzle of a disruptor bolt cut through the gloom, and the shaggy shape stumbled. Another shot and the shape ceased to move.

Drex had been so engrossed in the spectacle that he had stayed kneeling in the snow, which he now realized had been a bad idea. *I cannot feel anything below my knees.* Worse, the cold had seeped deeply enough into his bones that he no longer possessed the energy to care.

The blue outline approached him, but Drex was too weak to lift his head, let alone his weapon, but the desire to live, to find his father and avenge his mother, burned brightly in him and he once again groped at his belt, this time searching for his disruptor.

Time slipped past in uneven fits and starts and he knew the cold was truly burrowing its way into his brain.

Suddenly, he felt a spot of warmth bloom on his shoulder and flow down his arms and back. Moments later, Drex could flex his fingers, but then knew pins-and-needles agony as the blood in his hands once again began to flow. Looking up, he found that the blue-sheathed person stood before him, the two of them linked by the peculiar glow. The sounds of the wind now seemed muted, too, and Drex realized he could once again stand.

Darok, still touching Drex on the shoulder, handed him a small gray and silver box with a small blue dial on the side and an adhesive strip on the back. "When I let go of you, the shield will drop, so strap this onto your wrist first, but don't turn it on yet. Nasty disruption pattern."

Drex nodded, fumbled a little, his fingers still clumsy with the cold, but managed to get the box strapped on. Darok released his grip, taking the blue glow with him, and the cold immediately dug its claws into Drex. When he twisted the dial up to high, the cobalt glow oozed up his arm, then down his back and into his legs, banishing the frost.

"What is this?" Drex asked, standing, studying the device.

"Something Kahless had made. Anyone who didn't have heavy-weather gear was issued one. Somehow, he knew you wouldn't be dressed properly." Darok's face split into an uncharacteristic grin at some private joke. "My grandmother would have chewed your ear off about not wearing a warm garment."

Drex reached up and absently touched his ear. *Which one?* he wondered and made a mental note to ask his father about Darok's family. "How long will the battery last?" he asked.

"Long enough," Darok said. "If you find anyone who's in bad shape, just touch his shoulder or arm until he warms up, then send him back up to a ship or into the cavern entrance. It's just ahead," he pointed. "That way."

Drex nodded and drew his weapons. "Was that a Hur'q you killed?"

"Yes, but it was already half-dead from exposure, I think, or it wouldn't have died so easily. Whoever's in charge out here isn't paying much attention to the condition of their troops."

"Easier to kill, then," Drex said.

"The Hur'q, yes," Darok said. "But not the Klingons.

Kahless says we should try to save as many as we can."

"They're traitors."

"When you live to be my age—*if* you live to be my age—you'll someday see that we all betray something someday," Darok retorted. "Try to save as many as you can."

"Don't be a fool," Drex said, and turned away toward the cave. "None of them would stop to save you."

"That doesn't make me a fool," Darok said into the teeth of the wind, knowing Drex did not hear him.

Another blue-lined shape appeared out of the wind-swept snow and stood beside him. "It doesn't," Kahless said. "He may survive to understand that."

Darok grunted. "If he would learn to listen."

"Did you learn to listen?"

Darok paused, then answered, "Eventually. There comes a point where brute strength isn't enough, when you listen or you cannot survive."

"I know," Kahless said. "But, like you, I am a terrible old man. We know many things the young will not learn. Such as: Keep moving on a battlefield. Enemies are all around us and any second now this gale will die down and we'll have lost our cover."

"How do you know it's going to die down?" Darok asked, and it was almost as if voicing the question made it occur. Suddenly, the wind stopped and the sheets of crystalline flakes parted around them like the opening curtain of a stage play.

The force shields muted sound, but Darok didn't need to hear clearly to know that the half-dozen Hur'q ringed around him roared in happy surprise.

Kahless lifted his *bat'leth* and smiled grimly with

deep satisfaction. Darok, less happily, drew his disruptor and wondered if Drex would be able to identify his remains or even look for them. The general would be disappointed, but, ah—looking on the bright side—he would see the Lady Sirella again soon. Bearing that pleasant thought in mind, he carefully sighted down the barrel of his weapon and fired the first shot into the Hur'q's gaping maw.

16

"What do you call these beasts?" Martok asked. Seven stalls were lined up along each side of the long, narrow cave, and as soon as the fourteen of them entered, fourteen huge steaming noses were pressed against the slats of the stall doors.

"*Jarq*," Angwar replied, opening the first stall door. "This is Sithala." The beast bent its neck and touched its wet, quivering nose to the man's forehead and inhaled deeply. Snorting in welcome, the shaggy, four-legged beast pranced happily, its great hoofs clacking loudly on the cave floor. "We are old friends, aren't we, Sithala?"

Martok took a step back, then two, then three as Angwar led Sithala from his stall. The *jarq*'s coat was a dusky off-white, yellow at the fringes and a buttery gold at the roots. Its eyes and ears were well protected by long guard hairs, and the stub of a tail was bound with white thread. Heavily shod, its hooves struck sparks wherever it stepped.

But none of these things was the *jarq*'s most notable characteristic.

"By the Grand Nagus's credit chip," Pharh said, gripping his nose. "These things smell worse than my mother's private bathroom!"

Angwar asked, "If it's a private bathroom, why do you know what it smells like?"

"That's not the point!" The Ferengi waved his hand in front of his face. "I think I'm allergic! My nose is running!"

Angwar shook his head. "Don't worry. Everyone reacts that way at first. It will pass . . . eventually."

Martok's vision shimmered for several seconds and his sinuses burned, but the wave of nausea passed quickly. Sithala butted his massive head against Martok's chest, almost knocking him over, then lowered it.

"He wants you to scratch his ears," Angwar said.

Martok complied and the beast began to trill, a surprisingly soft sound coming from such a cavernous chest.

"Are they native to Boreth?" Martok asked, finding enjoyment in Sithala's obvious pleasure.

"*Nothing* is native to Boreth," Okado inserted. "Boreth is an icy rock. *Jarq* are well adapted to living here, if you feed them. . . ." He paused, listening, then said, "Our sister has defeated those who were pursuing us, but she has fallen. More are coming from outside." Drawing his weapon, he said, matter-of-factly, "I will go."

Angwar said, "Master, no. Let me."

"Don't be ridiculous," Okado said brusquely. "I'm old and ready to die. And I hate riding these things."

"Okado," Angwar said. "I would *make* you stay."

"You could *try*," Okado replied. "But then you would have to fight this mob one-armed and that would throw off your balance." He shook his head. "Stay with Martok and guide him. He will require your advice." To Martok he said, "She will try to trick you. Depend on it."

"I will be ready."

"No," Okado said. "You won't. That's why I'm warning you now. Do your best." He glanced at the Ferengi and said, "And keep your shield at hand."

Without another word, he pulled up his hood and slipped out the cave entrance into the main tunnel. The remaining eleven *katai* remained silent for several seconds, all of them listening for something Martok could not hear, then resumed tending the *jarq*.

"There are fourteen," Pharh said.

Angwar, who was in the process of lifting a bridle over Sithala's snout, said, "Yes."

"And there are eleven of you here."

"Yes."

"And then there is Okado and her . . . the girl."

"Yes."

"Who did the fourteenth belong to?"

"To my son, Grot."

"Where is he?" Pharh asked.

"He died yesterday while leading a search party here."

"*Leading* a search party here?"

"They did not know they were being led and he killed twenty of them to make it look proper," Angwar explained while dropping a high-backed saddle onto the *jarq*'s back.

"Why did you want anyone to find this place?" Pharh asked incredulously. "You were all perfectly safe here."

Angwar did not reply, but looked at Martok for an explanation.

"Forgive him," Martok said. "He doesn't understand." Turning to the Ferengi, he said, "Pharh, their purpose isn't to be *safe*. Their purpose—our purpose—is to bring about a change. We cannot do that hiding here in these caves. We have to meet Gothmara head-on." Starn led one of the outfitted *jarq* to Martok and handed him the reins. The beast, surprisingly, did not shy away. Never having been much of a rider, Martok expected the obviously intelligent creatures to immediately pick him out as an easy mark and refuse to cooperate. "And who am I going to ride?" he asked, looking up into the *jarq*'s great brown eyes.

"Sithala," Starn told him. "She belonged to Okado, who considered her to be wiser than most creatures who walked on two legs."

Martok set his foot into a stirrup and pulled himself up into Sithala's saddle. The *jarq* danced from side to side, moving responsively to light tugs on the reins. "She needs only a light touch," Starn explained. "And she knows how to move on a battlefield."

"I am indebted to you all," Martok said. "Should I ride at point?"

"Sithala would not permit otherwise," Starn said.

Martok looked down at Pharh, who, for the first time since they had met, seemed quite small. "What about you, *kr'tach?* Will you ride?"

"I'm not sure if that's a good idea," he said. "These things don't come with handles, do they?"

"Only reins."

Pharh reached up his hand and Martok thought for a moment that they were finally parting ways, which, surprisingly, saddened him. Martok took the proffered hand and made as to shake it, then was confused when the Ferengi didn't release his grip. "What are you doing?" Martok asked.

"Trying to get up there, too," Pharh said.

"What?"

"It looks like it could carry us both easy."

"Pharh," Martok tried to explain, and somehow—un-accountably—pulled his friend up behind him on the saddle. "We're going into battle. We're going to fight Gothmara. . . ."

"Right," Pharh replied, trying to squeeze in behind Martok. "And you don't think you're going to need me? You still owe me for the Sporak."

"I'll pay you for the damned Sporak!"

"Damned right you will. Let's go finish this thing so I can get my money."

Laughing, Martok dug his heels into the beast's flanks and clucked at it. "All right," he said. "Let's do that."

As soon as she popped the latches on her helmet and yanked it off, Ezri immediately regretted that she had done so. The atmosphere in the transporter room was foul, gray with particulates and so thin that she could barely draw a breath. Alexander was standing behind the transporter controls.

"Shouldn't you . . . be on the bridge?" she gasped, finding it difficult to speak in complete sentences.

"Father sent me," Alexander said, having nowhere near as much trouble speaking.

Klingon redundant physiology, she thought. *Nothing like it in a crisis.* In addition to being smaller and less robust, her Trill physiology was also hampered by the fact that much of her system was organized around keeping her symbiont alive. Though overall, as a host, she greatly benefited from her relationship with the sluglike creature in her gut, this was one of the few shortcomings. Proportionately, the host needed more air to stay alive, but the symbiont would receive the last molecules after Ezri expired.

"We took a hit," Alexander explained. "Everyone down here is either injured, working on emergency crews, or . . ." He glanced down and for the first time Ezri saw the body of what must have been the transporter technician. "Come on. We have to get to the bridge."

Ezri took a step forward to follow, then paused, suddenly panicking. "The sword! Where is it?!"

"At your feet," Alexander said, pointing. "You must have dropped it." He approached her and lifted it up. "Let me attach it to your back so you don't lose it again. The suit has clamps."

Ezri turned around and waited to feel Alexander's hands on her back, but several seconds passed while nothing happened. "What's taking so long?" she asked as she turned to look at him. To her surprise, she saw Alexander holding the weapon in one hand, staring at it transfixed, and gently tracing his fingertips over the carved surface. "Alexander?" Ezri said as loudly as she could.

"It's . . . it's beautiful," he whispered.

"You should see it . . . when it's got a coat of polish on it," Ezri gasped, trying to invest her tone with some sarcasm despite the lack of air. She jerked her thumb at her back. "Strap it on me!"

Jumping as if slapped, Alexander did as he was ordered, then sheepishly led Ezri out the door. *What is it with Klingons and this damned sword?* she wondered.

The corridor from the transporter room to the turbolift was littered with equipment and bodies, both living ones working on repairs and others who were either dead or dying. Klingons did not bother with the niceties of clearing away the dead until the battle was won.

Inside the turbolift, Alexander fished out a small rebreather from inside his tunic, took several deep breaths, then handed it to Ezri, who did the same, then offered to give it back. "Keep it," Alexander said.

Ezri shook her head. "I have my helmet."

Alexander shrugged, but did not otherwise respond.

"How are we doing?" Ezri asked, tucking the rebreather into her belt.

"Not well. Father is keeping us ahead of Morjod, but only barely. He thinks Morjod is playing with us. His ship *should* be able to catch up to us."

"We're not being chased, but herded?"

Alexander nodded, waving his hand in front of his face. Even in the turbolift, the dense smoke made it difficult to see.

"Any ideas what he has planned when we get to Boreth?"

"Nothing except follow through with the original mission: Get the sword to Boreth . . ."

". . . And hope Martok is there to take it."

"Right."

The ship shuddered and the lights in the turbolift car faded. The car's momentum carried it as high as it could go, and then it began to slip back down the shaft.

"Free fall!" Alexander shouted, and began to frantically pat the walls to find the emergency brake.

As Alexander flailed about the car, Ezri calmly punched the switch and they shuddered to a halt.

Panting, Alexander asked, "How did you know where that was?"

"When Klingons find a design they like, they stick to it," Ezri said. "And I've been riding in these ships for ninety years." The lights flickered back to life and they resumed their journey up to the bridge.

Darok had often complained to Martok (and, in truth, anyone who would sit still for two minutes) that the young warriors of the day only seemed to know how to posture and pose with their impressive weapons, but few of them truly knew how to *fight*. When he had been a lad, back in the day when the empire and the Federation skirmished along their borders, the Defense Force and Starfleet were like packs of wild *gon,* snapping at each other's heels. *Those* had been the days.

A pair of ships would meet, they would fire shots at each other (nobody meaning to do much damage to anyone else), then bands of warriors would beam down to a planet and beat on each other for a few hours. Why, Darok had himself fought with one of the original *Constitution*-class captains, a savage man named Decker, who had been dishonorable enough to shoot Darok in the leg when they were locking hand weapons. Oddly enough, when the battle ended (not well for the Klingons), Decker himself had patched up Darok's wound and signaled the ship that he needed to be beamed up. Darok's shipmates had mocked him mercilessly until he had slammed a couple of prominent faces into bulkheads, but he had formulated an interesting theory that day: Fighting to win is not dishonorable even if you occasionally do dishonorable things along the way to victory.

Darok had tested his theory on many occasions since that day and every experiment had confirmed his initial impulse. As he shot the third Hur'q through the head (he had shot the first one in the knee and the second in the groin) he formulated a corollary: namely, there is no dishonorable way to kill monsters. The only thing that matters is that they die.

Unfortunately, as he had learned, monsters do not die easily and his disruptor's energy cell was almost depleted.

The monster's carcass dropped into the snow, its liquefied brains staining the ground. Right behind it, another Hur'q, this one less than ten meters away, sniffed the air and turned toward Darok. He lifted his weapon, but knew even before he brought it level with his eye that the warning light was flashing gold and blue: not enough energy for another shot on the previous setting. Quickly resetting the power level, Darok fired once, staggering the beast, then drew a disruption grenade from an inner pocket and tossed it expertly into the monster's path. As designed, the blast flashed upward in a field of three meters just as the Hur'q moved over the grenade, disintegrating it.

"Well done," Kahless said as he drew a small tricorder from his inner pocket. He had gracefully decapitated the first Hur'q who had attempted to gnaw on him, had severed the limbs of the next as it swiped at him, and had hamstrung the third as it attempted to kick him, all with a dancer's poise. Darok had never seen anyone who fought with quite so much artistry. There was a single word that came to mind and that word was "elegant." The general, too, had exhibited a peculiar beauty when he fought, but it was the natural beauty of a large animal in its natural setting. "Artistry" was *not* the word that came to mind and "elegant" was totally out of the question.

"How goes the battle?" Darok asked.

Studying the sensor display, Kahless said, "I cannot distinguish which are our Klingons and which are Gothmara's, but the number of Hur'q has dropped by several dozen. Unless Gothmara's warriors are killing them, too . . ."

"Don't discount that possibility."

"I shall not," Kahless said. "But unless they are, we are doing well enough." He pointed at an indistinct gray hulk that was slowly becoming visible through the thinning mist. "That way. Gothmara's stronghold is there."

Darok picked up his feet and trudged through the calf-high snow. The blue forcefield was wearing off. He could feel the cold slipping into his feet and legs. "And when we get there?"

"Find Martok," Kahless said. "Then find Gothmara if we can."

"What about Worf and the thing he went to retrieve?"

Kahless shrugged—elegantly—and said, "If he arrives after the fight is over, we'll tell everyone Martok had it all the time."

Darok was surprised. "That's a remarkably cynical attitude for you."

"My apologies," he said, then paused to wave at a pair of warriors whom he recognized from the *Ch'Tang*. "K'moth! Tong! Here! Form up on us!" The two warriors immediately made their way over the snow to Kahless.

Darok was dazzled. In the few short hours that the emperor had been aboard the ship, Kahless had learned the names of two-thirds of the crew. The only reason he hadn't learned the names of the remaining third, Darok felt, was because they had been asleep. One more shift in turnaround and the old man would have memorized them all. The emperor was, in short, everything the myth of Kahless indicated he should be.

"You were saying?" Kahless asked. "Oh . . . cynicism. Yes, well, I've had to learn to conceal it, but I *was* the ruler of an empire for many years. You don't last long in politics without developing some sort of cynicism."

"Is that what it was like even back then?" Darok asked. "Even the First Empire was ruled by *politics?*"

A trio of warriors fell in behind them, all of them breathing heavily as they marched through the snow. "My friend," Kahless said. "Every group of people living together involves *politics.* We cannot help ourselves. It is our meat and drink. Klingons often try to pretend they're above such petty things, but they are no different than anyone else."

"We are no different than anyone else," Darok corrected.

"We?"

"You said 'they.' "

"I did?" Kahless asked, genuinely surprised.

"You did."

"How strange."

A pair of Hur'q charged out of the mist at the small troop. Kahless and Darok did not even bother raising their weapons. Six shots rang out before the monsters were closer than ten paces.

"I think we're winning," Darok said as he stepped over a Hur'q's body.

"For now," Kahless said, and redoubled his pace. "But this feels too easy—calculated."

"I said that before." Darok looked back over his shoulder and saw that another score of warriors had joined them; on every side, more approached through the mists. Studying faces and forms with a practiced eye, Darok determined that their force had encountered resistance, but nothing beyond their skills. Their warriors had gashes and abrasions, a few broken bones and other minor injuries, but nothing serious. Of course, those with life-threatening injuries would have been left behind for pickup, but overall Darok thought their makeshift army looked strong and, more important, confident.

The rising sun began burning away the morning mist, revealing more about their position. Fifty meters before them was the gray hulk they had seen through the mist, now revealed to be a steep cliff wall almost two hundred meters high. To the right and left the cliff tapered away to less lofty heights, but these wings curved inward so that now the invaders stood near the center of a semicircular arena. All of Darok's warning senses jangled. "We don't want to be here," he said to Kahless, and a quick glance at the emperor revealed that he had already come to the same conclusion.

Kahless held his hand up, signaling for a halt, then made the gesture that indicated a quick retreat to the rear. Confused by the gesture, their warriors, now fifty or sixty strong, obeyed as best they could without the benefit of being organized into fighting units. *We were too hasty,* Darok thought. *Too confident in our ability to strike quickly. We're not organized for a long fight. . . .*

They almost managed to escape, but the troops at the back had not seen Kahless's signal through the mist and impeded the ranks from moving backward. Before they could be quit of the space in the center of the clearing, doors opened in the cliff walls on all three sides and the barrels of large disruptor gun emplacements were shoved out. "Break for the gap!" Kahless shouted. The warriors who could hear him reacted instantaneously, but too few could hear with the steady drone of wind in their ears; soon enough there was only the sound of shouting and screaming and gunfire.

Darok threw himself facedown in the snow rather than attempt to cross the clearing. He was too old to make the run, especially with all the others between him and safety. The gunners must have seen him and many others around him drop to the ground and, quickly enough, they found their range. Chunks of ice leapt into the air around his head and he could hear the sizzle and *pock* of the snow as it vaporized.

"K'pekt!" Darok shouted. *"I am not dying here!"* Rolling to his left just as a trace of disruptor bolts stitched the ground where he had lain, he scrambled to his knees, got his feet under him, and pushed himself up. Crossing the clearing in a zigzag pattern, he headed for the nearest gun emplacement, holding his nearly depleted disruptor in one hand and drawing his *bat'leth* with the other. He would reach the wall. He would find a throat to cut. He would, somehow, die with honor, even if no one ever knew of his deeds or sang a song about him. . . .

And then behind him, Darok heard a steady pounding noise approaching nearer and nearer. He dared not look back. With his target before him, he kept his eyes on the gunner, to try to guess where he might try to fire next. If the noise behind him was another gunner, one from the other side of the semicircle . . . ? Though it scarcely seemed possible, Darok had to know. *I will not be dispatched to* Sto-Vo-Kor *with a bolt to the back!*

But before he could determine how to look back and see what followed him, he heard another sound, one even louder than the pounding behind or the disruptor bolts in front, or the throbbing of his blood in his ears, a sound he had heard many times on the field of battle, a sound he knew well.

Behind him, Darok heard Martok laughing. The general had come to make war on Gothmara.

Reaching down within him, Darok found an untapped reserve and felt the fire of battle surge into his veins. He ran faster, determined that he would reach his target before his lord. He would show him: *Still some fight left in these bones.*

At the edge of the Boreth system, the *Rotarran* burst out of warp space, switched over to her impulse engines, and began wildly zigzagging back and forth, dropping a clutch of photon torpedoes behind her. Seconds later, General Ngane's flagship, the *Chak'ta*, emerged from warp, her fore guns blazing, shields glowing azure. Despite her great size, *Chak'ta* easily dipped and slid with precision between torpedo bursts, taking no damage, then flung a pair of torpedoes into *Rotarran's* path. Though neither missile made a direct hit, the smaller ship staggered and slowed. Her port warp nacelle glowed orange, then red, then violet. An alert engineer vented antimatter into space, but not before a shock wave ripped through the aft hull, tearing out bulkhead seams. Engineering fluids, gas coolants, and precious atmosphere that had been transported through the bulkhead spewed out into space.

Mortally wounded, the *Rotarran* commenced dying, her killer screaming in her wake.

In his short life, Pharh believed he had done many, many stupid things, among them being born into his family in the first place (which, yes, he actually considered his own fault). Somewhere in the middle of the pack was the whole leaving-home-to-make-his-own-way-in-the-big-bad-universe thing, which had eventually led him to Qo'noS. Toward the top of the list were all the many times in the past week he had insisted on accompanying Martok. Number one on the list—that moment, in any case—was actually *volunteering* to sit behind Martok on the smelly *jarq* as it bounced and rolled beneath them across the plain. Someone had started shooting at them a little while ago, which was terrifying, but not even Pharh was self-absorbed enough to consider that *his* fault. Stupidity wasn't the issue when people shot at you; ducking was.

Sadly, Martok did not appear to believe in ducking. Martok appeared to believe in shouting and laughing and brandishing his weapon and encouraging the smelly, four-legged sacks of suet to go faster. *Toward* the people who were shooting at them.

Talk about stupid, Pharh decided.

Though moving at what felt like a tremendous rate of speed, Sithala seemed to playfully weave in and out among the disruptor bolts, almost as if she anticipated where the gunner would place his next shot. Every miss put Pharh and Martok another ten meters closer to the wall. Clutching the bellowing Klingon's sides, Pharh risked a quick look over his shoulder to see what was happening to the *katai* and was surprised and happy to see that they were all still keeping pace, though maintaining a more stolid, dignified silence. They were not, apparently, quite so much the screaming type, though even across the battle-scarred field, Pharh could see Angwar's grim smile. Whatever else, Pharh guessed, the *katai* knew that this was the moment for which he had prepared his entire life. Pharh only wished he could say the same for himself.

But for what moment did *you prepare yourself?* he had to ask. And the honest answer (Pharh was nothing if not brutally honest with himself about his shortcomings) came back: *None! Which is how you end up clutching the ass-end of someone else in the middle of a war!* And the more honest part of his mind asked, *What do you do about it?* And the answer came back: *Hold on and stop complaining!*

They passed batches of Klingons fleeing from the crossfire, but as soon as they saw who was riding the *jarq,* the warriors turned around and heedlessly charged back into the killing field. Gunners, who moments ago had been mowing them down, were now distracted by the charging cavalry and seemed unable to find their targets. Encouraged, the foot soldiers formed up into wedges and pelted across the churned-up snow.

After crossing the field's center, Pharh saw only one Klingon ahead of them, a white-haired warrior whom he first took for Kahless. As they passed, Pharh saw it was actually old Darok, whom he had formerly considered the most sensible member of an insane race. And yet, here he was, staggering through knee-deep drifts up the short slope to the gun emplacements. Pharh turned around in the saddle and shouted, "What's wrong with you!?" but there was no way Darok could have heard him over the *whump-whump* of the guns and the exploding turf.

When Pharh turned back around, he was surprised to find that he could actually see what was in front of him, and this was simply because Martok was leaning down over his mount's neck, his blade lying flat against the beast's side. Suddenly, they were airborne, the gun muzzle was sliding under Sithala's belly, and Martok was bringing the point of his *bat'leth* up into the Hur'q that had been ordered to stay there to prevent precisely this sort of invasion.

The monster's entrails slid out through the slit in its gut, leaving an almost too-slimy landing spot for the dexterous *jarq*. Martok's mount skidded in the combined slush and blood, but kept its feet. Two Klingon gunners, both too surprised to react, stood stunned when Martok leapt out of his saddle and swung his blade one-handed in two bright arcs. Heads tumbled to the ground and their blood joined the Hur'q's.

Sithala danced about for a moment until his hooves found purchase. Martok pointed at Pharh. "Get down here."

"I'd rather not," Pharh said, looking down. "If it's all the same to you."

"It's not all the same. Get down here or I'll throw you face-first into the snow."

"Okay. Convinced." Pharh hopped down off the saddle, almost losing his balance because of the shield.

"Do you know how to fire one of these things?" Martok asked, pointing at the gigantic gun. There were numerous dials and sensor readouts, all of it in Klingonese.

"Unless there's a big, red button labeled 'Push me' that I'm missing, then the answer is no."

"Fine. Then you feed me the ammo charges. They're over there." He pointed at a pile of red cylinders. "Don't drop one. They're temperamental."

"What are we doing?" Pharh asked, slipping across the floor to the ammo pile.

"We're going to destroy the other guns," Martok said.

Pharh considered the layout of the cliff wall and the position of their gun, which was near the center of the semicircle. "How can we do that from here?"

"We can't," Martok said, picking up a piece of line from a pile of supplies at the edge of the small chamber, then tying an end to the *jarq*'s saddle. "We're going to drag it outside."

"Great," Pharh said and rolled his eyes. *When I have a moment to think,* he decided, *I need to reconsider my life goals.*

Gothmara's communicator chimed. It had chimed steadily for the past ten minutes, usually calls from various lieutenants and commanders requesting assistance. She had been watching the battle unfold on her sensor display and had been satisfied with the way the fight had been playing out until Martok and his friends had shown up on their fuzzy beasts. At first, she hadn't really considered it a significant change to the order of the battle; after all, there were only twelve of them. But then, when they made it across the kill zone to the gun emplacements and began using the weapons against Gothmara's soldiers, she remembered the mysteriously killed twenty-two warriors.

She had stopped taking calls a few minutes ago, having given up on this position. Other problems preoccupied her now, such as how to get to a ship she could use to escape. But she recognized this chime and answered it immediately.

"Mother?" Morjod asked.

"Who else, my dearest?"

"Are you all right?"

"I am now, my pet, now that you are here. Where are you precisely?"

She could practically hear Morjod preen at her words of praise. *"We've just entered the system and are pursuing* Rotarran *toward the planet."*

"Excellent," Gothmara said. "I'm currently engaged in an altercation with your father . . ."

"He's there? On the planet?"

"Yes, dear. Please don't interrupt. I've told you how much that displeases me."

"My apologies, Mother."

"How far are you from the planet? More importantly, can you begin beaming in troops now?"

Morjod paused, obviously to check with the navigator and transporter chief. *"In three-point-six minutes, Mother. Right after I finish off* Rotarran."

"Fine, Morjod. That's fine. You do that and then beam down as many men as you can to these coordinates." She transmitted the coordinates for a field near the battle site where Martok would not be able to see them. Gothmara wanted Morjod's father to have a few moments of false hope before she crushed him. "Then beam down yourself. The warriors will need to see you."

"*All right, Mother. I will. One other thing, Mother . . .*"

"Does it involve sending down troops, dear?"

Morjod hesitated. "*No. Not really.*" His voice sounded oddly petulant.

"Then it will have to wait."

Morjod said, "*All right. It can wait. Qapla', Mother.*"

"*Qapla',* my son."

17

She doesn't want to know, Morjod thought. *Fine. She doesn't need to know. There are things she doesn't tell me, so now there's something I won't tell her. I will make it mine—only mine—and then we'll see who will issue the orders.*

A sixth head had joined the five under the main monitor, one belonging to a navigator who had displeased the emperor. Morjod had removed the offending cranium with a single blow, a swipe so graceful that though many of the bridge crew had been surprised by its sudden, savage fury, many had also been impressed. Certainly they had all treated their emperor with even greater respect, even awe, since the headless body had slumped over his console. Sadly, she had been the best navigator aboard, and the second-best navigator—a *distant* second best—was struggling to maintain their course, though Morjod had been having difficulty understanding precisely *why*. How hard could it be to follow a ship whose warp signature you had recorded in your sensor logs?

"Time to planet?" Morjod asked.

"Six point, uh, seven minutes, my emperor," the first officer responded, his tone a little too hesitant for Morjod's taste. He liked his bridge officers to sound more assertive.

"Weapons officer—distance to *Rotarran?*"

"Ten thousand *kellicams,* my emperor!"

That was a little more like it. Enthusiasm would be a key virtue in the new Defense Force he would build when he had solidified his hold on the empire. Morjod rubbed his chin and looked around the bridge from his seat. He could not see everyone at once, which simultaneously made him anxious and also reminded him of old recordings he had seen of Klingon ships. In those images, the captain's chair had sat on a high platform— like a pedestal for a throne or a base for a piece of statuary. The idea appealed to him, and not only for his own sake but because it would benefit every captain in his fleet. "A captain should be like a god to his crew," he said aloud. "He should always know precisely what they are doing."

Sensing the crew's attempts to avoid nervously glancing at each other, Morjod smiled. He enjoyed their discomfort, reveled in his elemental unpredictability. *Not only a god,* he decided silently, *but a storm god.*

"Weapons officer," Morjod said. "Disable *Rotarran,* but do not destroy it. Understand?"

"Yes, my emperor!"

"Do you know what will happen if you do not?"

The weapons officer glanced at the main monitor, or rather, at the spot below it. "Yes, my emperor!"

"Excellent. Fire at will."

The weapons officer saluted crisply. "By your command, my emperor."

Morjod settled back in his chair, crossed his legs, and laid the blade of his *bat'leth* across his legs. Though he had told no one about it, he had become attached to this weapon, the one he had taken from Martok when his mother had captured him beneath the emperor's—that is, *Morjod's*—palace. The blade was heavy and cumbersome and not at all the sort of weapon an emperor should carry, which, in Morjod's mind, made it all the more desirable. Carrying it, he thought, made him eccentric. All the great emperors of the past had possessed some peculiar characteristic for which they were remembered. Someday, someone would ask Morjod why he used such a haggard, misbegotten old *bat'leth* and that would give him the opportunity to explain how he had come by it—taking it from his father while he had been trying to rescue his wife.

"And why do you carry this rather than the splendid Sword of Kahless?" that person would ask.

Modestly, Morjod would say something like, "Kahless's sword is for state occasions." Then he would pat the old piece of steel and say offhand, "It isn't the blade that makes the warrior, but the warrior who makes the blade." Everyone would nod approvingly, especially the grizzled old veterans. Someone would write down what Morjod said and repeat it later.

And if no one *did* write it down, Morjod would kill the entire audience and bring in a fresh one. Eventually, someone would get it right.

Studying his reflection in the polished blade, Morjod noticed a tiny nock in the edge, a subtle imperfection.

Probably the edge had been chipped on the collar of someone's uniform. *Maybe I'll throw this thing away after all,* he decided. Tiny flaws were, in their way, the worst kind of all.

Distantly, he half heard the weapons officer say, "A hit, my emperor. On the port nacelle. They're going in."

Martok enjoyed himself tremendously. He was not the chancellor now, not the general, and certainly not the glorious leader the *katai* had envisioned, but only Martok the soldier.

Sithala, as commanded, had dragged the disruptor cannon from the cave (with a little help from Martok and a *very* little help from Pharh), and he had destroyed several other emplacements before Gothmara's gunners had determined his position. Moving to a second gun farther down the row had been a simple feat, though the Hur'q in this cave had been a slightly greater challenge. Still, either Martok's abilities as a warrior had increased geometrically since he had left Qo'noS or, more likely, Hur'q did not adapt well to subzero temperatures.

After believing that he had laid a creature out with a pair of well-placed blows, Martok had turned to the gunner and his companion, only to be surprised by a smashing blow to the back of the head. Tumbling forward, Martok heard the monster bellow, no doubt winding up for a second attack, when a disruptor spat fire and the beast disintegrated before Martok's eyes. The two Klingons had stared wide-eyed at the warrior standing in the cave mouth, too surprised to either attack or even speak.

Pharh gesticulated wildly with his weapon and screeched, "You two! DROP YOUR WEAPONS!"

This would have been an impressive pronouncement if either of the pair had been holding weapons. Since they were not, Martok simply clubbed them with the blunt end of his *bat'leth* and ordered the quaking Ferengi to quickly bind them before they awoke. Quivering with hormone-provoked energy, Pharh sped to his task while Martok hitched the second gun to Sithala and repeated the process of setting up outside. This time, surprisingly, Pharh did not need to be ordered to bring ammunition.

They ran out of targets before they ran out of ammunition; none of the other guns found them amid the chaos at the perimeter of the bowl-shaped valley. After he had destroyed the three or four gun emplacements that he could reach, Martok had turned his attention to the tall silhouettes out in the field. He prayed that his shots were accurate enough to only destroy the Hur'q without killing any Klingons, but knew also that any warrior slain was more likely an enemy than an ally.

The tide of the battle drifted away from their edge of the semicircle and Martok was just beckoning to Pharh to bring Sithala when Angwar, Starn, and the other *katai* rode up and greeted them. *"Qapla',* Martok!"

"Qapla', Katai Masters," Martok replied. "What news of the battle?"

"Our numbers are evenly matched, but not our hearts," Angwar said. "Though Gothmara's beasts are as strong as ten warriors, they are few and fight poorly."

"The cold, I think," Martok said.

"She chose this field carelessly," Starn said with a nod. "What of her Klingon warriors?"

Starn frowned. He was not, Martok had noticed, quite as lighthearted as most of the other *katai.* "Traitors," he spat. "And worse—cowards! Already they begin to fall back to their caves. We will root them out and . . ."

"Starn," Angwar counseled. "Enough. Gothmara wields an unwholesome influence over them. Our goal is not to slay, but to liberate."

Scowling, Starn jerked the reins of his *jarq* and trotted off to the lower edge of the slope. Angwar sighed, but only said, "Join us, Martok. Your presence will be the final inspiration your warriors need to . . ."

"General!"

A solitary, panting figure staggered halfway up the slope, all the while clutching something to his chest, and collapsed facedown into the snowbank. Martok, recognizing the voice, slid down the hill, skidded to a stop beside the half-frozen figure, and pulled him up into a sitting position. "Darok," Martok said. "What are you doing here?"

Darok, too winded to speak, thrust the silver and black box he had been clutching into Martok's hand. It was, he saw, a Federation tricorder, forty years old if not more, the kind of prize warriors of Darok's generation frequently looted from slain opponents. Martok knew his retainer possessed such a device, but he had not seen it in years, especially since the empire had formed closer ties with the Federation.

"General," Darok gasped and pointed at the display. "Look. *Here.*"

Martok glanced at the tiny screen, but he had little experience with such devices. Darok was so insistent, however, that Martok persisted, squinting to focus on the tiny blips and dots.

"I became lost," Darok muttered. "Out on the field, so I used this to find my way." He tapped the edge of the screen clumsily. "We are here," he said. "And the mass of the warriors fighting are here." Martok understood what he meant: the mass of blue and purple lights crossing and recrossing in the center of the screen. Finally, at the edge of the screen, he noticed another mass of purple pulses.

"What are these?" Martok asked.

Darok nodded feebly. His general had seen what he wanted him to see. "Transporter signals," Darok gasped.

"How many?"

"Many. As many as are already on the field and they are coming this way." Pushing himself up weakly, Darok pointed at a narrow gap in the cliff wall across the field. "From there."

Martok looked up at Angwar. "Did you hear?"

"I heard," the *katai* said. "Mount your *jarq*. Draw your weapons. We will ride to meet them."

Martok nodded, then called to Pharh, who was standing in the mouth of the cave. "Stay with Darok. Get him into the cave. Protect him. Did you see how to use the gun?"

"I'll figure it out," Pharh said.

"Like you did the transporter?" Martok asked.

"Don't mock the guy with the big gun, Martok."

Climbing into his saddle, Martok said, "Good advice. I'll try to remember it myself." Spurring his mount, he cried, "Katai! *To me! We ride to battle!*" He did not check behind him to see whether the other riders followed, but hastened across the field toward the gap, Sithala skipping and leaping around and over combatants as if they were puddles that she did not wish to wet her hooves in.

As they passed near one of the spots where he had been shooting at a Hur'q, Martok noticed that the ground was cracked and water had welled up to the surface. The hole was beginning to scab over with ice. One of the dead monsters had fallen head down into the hole and, if he slipped inside, would be preserved just like the one Gothmara had found two decades earlier. Even as he rode, even as most of Martok's mind was preoccupied with the coming battle, he could not help but notice that field upon which the armies clashed was roughly circular. *A lake,* he realized. *So there might still be life of some kind on Boreth, below this icy crust.* For some inexplicable reason, this idea comforted him.

Morjod's troops continued to beam in, wave upon wave, row upon row. Gothmara would open the top of her car, and climb up to point the warriors who had recovered from the shock of the cold in the direction of the battle. For the first couple of hundred, she said a few words, exhorting them onward toward victory. Soon she became too cold and merely commanded them to follow the tracks in the snow, find their fellows, and destroy her enemies. When Morjod beamed in and approached her vehicle, Gothmara sighed with relief. She could depend on him to order the warriors around. Morjod was, if nothing else, an excellent orator, thanks to her modifications.

"What are your orders, Mother?"

"Find Martok and his followers. Slay them all."

"No capturing him alive then? No executions?"

"I tire of these minor distractions, my son. Please take care of this for me."

He nodded enthusiastically. "Will your pets obey me?"

"They will if you speak to them with the Voice. These have been conditioned."

Saluting her, he said, "We will be back presently."

Gothmara sat down, intending to close the top without another word and turn the heaters up to high, but a thought nagged at her. Standing again, she called to Morjod. "What happened to *Rotarran?*" she asked. "Was it destroyed?"

Morjod hesitated before he responded, something unusual for the boy. He had not, she saw, precisely followed her directions. Gothmara almost laughed when she realized that he was attempting to *plot a scheme*. Such an amusement was almost worth shivering in the cold for.

"Not destroyed, Mother," he said straining to sound casual. "But up above the planet, struggling to maintain orbit. I thought it would be . . . amusing to have some prisoners later. Worf, you know. The Federation's dog."

"But unable to escape?"

"We destroyed her engines. If the pilot is gifted he will be able to keep from burning up in the atmosphere."

"If not?"

Morjod shrugged. "There will be other prisoners." *Something on the* Rotarran, she realized. *Something he wants, but not prisoners.* He was so transparent, Gothmara could have used him as a window in her study. Unfortunately the moment to determine the precise scope of his scheme would have to wait until after Martok was defeated.

"Very well, Morjod. As you wish."

Turning away, Morjod ran across the mashed snow so he could "lead" his warriors into battle.

What could he possibly be attempting to hide from me? she wondered. After a fashion, the idea that her son would attempt to deceive her pleased her. *Almost like he's finally growing up.* Snuggling down into her wraps, Gothmara decided that should he survive the day—which she sincerely doubted—she would have to decide whether to try to ensnare his mind again or kill him. *The latter would be so much simpler,* she decided. *Yes, definitely time to dispose of this one.*

"How long can we maintain orbit?" Worf asked Leskit.

The helmsman rubbed a smudge of black char from his board and answered, "With our current vector? Two hours."

Worf grunted, then turned to his son. "Transporters?"

"Short-range only," Alexander responded. "The coordinate locking sensors were . . ."

Worf waved away the rest of the explanation. He was not looking for a technical treatise. All they needed was a way to get the sword down to Martok.

"Shuttlecraft?" he asked no one in particular.

"Shuttlebay was destroyed," Alexander answered. "Besides, *Chak'ta* is still out there watching us. She would not let a shuttle go far."

"Then why are we still alive?" Ezri asked, stomping across the deck. Though Worf would never say anything to her, he thought she looked preposterous in her oversized Klingon space armor, helmet clanking on her belt, the huge *bat'leth* clipped to her back.

"They must know we have the sword," Worf snarled. "We are being kept out of the way until Morjod or Gothmara comes to claim it." Rising suddenly, he crashed his fist against the arm of the captain's seat. "This must not be permitted!"

Ezri nodded, her head absurdly tiny in the giant collar.

I must focus my thoughts, Worf thought on the verge of snickering. *This is ridiculous. If this were Jadzia . . .* And the truth of the moment struck him: If this were Jadzia, who was always aware in some manner of how she appeared, she would have commented on it long ago, probably laughing at herself. This was only one of the thousands of ways this incarnation of Dax was different from the one to whom he had been wed. Ezri, whatever else he could say about her, was nowhere near as self-conscious as Jadzia had been.

"Then there's only one course open to us," Ezri said definitively.

Alexander, looking confused, asked, "And that is . . . ?"

"We take the sword down to Martok the only way we can."

Alexander looked around the bridge, obviously hoping someone would give him a hint. Finally, he asked, "Jump?"

"Almost," Ezri said. "Leskit, when was the last time you attempted a landing?"

Leskit turned to look at her. "A long time ago. Once, perhaps, in the past ten years."

"Worf? Would you agree that this is necessary?"

Worf took only a moment to ponder the options. *And even if we do not survive, the sword might still,* he decided. "Plot a course," he ordered. "Alert the remaining gun batteries. *Chak'ta* will try to stop us."

"And make sure the transporters stay online," Ezri added, looking at Alexander. "Just in case."

Worf agreed with Ezri, then issued the remaining orders, and settled back into the captain's chair. "And if we must die," he said loud enough for all to hear, "then let it be a death worthy of a song."

After dragging Darok into the small cave, Pharh had tucked some blankets around the old Klingon, found him a bottle of bloodwine that the previous tenants had been using to stay warm, then hunkered down in the cave mouth to watch as much of the battle as he could. Martok had been right: the battle moved away and there was very little to see from where they sat. Sighing with relief, yet experiencing a peculiar disappointment, Pharh began to check his parka for provisions.

Finding some kind of compressed ration bar in his pocket, Pharh peeled away the foil wrapper and began to munch. He turned to Darok to see if he would like something to eat and was surprised to find the Klingon slouched against the cave wall taking a long pull from the bottle and staring at him. "Want anything else?" Pharh asked, holding up the ration bar.

Darok shook his head, took another pull, then cradled the bottle in the crook of his arm like a child. "Why aren't you with him?" he asked.

"With Martok, you mean?" Pharh asked. "Because he told me to stay here with you."

"Don't worry about me," Darok said. "Old men like me never die in places like this."

"No?"

"No. We die in interesting places like, oh, brothels."

"I don't think a brothel is such an unusual place for a man to die."

"Crushed to death by a small spacecraft that falls out of the sky directly onto a bed at four in the morning, killing no one else?" Darok asked.

Pharh considered. "All right. *That* would be interesting. Has that ever happened?"

"My father," Darok said proudly. "When they found him he was only about a centimeter thick, but they could still make out the smile on his face."

"Well," Pharh said, trying to find the appropriate words. "How nice. For him. And you, too." He pondered the image for a moment, then said, "I have a question."

"Ask. If I know, I'll tell you. I'm feeling very generous right this moment. And then I'll ask you a question."

"Deal. Here's my question: What do Klingons think happens when they die?"

Darok took another drink (the bottle was almost half empty now), then said slowly. "If we die well—meaning usually in battle—many believe we go to a place called *Sto-Vo-Kor*. All the great warriors of the past live there and the good Klingons get to eat and drink and fight and whatever else they want to do as much as they want, whenever they want."

"And if not?" Pharh asked. "If they don't die well?"

"There's the less pleasant option reserved for cowards and traitors and well, you know, bad people. . . ." Darok's eyes began to droop.

Pharh perceived that Darok's injuries and a failure to eat that day had made him more susceptible to the bloodwine. *First the slurred words, then a few rousing battle songs, then maybe he'll pass out*, he thought philosophically.

"The Barge of the Dead and then after that . . . Mother."

"Mother?"

"She'll be there . . . somewhere."

"She's dead, your mother?"

"By Kahless's sword, I hope so! How about yours?"

"Still alive," Pharh sighed. "Last I heard."

"What do Ferengi believe happens to them when they die?"

"Is that your question?"

"It's *a* question. Just answer it."

"Most Ferengi believe we go before the Great Auditor and are grilled for three days and three nights about our business dealings. . . ."

"Ooo. A little of the old hot charcoals, eh?"

"What?" Pharh asked. "Oh. No . . . Not 'grilled.' *Questioned.*"

"Same thing," Darok said after swallowing half of what was left in the bottle. "Then what?"

"And the Celestial Board decides whether we are allowed to become Vested."

"Which means?"

"We can go on to the Divine Treasury and exist comfortably from what's in our portfolios."

"And if not?"

"The Vault of Eternal Destitution."

Darok made a face. "Neither sounds really appealing, does it? How do you think you're doing?"

"Not well," Pharh admitted. "I've never been good at business and I can't get too excited by the idea of being Vested. Oh, the Celestial Secretarial Pool sounds nice enough, but other than that . . ."

"*Sto-Vo-Kor* sounds like a lot more fun," Darok said.

"I thought so, too."

"Maybe you could ask Martok about it. He might be able to get you in."

Pharh was surprised. "You can do that?"

"If you're part of the family. Worf did it for his wife Jadzia."

"The Trill."

"Right."

"Interesting relationship there," Pharh observed discreetly.

"Phpht!" Darok said, spraying a little. "You don't know the half of it."

They both stayed quiet for a couple of minutes while Pharh finished his ration bar and Darok finished his bottle. After sucking down the last drop, Darok piped up, "Now, my question. . . ."

"Thought you asked a question."

"But not *the* question."

"All right."

"So why aren't you with him?"

"You already asked me that."

"Did you have a good answer?"

Pharh considered, then answered, "No, not really. Well, yes: Because I'm afraid to die."

"Don't worry about that, boy," Darok said. "Take it from me. I'm much older than you and have seen hundreds of people die. Dying is easy."

"And commodities are hard."

"Precisely. So you should go help him. You're his *kr'tach* after all."

"Oh. One of the *katai* told you that."

"They didn't have to. I know a *kr'tach* when I see one. Though I never saw one with such big ears."

Zipping up the hood of his parka, Pharh asked, "You'll be all right?"

"I'll be fine. Make sure you have the safety off the disruptor. Nothing as embarrassing as having the safety on when you need it off."

"I bet," Pharh said stepping out into the wind. "Thanks for everything. We'll come back and get you when the battle's over. You'll be fine here."

"I'll be fine."

Pharh left.

Ten minutes later, Darok closed his eyes, his heart stopped, and he died peacefully with a smile on his face, as if he had just seen someone whom he had been waiting to see for a long, *long* time.

Or, possibly, he had just avoided seeing someone that he feared he *would* see. There was really no way to know for sure.

18

Kahless took two steps through the knee-deep snow, slashed with his *bat'leth,* leaped to his left, slashed again, then slid under the legs of the Hur'q as it collapsed face-forward into the snow. To his right, Drex fired the disruptor he held in his left hand at a Klingon warrior while slashing at the throat of an opponent with the blade in his right. *Well,* Kahless conceded. *He is efficient. I'll give him that.*

Drex dodged a third opponent, tripped him up with an extended leg, and when the warrior went sprawling in the snow, Martok's son shot him in the back of the head. *Perhaps too efficient,* Kahless decided.

Pausing, the pair quickly checked the immediate vicinity and, deciding they were for the moment not in mortal danger, regarded each other. Inspecting the pile of bodies around them, Kahless asked the boy, "How do you know if the Klingon you're attacking is an enemy?"

Drex dabbed his hand against his cheek where it had

been slashed open. "If they're running at me, I assume they're enemies, so I kill them," he said, panting slightly.

"And if they're running away?"

"They're enemies and I kill them."

Kahless shook his head in baffled amazement. He had been focusing his attentions on the Hur'q, partly because they did not unnerve him the way they seemed to with some of the others and partly because he did not like killing Klingons—*any* Klingons. Drex, on the other hand, more than made up for the emperor's hesitation.

Somewhere during their passage across the wide plain, they had lost Darok, which worried Kahless. He had seen mounted warriors ride past just as the battle had been joined and, assuming Martok must be among them, pursued them. Cannon fire had begun and Kahless had thought his troops were lost, but then someone—the riders, perhaps?—had obviously taken control of one or two guns and made short work of guns manned by Gothmara's troops. Then, the remaining guns had turned their fire on the Hur'q and killed many of them. All in all, despite what seemed like an early advantage for Gothmara's forces, Martok's side was doing quite well.

Now, having pursued opponents farther and farther away from the main flow of the battle, he and Drex found themselves at its fringe near a narrow gap. Not wishing to be surprised by new assailants, yet curious about what might lie beyond, Kahless rested and considered. Drex drank from a flask of bloodwine he had brought and grinned maniacally. "A good fight, eh, Emperor?"

Kahless nodded. What else could he do? It *was* a good fight. His blood, he knew, should be singing, his heart aflame with battle fever. He was a Klingon, some would even say *the* Klingon. By the evidence of his senses, he was an adequate warrior, but still a shadow of the original. And yet, and yet . . .

Perhaps the legend of Kahless being the greatest warrior the empire had ever known was true, but why had everyone assumed that the emperor should *enjoy* battle? He knew he was only a clone, that the memories he possessed of his life in the dawn of the empire were really only tales extrapolated from myths of a bygone era. But his heart was the heart of Kahless, his blood Kahless's blood, and it was not aflame nor did it sing. Could it be possible that Kahless, the *true* Kahless, had not enjoyed battle for battle's sake, but only done what he had considered to be his duty? Could this be the one true memory of that life? He shook his head. A weariness had been growing upon him despite the press of duty. He had been feeling it in his bones for many weeks and months. If Gothmara succeeded in her nefarious plans, then the point was moot. If Martok's forces were victorious, then he would have a choice before him. . . .

"But not today," he muttered, lifting his blade and checking the edge.

"What?" Drex asked.

"Not your concern, boy," Kahless said. "We need to get back to . . ."

A disruptor shot sizzled through the gap, snagging Drex's shoulder and tumbling him facedown into the snow. Though half-conscious from the impact, the boy began to scream, though whether in pain or anger Kahless did not know.

A figure stalked out from the narrow gap, a Hur'q carrying a large disruptor rifle. Kahless raised his blade and took a tentative step forward, but then he felt a rumble beneath his feet. *Damnation,* he thought. *I've been feeling this for the past five minutes, but I've been too preoccupied with my ridiculous musings!*

Another Hur'q pressed through the gap and then a third. All three of them spotted Kahless simultaneously and lifted their rifles to their shoulders. No escape presented itself. Ridiculously, Kahless found himself thinking, *A decision I won't have to make,* then prepared himself to find out whether clones go to *Sto-Vo-Kor.*

One of the monsters dropped its rifle, its eye pierced by a disruptor bolt. Screaming, it lashed out, spoiling the aim of the other two. Kahless tore his eyes away from his attackers to see Drex propping himself up with one arm, the muzzle of his weapon laid over his knees to hold it steady. *"Ha'DIbaH!"* he shouted, then fired again, but this shot went wide of the mark by several meters. Trembling with shock, he sagged back to the ground and dropped the weapon, the snow turning magenta with his blood. *The bolt didn't cauterize the wound,* Kahless realized. After slinging his blade onto his back, Kahless crouched, grabbed the boy's uninjured arm, and pulled him up over his shoulders, then turned and trudged as fast as he could in the churned-up snow.

Behind him he heard the beat of drums and beneath his feet the ground began to tremble. Experience on a thousand battlefields told Kahless that countless warriors approached. Having to squeeze through the gap would slow them down, but not for long; the emperor had no idea what he would do when they reached the circular plain.

Running down the narrow valley, the drums and footsteps growing fainter behind him, Kahless suddenly became aware of another pounding beat before him. *Could some of them have circled around before me?* he wondered, but no sooner had the thought crossed his mind than he recognized the source of the thunderous beat.

At the mouth of the valley, he saw a dozen great, shaggy beasts headed toward him and astride them twelve warriors. At the fore rode Martok, his *bat'leth* held high glittering in the sun, hair streaming behind him, his cloak snapping and rippling. Though Kahless knew a host of demons was behind him, still he had to stop and stare in awe and wonder.

As they swept past him, the clods of snow cast out from behind their mounts' hooves struck Kahless and Drex in the back. As the thunder of their passage receded, Drex whispered hoarsely, "Put me down. Go fight."

"I can't leave you . . ."

"If I cannot survive on my own," he hissed, "I do not deserve to live." Then, more softly, Drex said, "My father needs you, warrior." Not "Kahless" or "Emperor," but "warrior."

Kahless trudged to the edge of the canyon and deposited Drex in a crack in the rocks. After quickly binding the boy's shoulder with strips of cloth torn from his cloak, the emperor made sure the forcefield generator still functioned and was turned up to full. Kahless did not like the fact that Drex had no color in his face, but the boy was conscious and appeared lucid. "You're taking too long."

"Don't give orders to the emperor," Kahless said. "Everyone has been doing that to me lately."

"Perhaps if you acted more like an emperor," Drex muttered, "and less like . . . like . . . the humans have a word for it. Someone who entertains by performing tricks."

"Priest?" Kahless asked. His knowledge of Federation Standard was good, but his command of idiom was poor.

"No. Not religion. The other kind of trick . . . clever sleight of hand."

Kahless thought about it. This was eating up valuable time, but now he felt like he had to know. He tried to recall some of the human entertainments he had read or seen, but they were usually incomprehensible to him. There had been one old story, though, that he had liked and the characters in it had sung often enough to please him. One character—an old man with white hair who was always a little smarter than everyone else . . . What had they called him? "Wizard?" Kahless asked.

Drex's eyes started to glaze over with pain, but he said, "Something like that. Yes . . . Don't be one of those. Be a warrior now. Father needs warriors."

"A lot of them, I warrant," Kahless said, and patted the boy on his good shoulder. "Stay here and I'll find some."

And thus, rather than follow Martok and his riders into the gap as he would have preferred, Kahless ran back to the field to gather as many allies as he could with his tricks and sleight of hand. But, as he ran, under his breath, he muttered, "Wizard, eh? Then maybe if this all ends well, I'll need to do one more trick."

Riding into battle, Martok felt young. Years fell away with every heartbeat, with every jolt from the saddle up through the base of his spine. He was a man of fifty, no forty, no *thirty* again. Snow whipping into his face, his blade held high, he laughed for the pure joy of speed and strength and vigor. To his right, Angwar bellowed a war cry. Grim Starn at Martok's left rose up on his stirrups, held a horn to his lips, and blew a blast so loud and reverberating that it threatened to shake the ice from the canyon walls.

A hundred meters before them, a pack of Hur'q bunched around a narrow crack in the canyon, two trying to squeeze through simultaneously while a pair of Klingon warriors crouching in the snow attempted to set up some kind of mortar cannon. Martok turned to see if Angwar saw it too and, yes, obviously he did. The *Katai* Master drew his disruptor, a huge antique-looking piece of hardware, was able to take aim on his galloping beast, and fired.

The ground in front of the mortar exploded into the Klingons, throwing them backward, slashing them with splintered ice. A thick sliver of rock calved away from the canyon wall above the crack and tumbled down onto the neck of a Hur'q, practically splitting the creature in half. The other Hur'q turned round and round in bafflement, each of them stunned and unable to see where the attack came from.

"Hah!" Martok shouted above the fray. "One shot! Brilliant!"

Hearing voices, but uncertain about their source, the confused monsters began firing their weapons at random.

"Back!" Angwar shouted even as he set his spurs to his *jarq,* but Martok, never an experienced rider, fumbled his reins even as he saw the danger before them: the damned idiot Hur'q had his weapon pointed at a case of mortar shells.

The concussion from the explosion threw Martok and his mount ten meters down the canyon even as the ground rose and bucked underneath them and splinters of ice flew like spears. When he could once again determine up from down, Martok was lying half under Sithala, who wildly thrashed the air with his front legs while his back legs feebly twitched.

Angwar, still in his saddle, circled Martok shouting *something,* but Martok's ears rang so badly he could not say what for sure. Pointing his disruptor again, he fired a single shot into the *jarq's* head, killing him. Sithala's dangerously flailing limbs ceased to move.

Martok dragged himself out from the carcass, took one second to pat its side, and performed a quick inventory to make sure he was intact. *So much for feeling thirty again,* he thought as aches and pains assailed him. Looking up at Angwar, he shouted, "Nothing broken!" then realized the explosion might not have affected the other man's hearing.

Angwar gave him an acknowledging wave, then pointed frantically toward the end of the canyon. Staring through the swirling snow and dust and expecting to see nothing more than dead Hur'q and a pile of ice, Martok took first one step backward, then another.

The crack in the wall had been pried open. What had been a mere gap was now a passageway and beyond, indistinct through the haze, Martok saw a glittering sea of bright eyes and shining weapons. A standard-bearer held up a banner emblazoned with the Klingon letter "M," and Martok knew it was not meant for him except perhaps as another way to beat him to death. Morjod, apparently, had decided now would be a good time to attempt to bring back one of the ancient customs, because Martok heard the sharp rumble of drums against his skin.

Extending his hand, Angwar mouthed the word "Retreat." Martok mouthed a word in response, but he also held up his hand to be pulled up behind Angwar on his mount. The chancellor of the empire knew he was a proud man and by some accounts a great warrior, but he was not as foolish as his wife often accused him of being. Now would be a good time to leave.

Morjod, standing on the back of one of the armored vehicles, had the best vantage point of anyone in his attack force, but even he had no clear idea what had just occurred. After an explosion, a great deal of falling ice, rumbling ground, and now, suddenly, the crack in the ice wall that had been slowing down his force was gone. True, a score of warriors and a handful of Hur'q who had been waiting to get through the gap were now buried under tons of ice and stone, probably dead, but the loss of so few meant little in the grander plan.

His communicator chirped. Only his mother would be calling him now and he considered ignoring the call, but it was difficult, very difficult to ignore Mother. He held the com to his mouth. "Yes, Mother?"

"The ground rumbled. What are you doing?"

Just like her, he thought, *thinking it was my fault.* It felt odd to be having such ungracious thoughts about Gothmara, but there they were and there was no denying them. "There was an ex . . ." he began, but then changed his mind. "We're using explosives to clear a way into the canyon."

A moment of silence, then his mother said, *"Good idea."*

"Anything else, Mother?"

"Good hunting."

Dust and snow settled and Morjod lifted his field glasses to his eyes. Beyond the gap, he caught glimpses of fleeing figures. "Excellent," he said, grinning, then shouted, "BEAT THE DRUMS AGAIN! FORWARD!"

The mass of warriors and monsters moved as he commanded. Morjod enjoyed watching them march, loved the feel of the drums in his belly. *Why did they ever stop using drums?* he wondered. *Telling your enemy that you're coming to kill them is the most satisfying thing I can imagine.*

"KEEP THE NOSE UP!" Worf shouted at Ezri, who barely spared him a look, let alone a word in response.

Father is venting, Alexander thought.

Pointing at Alexander without looking at him, Worf roared, *"ANOTHER SPREAD OF TORPEDOES!"* *Rotarran* had precisely four remaining in her tubes. Alexander doubted that this constituted a "spread," but there was no sense in bothering the captain with facts that would only aggravate him; Alexander double-checked the firing solutions and popped the tubes.

On the main screen, the smooth, silver-white ball that he had come to know as Boreth resolved into a grayish blue, cracked and scalloped landscape. Flashing indicator lights laid over the image indicated that they were roughly on target. Somewhere down in those icy wastelands were a great many Klingons, and Martok might even be among them. *Of course he is among them!* Alexander told himself. He had to believe that Martok still lived, otherwise he would collapse beneath a crushing sense of futility.

Before him stood Ezri, unable to sit in the heavy space armor, the sword shining brightly even through the gloom of the bridge's grease-choked atmosphere. The gauntlet's chunky fingers made handling the controls nearly impossible. Alexander heard her muttering something about fire and ice as she struggled; he wondered if it was some kind of Trill prayer.

Prayer or not, invoking fire and ice fit the *Rotarran*'s current situation. The edge of the main viewscreen was tinted a flickering red and Alexander checked the exterior hull temperature. Bad, but not unbearable. Leskit had inserted *Rotarran* into a perfect approach despite the practically nonexistent sensor data and then gotten them a fair way toward the surface before their pursuers caught up and started firing. Amazingly, *Chak'ta* and the others did not seem to want to destroy them, but only to discourage them from continuing toward Boreth. As they neared the surface, however, their enemies' discretion began slipping. The most recent barrage had almost killed Ortakin and so now Ezri had the helm.

"TRANSPORTERS?" Worf hollered.

Alexander checked the status lights and was relieved to see that the carefully marshaled energy was still where he had left it. "Nominal," he responded, though he wasn't certain if his father really listened.

The engineers had been instructed to leave it until the last possible second, until the belly shields were just about to give in, but that didn't seem likely until they broke through to the lower atmosphere and (theoretically) began to slow down and level out. Fortunately, they needed to put minimal energy into the impulse drive. Gravity was their engine. As his old friend and former shipmate Data might have put it, "Isaac Newton is driving now." Alexander had met up with one of the bridge officers from the old *Enterprise*-D on DS9 several months ago, who had related the story of the day Deanna Troi and Data had successfully piloted the crippled saucer section onto the surface of Veridian III. "Such language!" the officer had said in response to Data's now-legendary comment as he had felt gravity's final, inexorable tug on the seat of his pants. "He just hasn't been the same since he got that emotion chip!"

Data with emotions: Alexander fervently hoped that he would have a chance to see that before he died.

A tremendous explosion rocked *Rotarran*, sending Alexander tumbling to the deck. Alarms blared, panels flashed warning lights, and every station on the ship called the bridge asking for advice, instructions, or simple reassurance. Alexander righted himself (Ezri didn't look like she had moved at all), started to respond to the first call, but then saw the two blinking messages on his status board:

In one minute the ship would be within their damaged transporters' limited range.

And, more pressing, *Chak'ta* had shot off their port nacelle, requiring that reserve power be fed into the shields.

All the energy Alexander had set aside for the transporters would be gone in seconds.

Gothmara watched the tiny symbols that represented her son's forces move through the narrow valley toward the circular plain where Martok's pitiful band waited. She recognized the place from her explorations, the only unfrozen body of water on Boreth. A geothermal vent at the bottom prevented the lake from freezing solid. When she had been searching the area for other Hur'q, she had also studied the lake bed, hypothesizing that the Hur'q had used the geothermals to power their bases, but had never found any evidence to support that supposition.

While the lake was not a particularly deep body of water—hardly a "bottomless pit"—she wondered what would happen if a large explosion took place at its center. If, against all expectation, Martok's forces began to win, she might have to crack the ice. She had tried every other way she knew to kill the man; drowning might have to do.

Again, her communicator beeped, but she knew it wasn't Morjod. She knew his signal intimately. One of the ships in orbit was trying to contact her, but Gothmara did not wish to be bothered. Leaning closer to her sensor board, she absently reached over and switched off the channel. Nothing happening in space right now could be more interesting than what was occurring before her.

Halfway down the canyon, the *katai* encountered a column of perhaps two hundred running warriors led by Kahless. When they spotted Martok, the troops began cheering, but Martok, seated behind Angwar, silenced them with a chopping motion and pointed them back toward the lake. "Did you take out the guns?" he questioned.

Several of the commanders looked at each other and then one of them spoke up. "I think so, General. Most of them."

Martok cast his glance heavenward in frustration. *Gods of Qo'noS preserve me: Most of them!* "Go back and take *all* of them! Stop acting like a rabble! Be an army!" He pointed his *bat'leth* at the emperor and shouted, "Kahless, array them in the Columns of Koloth."

"It shall be done, Chancellor!" Kahless turned to the two warriors beside him and said, "Carry out the chancellor's orders: Six columns with sixty men each arranged in wedges. Array them around the perimeter where the enemy will enter the field."

One of the two warriors hesitated. "Three hundred sixty, sire? I don't know if we have . . ."

"Do your best, then," Kahless said. "And take the guns!"

Kahless rushed up to Angwar and Martok and asked in a low voice, "How many?"

Neither man answered at first, but finally Martok had to say, "We do not know for certain. The way the ground shook, I'd say easily two thousand and perhaps more."

Kahless looked grim, but was undeterred. "They will fight for you, Martok. You know that."

"They may *die* for me, Kahless, and no one will ever know because Gothmara will see to it that there is no empire left."

"We must prevail," Angwar said.

"We must *move*," Stern shouted over the rising tide of drumbeats. "If we are to do anything at all."

Angwar nodded and spurred on his *jarq*. Martok left behind the emperor and the bulk of his column to see what he could do with those remaining on the lake. *No doubt I will find my son there,* he decided. *And perhaps I will discover what happened to Worf.*

As they rounded the last corner that led to the lake, Martok thought he saw the body of a man wedged between two rocks, but the *jarq* moved too fast and he could not see if the warrior was alive or dead. *One more unknown warrior if we do not succeed,* he thought, then bent his will to the coming battle.

On *Rotarran*'s smoke-choked bridge, Ezri Dax lifted her helmet and, just before locking it down into the collar, shouted, "WE'RE GOING IN!" She didn't know why she said it. Anyone still alive on the bridge knew the destination; it just seemed appropriate to announce their forthcoming doom.

On the monitor she saw a circular plain covered with tiny scurrying dots. Some ran to the left, some to the right, and others stood stock-still, no doubt more than a few of them pointing up at the red and smoking point of light headed their way.

Get ready, Martok, she thought. *Special delivery coming your way.*

19

About a quarter of the way across the ice plain, Pharh guessed that the mass of battling warriors were about two hundred meters away, all of them manfully (or womanfully) bashing one another. Going *toward* them, actually attempting to find his way into the mass of these fighters, even with the shield the *katai* had given to him strapped to his arm, ran counter to every instinct he possessed. Well, not instinct really. *Instinct has nothing to do with it,* he thought. *Common sense tells me that running into a mob of Klingons and giant monsters is a bad idea; I don't need instinct to tell me anything.*

But Pharh went forward anyway. Reflecting on what Darok had said, he realized that he still had no definitive reason for his behavior *except* that he didn't have any other ideas that would make a bit of difference. Would finding Martok and standing by him make a single bit of difference? Pharh had no clue, though he knew for a fact that *not* finding Martok and *not* standing beside him would make *no* difference at all. And with everything that had happened to him over the past several days, the idea of *making a difference* had become important to Pharh.

He earnestly trudged along for several minutes—he was not a fleet-footed Ferengi—but concluded that he wasn't getting any closer to the mass of the warriors since the fighting appeared to be moving farther away. Feeling ridiculous, Pharh stopped, panting heavily and sweating through the inner layers of clothing despite the freezing wind. He squinted, studying the figures against the blue-white background of the ice-encrusted canyon walls. Was he seeing an optical illusion?

The sun had climbed high enough in the cloudy sky that most of the ice field was bathed in an eerie luminescence, as much light reflected back up to the eye from the ground as fell from the sky. In between his gasps, he heard distant, isolated grunts and cries as tricks of the wind carried random sounds to Pharh's sensitive ears.

Frax it all, they're getting farther and farther away! Where in Eternal Bankruptcy are they going? Squinting, he thought he saw a gap in the far wall, but why would the warriors be going that way? As Pharh approached the center of the plain, he passed isolated couples of combatants who still circled one another warily, like pairs of lovers in some archaic dance. The Ferengi gave these pairs and trios as much space as he could, but, in truth, he did not have to try very hard. Even to his untrained eye, he could tell that anyone still fighting for Morjod was doing so for ego's sake. Klingons, he understood, were like that sometimes.

All the Hur'q, Pharh noted with satisfaction, were dead, their bodies half-buried in the snow, their backs and necks chopped repeatedly. Apparently, when a Hur'q fell, warriors on all sides made sure it *stayed* down.

Starting across the field again, though at a less determined pace, Pharh saw that most of the warriors had passed into the canyon. *Martok must be in there,* he decided, and altered his course slightly to the west in order to go that way, though his Ferengi common sense was asserting itself more strongly. *It's one thing to think you can cross a field of warriors, maybe ducking and weaving in and out between fighters until you find your . . . your . . .* He was stuck. Though he knew he was the *kr'tach,* Pharh did not know what the other guy in the pair was called. He shook his head. *Whatever . . . Pushing through a bunch of packed-together warriors will be a completely different problem, especially since most of them don't know who you are. . . .*

Confidence ebbing away even as the cold began to ooze up into his boots, Pharh halted. "Well, *skritz,*" he said, facing the trial every well-meaning but sensible person faced under similar circumstances. "This isn't nearly as heroic as I'd hoped."

No sooner had the words left his mouth than he heard an explosion ripple across the plain. Though the crack wasn't fantastically loud at his location, Pharh's sensitive hearing told him that the sound had been amazingly loud wherever it had begun. Turning his head from side to side, he attempted to track the thudding vibrations back to their source and found he was tipping his head backward and facing into the east, out toward the wide gap that led onto the circular plain.

Up there, he thought. *Quite a way above the horizon. It's a gray dot.*

If it was a missile, it was the slowest, worst-directed missile imaginable. Weaving back and forth across the sky, the gray dot trailed a thick, black tail of smoke, the kind he associated with the smokestacks of loading equipment that was destined to become part of someone's insurance claim.

He heard another dull thud—the *wump* of a ship without shields breaking the sound barrier—and the gray dot hopped, skittered to the left, then recentered itself.

He thought, *That leaves out a meteor.* Whatever this thing was, someone was *driving* it. Someone was trying to bring in a ship, though slowing down enough to make a safe landing would be problematic. He cocked his head to the side and realized the dot was growing a lot faster than he preferred seeing.

Again, Pharh considered the wide open plain and, finally, all the tumblers clicked into place. "*Skritz* again," he said, and scanned for possible escape routes. Turning toward the canyon, he headed down the only path that offered even a chance of salvation. As he turned, he ran into the first of the Klingons who fled the valley. Pharh spun around, desperate to keep his balance, because right behind the first Klingon he spotted Klingons number two through three hundred hot on number one's heels. Everyone was leaving the canyon as quickly as they could.

Pharh tried getting their attention, waving his arms and fending them off, but the warriors ignored him. Probably that was a good thing; if anyone *had* paid him any mind, they would have sliced him in half. He noticed that while the Klingons were running, they weren't precisely *fleeing.* Most of them had a very specific goal in mind.

"STOP!" the Ferengi shouted over and over. "LOOK

TO THE SKIES! UP THERE! LOOK! LOOK!" No one spared him a glance.

Finally, one of the lady *katai* reined in beside him on her smelly beast and asked, "What is it, *kr'tach?* Why are you here? Why aren't you with your *kr'mact?*" (*One question answered,* Pharh thought.)

"I *would* be if I could find him," Pharh shouted, "but, listen, we have more important problems right now."

"Such as?" the *katai* asked sardonically.

"That!" Pharh shouted, pointing up into the sky.

She looked where his finger pointed and he had the grim satisfaction of watching her eyes widen. She said a word he suspected that nice lady Klingon warrior priestesses aren't supposed to know. After fumbling at her side for what seemed an eternity, she drew a bone horn decorated with silver filigree letters around its border and blew as if her life depended on it, which it did.

Everyone within a hundred-meter radius turned to look at her. *Naturally,* Pharh thought, and she pointed heavenward.

Approximately one hundred and fifty Klingon warriors—maybe more since it's always difficult to estimate under those kinds of circumstances—uttered the same word the warrior priestess had used (or slight variations) and began running like *frinx* for the edges of the circle.

And Pharh, easily the slowest person on the ice as he pelted for the perimeter, had the satisfaction of thinking, *At least I did something important.*

Wings stretched wide, thrusters screaming, *Rotarran* slashed through the lower atmosphere, hull burning, her damaged warp nacelle sputtering coolant that turned into black smoke upon contact with the oxygen-nitrogen mix.

Ezri braced herself against the navigational console, the fingers of her clumsy gauntlets almost too large to manipulate the control surfaces. The question was no longer if she possessed the necessary piloting skills, but whether Klingon engineers built airframes tough enough to take the punishment she was asking *Rotarran's* to endure. Watching the flight-path indicator overlaid on the main monitor, she pointed the ship down the pipeline and tried ignoring the alarm Klaxons that told her she was flying too fast, too low, with too little reserve energy in the shields. She possessed the piloting knowledge, if not the skill, of the fifth Dax host, Torias, which told her that the ship could stand the strain. Of course, there was the nagging doubt of what Torias could possibly know about Klingon ships, but Ezri told that little traitor voice to *shut up.*

At the edge of her vision, the armor's indicator lights nagged her about the rise of carbon-dioxide levels in the suit, but Ezri switched off the sensor. Suffocating was the least of her worries. In fact, considering her other options, asphyxiating inside her armor was one of the more pleasant prospects facing her.

At least the *Chak'ta* was leaving them alone. Couldn't take the g's, she guessed. "Ha!" Ezri shouted triumphantly. "Coward!" No one else on the bridge seemed to find any of this remotely amusing, which led her to wonder if the carbon-dioxide problem might already be worse than she had guessed. *No time to check now,* she decided, feeding the rest of the reserve power into the landing systems and bringing the nose up. *Let's find out how well they built this thing. . . .*

* * *

Standing on a high shelf overlooking the mouth of the canyon, staring out over the frozen lake, Martok was unexpectedly reminded of a youth who had lived in Ketha when he was a boy. This boy—Gort, if memory served—had taken a particularly savage delight in focusing a beam of sunlight with a piece of quartz onto the nests of colony insects called *tak*. Oh, how the *tak* would scurry when Gort managed to set a twig or leaf aflame. The tiny bugs would run hither and yon in a panic, none of them able to comprehend the baffling fate that had befallen them. Gort would laugh and laugh as he watched, then sometimes stamped the fire out so he could start another. Other times he would let it burn, but, honestly, in Ketha, who even noticed another fire burning? More particularly, who cared about some maddened insects?

As Klingon warriors, *katai,* and Hur'q monsters exited the canyon, they all behaved similarly: brake to a halt, stare up into the sky at the smoking fireball, then frantically look for someplace to hide. Desperate, a few struck out for the caves on the opposite shore. Quite a number tried turning around and heading back down the canyon, but Morjod's forces flowed out too quickly and any warrior who attempted to force his way past was facing a test not unlike trying to swim up a waterfall. The bulk of the, Martok guessed, two thousand warriors, simply fled to whatever spot looked well protected.

Knowing that one spot was no better than another, Martok decided to stay where he was. After conceding that there was nothing he could do about the situation, he resolved to stand and watch it play out, if for no other reason than to honor whoever was aboard the plummeting ship. A mighty struggle was taking place above him, he knew. He had seen many a crashing ship in his day and he knew that the vessel he watched was not out of control. Someone was guiding in a Bird-of-Prey to this exact spot under the worst possible circumstances. Martok thought of only one person who would be insanely confidant enough to attempt such a thing.

The ship had to be *Rotarran* and his mad brother Worf had to be at the helm.

Despite initial appearances, the ship had enough room. The pilot had started his run far enough back that he would be able to fire his reverse thrusters in time and grind to halt on the plain just shy of the entrance to the frozen lake.

"Wings up now," Martok muttered as the ship's flight path leveled out. "And keep the nose up." Worf must have heard him. Just like a living raptor, the wings flared back as the belly came down and the nose of the ship was jerked back. "Good!" Martok cheered. "Now fire thrusters."

But there was no slowing the ship down. Instead, the ship's belly skipped across the surface of the ice, slid to port, somehow straightened, then overcompensated and slid to starboard. A wave of chipped ice flew up in *Rotarran*'s wake and chunks of ablated armor spun off to either side where the shields failed.

Against all hope, Worf managed, briefly, to keep the nose up and the belly level. As the Bird-of-Prey sluiced back to port, any pretense of a controlled landing was forgotten; the ship rolled up onto her flank, shearing off the wing at the base. Now physics would play out until the inertia was used up.

Skipping and sliding like a child's sled that had es-

caped on a steep hill, *Rotarran* twirled across the plain
stern first, then the bow again, then the stern. Finally,
the lower hull screeched up over a low bank, sheets of
hull plating peeling off like scorched skin, and for a
stunning moment, the ship was briefly—and for the last
time—airborne. When it crashed back down again, the
icy surface of the lake splintered, mirrorlike, and crumbled. The sound of the hull screeching as it slid under,
the slosh and burble of the waves, and the crunch of the
floes against one another, all these sounds echoed un-
naturally in the frozen valley.

Frigid water lapped up over her nose and *Rotarran*
sank with barely a ripple.

Pharh gaped openmouthed as a crack in the ice crept
right up under his feet and continued on toward the
shore. He looked over his shoulder and considered re-
treating back toward the mouth of the canyon, but, no,
Klingons were still pouring out, drawn by the sound of
the crash. Unfortunately, he couldn't tell who was loyal
to Martok and who to Morjod, though he had a suspicion *they* knew, because small constellations of soldiers
clustered together into larger, denser clumps as they
joined their comrades.

Steam rose up from the giant hole. As Pharh watched,
chunks of ice around the rim of the gap broke away and
the crack under his feet grew wider as the heat from the
engines and the friction on the hull thawed this part of
the lake. Everyone seemed to grasp this fact at the same
moment and moved away from the hole, farther and farther apart until the mass of Klingons was either pressed
back into the canyon or fanned out on the still-frozen
portion of the surface.

Only one figure, standing right at the edge of the crumbling shore, about fifty meters away, did not move. Pharh squinted against the glare of reflected sunlight, but he didn't need to see the figure's face. The slouch of the shoulders and the spread of his legs told Pharh everything he needed to know: Martok.

The general appeared to be straining to hear something, his head cocked to the side, his left ear down. The ice directly before him broke away and spun off into the lake, forcing Martok to take a half step backward, but he didn't change the tilt of his head.

The wind from the plain whipped across the lake, churning up shushing and crashing whitecaps. No one spoke; no one stirred or changed stances. Every warrior stood still, watching the man who literally stood on the brink of oblivion, and listened.

A foot crunched in the snow behind Pharh and he turned his head quickly to see if he was being attacked, but the Klingon was staring out at Martok as intently as the Ferengi had been. Unlike every other man and woman on the ice, this warrior wore no robe or coat, nor glimmered with a blue environment field. In fact, if anything, he appeared a little warm—charred, even. Much of the hair on the left side of his head was burned away and there were raw, red marks on his cheek. He glanced at Pharh, grinned sheepishly, whispered, "Hi," but immediately returned his attention to the lake.

"Alexander?" Pharh asked.

Alexander nodded, but didn't look at him. Pharh turned to look over his other shoulder and saw Worf standing behind him. He, too, looked a little the worse for wear, but when Pharh considered the ship on the bottom of the lake was probably *Rotarran,* maybe not too bad. "How did you . . . ?"

"Shh," Worf hissed. "Watch."

Pharh obeyed.

Martok now knelt at the edge of the crack, his feet half submerged in the icy water that lapped up over the frigid shore. Opening his hand, he dropped his weapon into the snow without a backward look and then remained motionless, waiting, silent, every sense straining.

And then a shaft of light broke the surface of the lake and danced before him. A silver hand equally dazzling held the lightning bolt, the two so bright that Pharh turned his face away, stripes and glimmering aftereffects prancing behind his closed eyelids. When he turned back around, the shaft of light rose up out of the waters and Martok backed away from its brilliance toward the firmer shore. The silver glove was followed by an arm, then a burnished head, then a barrel chest, then two legs, which moved slowly as sheets of water sluiced down, forming broken puddles.

Martok stood erect now, his arms held wide, and hair blown back from his face by the icy wind. The armored figure knelt before him and presented the general with the shaft of light.

Pharh suddenly realized it was a blade, a *bat'leth,* but one unlike any he had ever seen. Even he, a Ferengi, could sense the astonishing craft that had gone into the creation of this weapon, this work of art. For the first time, Pharh understood the expression "A Klingon's honor shines only as brightly as his blade."

Reverently, Martok reached out and gripped the blade by its handle and slowly lifted it out of the armored figure's grasp. As he did so, every warrior who saw him exhaled as one and Pharh realized that he, too, had been holding his breath and was once again breathing with all the others. Friend and foe alike seemed suspended, unable or unwilling to move, and yet, despite the reverential stillness, Pharh began walking. Lifting his foot was like trying to loosen it from setting concrete, but as soon as he had one foot up, the other followed behind as if it had a will of its own. One step, then the next, then the next until he felt like everyone on the plain was frozen in time and he flew between seconds. A voice in his head exhorted, *Run, little warrior! Run as fast as you can!*

As Pharh ran, he never took his eyes off Martok, who stared transfixed at the blade, seemingly unwilling to blink for fear the *bat'leth* would dissolve into motes of sunlight. All around him, Pharh heard a low groan, the first note of a thousand-throated roar, and knew that Martok was about to lift up the blade for all to see. *And that will be the sign,* the voice said.

The thunder rose all around him and Martok flexed his shoulder, tilted back his head, his mouth split in a victorious grin.

Pharh plodded through the snow, crashed into a huge Klingon who was lifting his own sword, bounced off him and collided with another. His feet slipped in the icy slush, but he regained his footing. He found himself remembering that night on the roof of his house when he had rolled over the edge and had to almost dance on motes of air to keep his balance. Gripping the handle of the small shield the *katai* gave him, Pharh recentered himself, dug his feet into the slush, and pushed off.

The roar rose up, the *bat'leth* gleamed in the air. Martok opened his mouth wide in a wordless bellow of profound certainty.

Here it comes, the voice whispered in Pharh's giant ear. *Are you ready? Can you do this?*

Pharh measured the distance between himself and Martok, counted twelve paces, and pumped his legs as hard as he could. Time slowed down just for him and with it sound and motion, but soon it would all speed up again. He didn't have much longer.

I can do this, he thought in response to the voice.

The voices—the storm—rose, cresendoed, then broke. A roar—a name—his friend's name. The Klingons, the stupid, stupid Klingons who couldn't pay attention to what was really going on around them when there was a spectacle to be watched, a moment, a little bit of legend played out. Only Pharh knew, only little Pharh, except Pharh wasn't so little, and Pharh had excellent hearing.

Six paces now . . .

Back toward the canyon, he heard another voice, one other voice, and it was not shouting his friend's name, he was bellowing, *"NOOOOOO!!"*

Morjod stood on a small hillock where he had been gathering the last living Hur'q for the final assault, just high enough to see over the heads of all the others, just high enough to see Martok's men and even quite a few of his own watching his father.

Three paces now . . .

Two . . .

Pharh knew Morjod was there on his hill with a disruptor rifle, though Pharh didn't know how he knew.

I can do this, he thought and, shield stretched out before him, he jumped.

* * *

Ezri was freezing. Her teeth chattered and the blinking telltales inside the armor told her, in no uncertain terms, *Get some oxygen!* Martok had his damned sword and now she was down on her knees before him, the batteries in the suit drained down into their reserves. Soon, occupying this spot on Boreth was going to be several hundred kilos of soggy, immobilized Klingon machinery with a frozen Trill at its center.

Pop the helmet seals while you still can, Ezri, she said to herself, her gasps echoing hollowly in the shell that was about to become her coffin. She fumbled with the release switch, but the light blinked red: not enough battery power left. *Okay, the manual release.* Her fingers were so clumsy, though, that it was hard to find the lever. Ezri tried to see what was happening two feet in front of her face, but condensation ran down the inside of her faceplate. Dimly, she heard a rumble rise up around her and the ground seemed to shake, but she couldn't stop to see what was happening. *Damned Klingon spacesuit!* She wanted to scream. *Why don't these people put the release switch in a spot where you can find it?!*

Something crashed down in front of her, but Ezri couldn't see what it was. *Why wasn't anyone helping her?* Were they fighting? Had she arrived in the middle of a fight, interrupted it long enough to give Martok a new weapon just so he could go back to breaking heads with a more decorous blade? It made her unaccountably angry to think this might be happening. *And what about the rest of* Rotarran's *crew? Had any of them survived the beam-out?* She had barely survived and look at what she wore. . . .

Her finger caught on something and she yanked at it. Instantly, she could hear other voices and not just her own breathing. Almost afraid to take the chance, Ezri let go of the lungful of air she had been holding and inhaled deeply.

Air! Blessed air! The inrush of sweet oxygen almost froze her lungs, but thank the Womb, she could breathe! Her arms collapsed under her and her head fell forward, helmet tumbling from the collar ring. Gasping, eyes shut, snow melting against her forehead, Ezri felt nearly frozen water trickle down her cheeks and drip off onto the ground. Hearing wavered in and out, voices shouting, feet running, but nearer, almost beside her, two voices spoke in low tones. One, she realized, belonged to Martok and the other, softer, and high, sounded familiar. She knew she had heard it before. . . . The Ferengi. The one Martok had brought with him from Qo'noS. What was his name?

"Pharh?" Martok called, cradling the Ferengi's head. "Can you hear me?"

Warriors stood ringed around them, eyes out, searching for more snipers. Whoever had fired the shot had disappeared, but Martok's men were watching. Nearby, Ezri Dax was clawing at the helmet to her armor and Martok was just about to order one of the men to pop the seals for her, but the Trill apparently knew what she was doing. She yanked the manual control, the seals parted, and the helmet tumbled down into the snow. Dax was breathing, Martok saw, so he turned his attention back to his *kr'tach*.

"I can hear you," Pharh said, but almost too softly to be heard over the increasing sounds of battle. "Did I make it?" he asked. "Did I get my shield up in time?"

Martok looked down at the small, undamaged, and

probably useless shield that was still strapped to the Ferengi's arm. Then he looked at the charred hole bored through his friend's lower abdomen and the ever-widening stain on the snow beneath him. "You did fine, Pharh. Yes, you got your shield up in time."

Pharh grinned a snaggletoothed smile and said, "You are such a liar, Martok." He scrunched his eyes shut, overcome by a wave of pain, then gasped. "This really hurts. Has anyone ever mentioned that working for you can be really painful?"

"You are the first to dare comment," Martok said, his voice mock stern. "I do not think there is anything I can give you for the pain." He paused, uncertain if he should go on, but then decided Pharh knew what was coming. "Is there anything I can do to compensate you for your service? You have been a reasonably competent *kr'tach*. I could notify your family that you have been of service to the empire. . . ."

"Assuming you *live*," Pharh said sarcastically. "I don't think they would care much and even if they did . . ." He shrugged. "I don't think I'm going to give 'em the satisfaction." Pausing, the Ferengi's breath suddenly grew sharper and he gasped, "But there is one thing . . ."

"What?"

"Darok . . . he said . . ." Pharh coughed and there was blood between his teeth. Martok wiped it away with his sleeve. Behind him, he heard the cries of warriors as they ran into the plain.

"I have to go soon, Pharh," Martok said as gently as he could.

"So do I, Martok," Pharh said. "And I really don't want to go to the Final Audit. I don't think I'm going to do well. . . ."

"So?"

"Darok said Klingons could maybe buy their friends a spot in the Ko-Vo-Store."

Ko-Vo-Store? Martok wondered, then moved the sounds around and got it. "Yes," Martok said. "If we dedicate the victory to the fallen. But it only is necessary if the warrior does not die in battle."

Pharh furrowed his brow. "Do you think this counts?"

Martok considered, then answered, "Probably. But I'm not sure."

"I don't think I want to take any chances," Pharh said. "Could you take care of this for me?"

"For the opportunity to have you haranguing me and asking me stupid questions throughout eternity?" Martok asked. "Absolutely. It will be done, my friend."

Pharh's anxious expression relaxed and he began to weakly fumble at the front of his tunic. "Good," he said. "I have the down payment." Patting his shirt, his movements became both weaker and more frantic and the familiar lines of worry creased his brow. "I can't find it. Help me, Martok."

Martok reached down and patted the front of the Ferengi's shirt, uncertain what he was seeking. Then, he found it: a small, hard lump inside the tunic lining. "What is it?" Martok asked.

"It's yours," Pharh said weakly. "Cut the cloth if you want. I don't care."

Martok pulled off his gloves, then drew his blade and carefully slit open the tunic. A moment later, he touched a cold, metallic lump and his memory raced back to the strip of narrow dusty road a few kilometers outside the First City.

"I've been holding on to it," Pharh said. "Just like you said."

Martok stared at the chancellor's ring in the palm of his hand and tried to think of the appropriate words of thanks, but knew there were none. "I had forgotten . . ." he murmured.

"I know," Pharh replied, his voice barely discernible above the whispering wind. "I figured you would. What are you going to do without me to remind you of these things?"

Another wave of pain rippled through the Ferengi's thin body and Martok heard him whimper. "I'm really not very brave," Pharh said softly, his eyes shut. "It's very dark in here. . . ." His breath caught in his throat and he suddenly grew rigid.

Martok leaned forward and roughly pushed the Ferengi's eyes open with his thumbs. He whispered sternly into his ear, "Don't let them see your fear, my son. Klingons do not fear the gods. . . ."

And with his last breath, Martok's *kr'tach* whispered, "They fear us."

Ezri was roused from her stupor by a shout of rage and grief and defiance. She looked up and saw Martok kneeling beside the Ferengi's body, his thumbs holding Pharh's eyes open and bellowing to the heavens. The cry seemed to go on and on and all around the chancellor, his warriors, at first puzzled, were moved by the shout and took it up until half the hillside howled up into the sky.

At last, the cry died away and Martok stood, the Sword of Kahless in his hand. He pointed at the canyon where Morjod waited with his army. "This battle," he cried, "is for the right of this warrior to enter *Sto-Vo-Kor!* WILL YOU FIGHT FOR HIM?!"

The hills shook with the response: *"KAI!"*

Martok held the sword aloft and roared, "TODAY IS A GOOD DAY TO DIE!"

And the storm, at long last, broke.

20

"Mother," Morjod said. "He has the sword."

Sword? Gothmara thought. *What sword?* But she did not want to say that to her son, having learned that children should always be under the impression that their parents know everything. So instead she asked, "Who brought it to him and how are the warriors reacting?"

"How are they *reacting?*" Morjod said, his voice practically a screech. "How do you think they're reacting. It's the damned Sword of Kahless! Or so they think!"

The Sword of Kahless! How did Martok get it? And how does Morjod know about it and I do not? Her son, she sensed, had been hatching plots, a very bad sign.

"*Rotarran* brought it to him," Morjod continued. "They crashed the ship and someone brought it to him from the wreckage. Damnedest thing I've ever seen. You could hear the ice melt while he was staring at it. I had gathered the monsters up on a bluff so everyone could see me with them, but *no one was paying attention.* They were all watching Martok play with his new toy."

That explains the seismic activity, Gothmara thought, glancing at her sensors. *And now he has the symbol he'll need to wrest back control of the empire . . . unless we can claim it.* "Can you take it from him?"

"OF COURSE!" Morjod shouted. "I tried shooting him, but some mongrel-lover threw himself in front of the shot and now Martok's surrounded!"

Gothmara realized that any semblance of self-control the boy might have once possessed was long gone. Indeed, any semblance of control *she* had over him had all but disappeared. *The time has come, I think.*

"Have you assembled your men?"

"Yes," Morjod reported. "As many as I can. Some of them . . . have changed sides, I believe. It's because of the sword. The damned sword! It has some kind of power!"

It's not the sword that has the power, you little fool, she thought. *But the wielder.* An uncharacteristically parental thought intruded and Gothmara wondered, *Did I ever try to explain that to you?* She shrugged. *Too late now. This battle may be lost, but if I can kill Martok the war is won. Time to play my trump card.* "My son," she purred seductively. "You must show your mettle and prove your love for me. Break through the lines, find Martok and fight him. Use any resource at your disposal. I will come and find you so I can watch your victory." She used the Voice then and set her seal on her son. *"You must defeat him, no matter the cost. Do you understand?"*

Morjod hesitated as if in a stupor, as Gothmara knew

he would. "I . . . I do understand, Mother. It shall be as you say."

"Excellent. Go find your father. Kill him."

"I will," Morjod said, and cut the circuit.

You won't, Gothmara thought. *Not right away in any case.*

She wrapped her furs around her and ordered the driver to take her as close to the battlefield as they could get. Gothmara would have to get out and walk through the canyon, but not right away. And there was a cave nearby, if she remembered correctly, one she had outfitted during her explorations. She would be able to rest there and, if necessary, even hide until the battle ended, regardless of who won. Her plan might not be working as she had envisioned it would, but the battle was not yet over.

Alexander's father fought joyfully, with skill and abandon, like a warrior out of legend. No blade or disruptor bolt could come near Worf. Three or four warriors would attempt to bring him down, but every time Alexander watched his father shrug off attacks like rainwater. The display of his glorious battle powers was, at once, wonderful and frustrating, because Alexander Rozhenko knew that he would never have his father's skill. *On the other hand*, Alexander thought, *neither will anyone else. Not even Martok or Kahless could beat him.* Then, uncharacteristically, as he drew a bead on an attacking figure, he preened with pride and decided, *But I have skills of my own.* Though born out of desperation, his idea to charge the transporter by hooking the system into turbines on *Rotarran*'s wings had been inspired. The chargers were almost never used, but that was one of the values of being the one assigned to clean the little-used pieces of any ship: You learned where everything was.

And so they were alive so that they could fight and die for their chancellor, his father's brother. Maybe it *was* a good day to die, but Alexander hoped not. He wanted very much to taste his grandmother's borscht once more and take a long ramble through the streets of the First City (a place he had grown to like before the stupid bastard had crushed part of it). Maybe he could even find a nice girl who would love him the way he loved her. All these ideas motivated Alexander, but they did not make him desperate or hasty or stupid. He pressed the firing stud on his disruptor and the enemy who had been studying his father's back fell to the ground.

In his heart, he decided that if he survived this day, he would ask the chancellor to consider amending the ancient battle cry to "Today is a good day to die, but, all in all, it's good to be alive." He seriously doubted if anyone would listen, but it never, in Alexander's experience, hurt to ask.

Worf, son of Mogh, slid a half step to his left, pivoted his hip, and kicked back with a heavily booted foot. The pelvis of the man who had been attempting to attack him from behind shattered into three pieces and, naturally, he fell to the ground. Bending his right knee, Worf tumbled to that side, rolled onto his shoulder, and popped up out of the tuck with his *bat'leth* held high to block the blow that had been whistling toward his head. The warrior who had been attacking him appeared confused, as if he could not believe what had just happened.

Worf could not forgive the man's inflexibility, knocked his blade back with a quick twist, then slashed open his abdomen with another.

Feeling a stir of air behind him, Worf tugged a small throwing knife from his belt, palmed it, spun, and threw it into the lower back of a warrior who was attempting to outflank his son.

Alexander was doing quite well, he noticed, methodically picking the most dangerous targets and bringing them down with, at worst, two shots. Worf, naturally, could have hit each with one, but they were not, as Jadzia had patiently explained, the same person.

Do not allow yourself to be distracted, Worf chastised himself. Scanning ten meters on all sides, he picked his next target. And his target after that. And after that. The day was not yet won for his brother, but Worf would do his part to assure victory.

Martok wished to fight, but instead, watched the battle unfold. This is not to say he did not kill enemies. He could not have done otherwise, considering the number of warriors who ran straight at him apparently with every intention of disconnecting his head from his shoulders. Few made it close enough to try, and any that made it past Martok's guards were quickly dispatched. When the third man made it through, Martok began to suspect that his ring of protectors simply enjoyed watching him use the sword. No denying, the blade was a thing of beauty. Lighter than air, it was as quick and responsive as a living entity. Martok even began to wonder if perhaps the blade was in fact some sort of bound spirit, but then rolled his eye at the ridiculous fantasy. A sword was a sword and nothing more. *This* just happened to be a very *good* sword.

Behind him, in the center of the circle, lay Pharh's body, watched over by one of the guards, no doubt confused by the honor being bestowed on the Ferengi, but none could deny the little alien's courage. How had Pharh known what Morjod was planning? Martok was baffled, but so many strange things had happened in the past couple of weeks. The old gods of Qo'noS, if that's what they were, had made themselves felt in ways few would have believed possible. Martok now felt that he might have been more correct than he suspected when he had said, "Klingons may not rely on gods, but we ignore them at our peril."

Angwar rode up to Martok and brought his steed to a sudden halt with a shower of slushy snow. "Hail, Chancellor."

"Hail, leader of the *katai*. How goes the battle?"

"We will take the day, Chancellor, if all continues as it is now. Morjod's forces have lost heart. Many have left the field and some have even thrown down his colors and now fight against their former comrades."

"Make note of their faces," Martok said. "And make sure to point them out to me later."

"As you say, Chancellor."

"What of the Hur'q?"

Angwar's face radiated satisfaction. "They are gone. Defeated in a last stand not ten minutes ago."

That at least is over, Martok thought. *Gothmara may have a few in reserve, but she would have used the bulk of them in this attack.*

"Have you seen Morjod or Gothmara?"

"The witch? No. Her son? Yes. He was positioned on a small hill near the canyon mouth and fights like a demon. Whatever else you may wish to say about Gothmara's spawn, his prowess as a warrior is extraordinary."

Martok gripped the sword's handle and muttered, "Truly?"

"Starn fell before him, as did two of my brothers."

Stunned, Martok felt his mouth hang open. "I can scarcely believe anyone could defeat a *katai*, least of all Starn."

"And yet, your son did."

Martok considered his options. A general might battle side by side with his warriors, but a chancellor was responsible for more than merely winning a battle. Sirella's voice rang in his head: *"You have a responsibility to your people. . . ."*

"What kind of a leader can I be if I stay here while others die?" Martok asked in response.

"What?" Angwar asked.

"Where is he," Martok asked. "My son—Morjod. And for that matter, if you see my other son . . . But wait, you've never met him. His name is Drex. He is somewhere on this field. A good warrior, but neither as seasoned nor as patient as either of us old men."

"There are many like that here today," Angwar said. "But I will watch for him."

He pointed up the slope to the cleft that led to the canyon. "Morjod is up there. I wasn't going to say, but he calls for you."

Martok lifted the *bat'leth* and said, "Stay here with my *kr'tach*, Angwar. And my friend who brought the blade." He pointed at Ezri, who sat nearby, teeth chattering but otherwise unharmed. "They must not be molested by the battle."

"As you wish, my chancellor."

Martok pushed between two of his guards, both of whom looked as if they planned to follow, but he waved them back. Finishing the fight in this manner required that he battle Morjod alone.

Though several guards remained behind as they had been ordered, others joined Martok as he walked toward the canyon. Without warning, Worf was there, flanked by Alexander. *Still no Drex,* Martok thought. *And no Darok. This does not bode well.* But he pushed the thoughts away and continued his trek, deciding to slow his walk so that others could see and join the throng.

Nerves up and down Morjod's spine prickled and burned. His arms felt light; his legs seemed to move of their own volition. He fought better than he had ever fought in his life, and he was, by any measure, a fine warrior. The Hur'q had been dragging the bodies away as Morjod defeated them, but he was certain that if they hadn't he wouldn't be able to move without climbing over a pile of them. Looking down the small slope, Morjod saw a crowd of warriors milling about and decided to taunt them: "More blood! Bring me more!"

The smell was intoxicating. As he watched the monsters make away with the corpses, he couldn't help but think about the last time he had eaten. During his fight with the horseman, his blade had nicked one of the beast's arteries, spraying him in the face with a geyser of blood. Morjod had wiped away the sticky syrup with the sleeve of his tunic, but then had surreptitiously sucked on the sleeve when he thought no one was watching.

Suddenly, the milling at the bottom of the slope

ceased and the warriors formed themselves into a line. Moving slowly, the line moved up the hill, the figure at the center two paces in front of the others.

"Father," Morjod whispered expectantly, and knew fate came to greet him.

Morjod ran down to Martok recklessly, heedlessly, without any semblance of skill or finesse. *How has he survived this long?* Martok wondered, lifting his blade.

His entourage fell back as the usurper came at him screaming wordlessly. *Madness has consumed him,* Martok decided. Then, unexpectedly, three steps away, Morjod switched grips on his *bat'leth* and swung under and up, a difficult and dangerous maneuver for a running attacker to perform.

However, Martok's experience with a blade was unrivaled and he changed his position with no more than a quick shuffle step and a twist of his wrist. The two blades struck each other at their midpoint and Morjod's shattered into a dozen shards. Several splinters bounced back and cut the boy on the face, but he seemed oblivious to his wounds.

Undaunted, Morjod picked up two slivers of metal and first threw one at Martok's head, then attempted to stab him in the thigh with the other. After deflecting the first attack with his *bat'leth,* Martok sidestepped out of range and butted the bastard on the back of the head with the blunt side of his weapon.

Martok meant for the blow to knock Morjod unconscious, but his now weaponless attacker instead stumbled back, unaware of the narrow seam creasing his skull, and began to gibber nonsense about the fight not being fair if he didn't have a weapon, too.

"Fair?" Martok asked. "What is fair about the thousands killed in the First City? Or my dead daughters?"

"I didn't kill your daughters!" Morjod shouted, pointing back over the mountains. *"She did it!"*

Gothmara is near, Martok realized. He had expected she would have escaped by now, but perhaps not. He knew now that her goal had never been victory for Morjod, but only that he, Martok, die. To find Gothmara, Martok would have to finish off Morjod, but his warriors would be displeased if he simply shot the madman or ordered him captured. Final victory stood on the edge of a blade, Martok knew.

He stabbed the sword into the ice and called back over his shoulder. "Give me another blade," he said, never taking his eyes off his son. "And give him one, too."

Morjod grinned happily. Blood dripped from a half-dozen wounds. When a warrior stepped forward and handed him a *bat'leth,* the boy swiped at the messenger as soon as he gripped the haft. The crowd groaned at this dishonorable display and Martok suddenly felt the pinch of anxiety: *He seems like one of his mother's ravenous beasts! What foulness has come upon him?*

Without thought, without planning or pausing to measure his foe, Morjod ran forward, savagely swinging his blade from side to side. "MOTHER!" he cried. "FOR YOU!"

Martok easily blocked every blow and focused on pushing his attacker back against a wall where he could be disarmed. Unexpectedly, Morjod did not employ any of the fundamental blocks that even the most inexperienced fighter would have tried, and took three or four cuts on his forearms as a consequence. Rearing back, Morjod repeatedly struck at Martok, attempting to overpower his father with brute strength; Martok parried every attack.

The crowd had formed a half circle around the fighters, and the open space they enclosed shifted across the ice as Morjod made his next flailing attack and Martok countered, usually by taking a half step to the side or behind. Each time Martok blocked one of Morjod's moves, the boy was cut again; a dozen seeping wounds marked his arms, chest, and face. *This is ludicrous,* Martok said. *I sought an honorable fight, but what honor is there in an opponent slowly bleeding to death?*

In his next pass, Morjod swiped at Martok's knees, the clumsiest, most amateurish attack in the book. "Enough," Martok muttered, jumping up as the blade swung down. He landed squarely on it, burying the tip in the ice. A sharp kick and the *bat'leth* snapped in half, leaving Morjod defenseless again.

"Surrender, usurper," he said. "And I will let you live." Grumbles from the crowd indicated that this was not a popular idea, but Martok cared nothing for the crowd's opinion. Strangely, he was beginning to think like a father, wondering what horrors the boy's mother had perpetrated on him.

Morjod laughed madly, then shouted, "Let me *live?* To cage me and mock me? *I think not, Father!"* Yanking back on the broken stub of his *bat'leth,* Morjod slashed at the backs of both of his legs, opening large vessels that immediately gushed thick arterial blood. The boy tumbled forward, blood pressure in his brain plummeting to nothing in only seconds.

"Medic!" Martok shouted, though he knew there were no medics on Klingon battlefields. Instead, he tore strips of cloth from his tunic to make a tourniquet. Morjod flopped around feebly on the ice. Unless his blood pressure was stabilized, Martok expected Morjod would go into shock, followed quickly by cardiac arrest. The crowd closed in around him, cutting off the light and adding confusion until Martok shouted them all away unless they offered him assistance. Worf pressed through the mob and began helping, but even as he began to wrap the first strip around Morjod's legs, he drew his head back, eyes wide.

"Martok," he called, voice husky with surprise. "Something is wrong."

"Of course something is wrong," Martok said, slashing off another strip with his *bat'leth*. "He's dying from blood loss. . . ."

"No. Something else. Look!"

Martok looked. Morjod had not lapsed into shock. If anything, his movements, jerky before, were becoming positively spastic now. His arms and legs, his entire body, vibrated. Even as they watched, flesh split and reknit around bones that were growing longer and thicker. Martok heard a stretching and snapping noise that could only be tendons.

Morjod began to groan, shaking his head back and forth in quick, sharp wrenching movements. He reached up to his face, but could not move his arms.

Martok tried holding the boy down until the spasms passed, but the tremors became worse. The cuts on Morjod's face had healed, but now new ones formed as the muscles beneath grew at a furious pace. His teeth shattered as his jaw re-formed; sharp new incisors pierced the raw, pink flesh. The orbits of Morjod's eyes turned into putrid butter, sloughed away, then seemed to reharden as the eyes themselves grew wider and darker.

"Get away, Worf," Martok shouted. "A weapon! I need a weapon!"

Whatever hint of intelligence that had once been in Morjod's eyes faded before the transformation completed. When the body ceased to shiver and shake, the creature, the Hur'q, climbed to its feet and tore at the tatters of clothing still hanging on its lanky body.

Martok rolled to his feet even as the beast that had been Morjod first tried balancing itself on its long legs. No sooner was the Hur'q standing than it swiped one of its long-clawed hands at Martok's head. The general lifted his arms to block and found that someone had put the Sword of Kahless in his hands. Daring only to glance behind himself for a moment, Martok saw a bent, white-haired warrior step back into the crowd. *Darok?* he wondered.

Warriors all around them drew their disruptors and aimed at the monster's head and chest, but Martok shouted, "No one fires!"

No one did. The Hur'q looked from side to side, searching for a way out of the ring, but, finding none, began to hiss at the faces and shining weapons. There was almost, *almost* a kind of desperate knowledge behind the monster's movements, as if some sliver of identity still lived within it.

But that could not be true. Martok could not accept that.

Martok stepped forward and the creature stepped back. It raised a weapon and slashed at Martok, but only succeeded in cutting itself on the sword's edge.

Wounded, it howled and drew back, the warriors behind it shuffling out of range of the long, clawed feet.

Then, leaping to the right, Martok waited for the monster's eyes to track after him so he could flick the blade, shining reflected light into its eyes. Squinting, the Hur'q turned its head away and at that moment, Martok rolled forward under its sweeping arms, leapt up, and pierced its heart with the tip of the blade.

When he had fought Hur'q back on Qo'noS, he had barely been able to cut their flesh with a *bat'leth*, though admittedly it had been an old blade he had recovered from a city guardsman. The Sword of Kahless, though, easily sliced into the beast's flesh.

Martok struck a vital organ and the beast that had been his son gasped, falling forward, leaning its weight into the blade. Blood flowed out around Martok's hands and he saw that it was now a deep indigo blue. *She changed even the color of his blood,* Martok thought. *I will find you, Gothmara, and you will hope that the* Fek'lhr *of* Gre'thor *treats you with more mercy than I.*

Tugging on the *bat'leth*, Martok twisted his son onto his back and tried to lower him to the ground as slowly and gently as possible. More blue-black blood gushed up between the creature's lips and Martok believed it actually sobbed. It extended an open hand, and Martok saw that it held a communicator. Its oversized lips and jaws moved spastically as it tried to form a word, but could not.

Even now, he calls her. Martok took the communicator from his son's hand. "I am sorry, boy," he whispered, cradling its head. "I will make it right."

* * *

In the crowd around the chancellor and his dead son, one of the younger warriors began to raise a cheer, but others turned on the poor, ignorant soul and hushed him. Others waited for Martok to hold open the creature's eyes and begin the howl, reasoning that as he had done it for the Ferengi, would he not also do it for one who had once been a Klingon? But Martok did not. Instead, he sat for a long, long time with the creature's head cradled in his lap, head bowed, blood leaking down over his hand and over his legs. He did not mourn openly, not even in the stilted way that Klingons do for the loss of loved ones to illness or untimely death. He appeared to only be meditating, though about what no one would ever be able to say.

Finally, after a time, the wind pierced through even the thickest armor and the assembled warriors began stamping and patting their arms and legs for warmth. The sun headed toward the horizon, though none knew for sure how long it would take to set. To all the day had felt endless.

"What will you do now, my brother?" the Federation diplomat asked at last.

The chancellor lowered the head of his son to the ice, picked up a piece of tattered banner, and cast it over the corpse. Looking at his brother, he growled softly, "Find his mother."

For the first time since Morjod's death, Martok saw those standing around him, waiting patiently for their orders. "Go," he said. "Gather the dead and tend to the wounded before they freeze. The battle is over. We have won."

And everyone looked around at the cliffs, down through the cleft, out to the plain, and saw the frozen bodies of their brothers and sisters, and realized it was true. But, still, strangely, no one raised a victory shout. They had won, but all understood the price.

Historians said in future ages that this was the moment when the second age of the Klingon Empire began. A single figure, an older man cloaked in gray watched the moment pass, nodded in approval, and began tending to the dead.

21

Martok showed the communicator Morjod had been clutching to Worf and asked, "Assuming he used this to speak to his mother, can you determine where she was?"

Worf studied the device, crumpled around the edges where the mutated Morjod had been clutching it, and put on his pensive face. "A *Khac* mark seven," he mused. "Not very durable."

"I'm not asking for a quartermaster's review," Martok replied through gritted teeth.

"I understand, brother," Worf said, and sighed. "But the casing has been crushed, the interior electronics exposed to the atmosphere . . ."

"And . . . ?"

"I do not know if there is anything . . ."

Alexander, who stood near his father, extended his right hand and asked, "May I?" Worf handed him the communicator. Alexander popped the outer casing away from the electronics, studied the interior for a moment, then pulled out his tricorder. After attaching a pair of leads to the communicator, he tapped on the communicator controls for several moments until a thin wisp of smoke emerged from it.

"You're burning out the power source," Worf said.

"I know," Alexander said, studying his tricorder. Satisfied, he handed both devices to Martok. "All the data is on there."

Martok looked at the tricorder display. The frequencies of the communicators that last spoke to Morjod's were listed along with a time and location stamp. "These coordinates?" he asked.

"About three klicks back through the canyon," Alexander replied, pointing.

Regarding Worf questioningly, Martok asked, *"This* is the son you're always worried about?"

Worf, surprised but obviously pleased, shrugged. "Once," he replied. "But not as much anymore."

"Good. Assemble the *katai* and ask them to join me here. To find Gothmara, I will need their familiarity with the terrain."

Worf nodded and grinned fiercely. "As you command, Chancellor." He ran down the small slope and quickly disappeared into the deepening gloom.

When he was gone, Martok slipped the tricorder into his belt. He asked, "How much cold can this take?"

"More than you can, sir," Alexander replied. "You're going after her?"

"Yes," Martok said, turning up his collar against the wind. "Unless you think you can stop me."

"I wouldn't dream of it, sir. But I will be obliged to tell my father when he returns."

"I know. But it will take him a little time to catch up. When he does, this will all either be over or . . ."

"Right, sir." Alexander extended his hand in the human fashion and Martok took it. "Good luck, sir."

"Thank you, Alexander. In the past several years, there have been few acts that I have felt were as uncompromisingly correct as taking your father and you into my house."

The boy smiled shyly and then his expression turned serious. "Why are you doing this, sir? Why risk yourself? After all, you are the . . ."

"I'm the chancellor," Martok said. "Yes, I know. If my wife were here, she would . . ." He paused then and considered. What *would* Sirella say? He would have to grow accustomed to asking himself that for the remainder of his life. "I believe she would inform me that I am a fool, which is something I already know. All men are fools eventually for something. It's how we know we are men."

Alexander laughed at that. "So, the man first and chancellor after?" he asked.

"I would not trust a chancellor who was not a man first. Would you?"

"No," Alexander said. "Not unless she was a woman."

Now Martok laughed, then clapped the boy on his back. "You should spend more time with my son, Drex," he said, wrapping his cloak tighter around him. "He could learn a few things from you."

With that, he turned and headed up through the cleft to the canyon and the plain beyond. *Three kilometers,* he thought wistfully, bowing his head against the wind. *I am too old for this sort of thing.*

None of the ships responded to her call. As the vehicle bounced the last several hundred yards to her hidden compound, Gothmara allowed herself, for the first time that day, to worry. Moments ago, when she had ordered the driver to proceed, she had discovered that he had disappeared, because of desertion or a misunderstanding Gothmara could not guess. Her immediate thought had been *I can drive a vehicle,* so she climbed in the cab and activated the controls. Unfortunately, she had never figured out how to activate the heater and was now chilled to the bone. Even her fur-lined gloves could not keep out the cold; she worried that her fingertips might be slightly frostbitten. "Fingers are simple enough to repair," she said to herself. "Once I get back to the lab."

But was returning to the lab a good idea? Martok knew its location. If Morjod had not been able to defeat him in single combat . . . Even if the mutation had occurred as she had planned, Gothmara conceded that Martok might have defeated him. *Very frustrating,* she thought, fuming. *I can't go back to the lab. Then where?*

Ah. Of course. As she had been thinking earlier, her cave compound was not far from here. *Much safer in many ways and, best of all, secret.* She would use the communication equipment to contact one of the ships and use the Voice on an officer, convince him to beam her aboard. *And then?* she thought. *And then I will fight another day. . . .* First, she needed to warm up and regroup. Gothmara checked the coordinates on the navigational array *(This I can figure out,* she seethed, *but I can't find the heater!)* and changed the vehicle's heading.

Fifteen minutes later, Gothmara pulled up before the cave mouth and slid out of the driver's cab, her feet as frozen numb as a pair of ice blocks. Stumbling clumsily, she staggered to the compound's hidden door and spoke the password to the voiceprint security module. Seconds later, the door opened, releasing a cloud of deliciously warm air. Gothmara hobbled inside and stood before the heating units, her fingers and toes pinched by a not entirely unwelcome ache as blood began flowing again. After several minutes of basking, she whispered, "Thank the gods," an almost playful squeak of pain in her tone.

"The gods have had nothing to do with this, Gothmara," Martok said.

Feeling foolish, she closed her eyes. *The door,* she thought. *Very careless, but then, discomfort always makes me less cautious.* "Then, our son . . ."

"Morjod is dead. Though you hardly have the right to call him son," Martok intoned portentously. "He gave me this before he died." Something silver and electronic clinked on the ground near Gothmara's feet. "I think he wanted me to find you."

"Why?" Gothmara asked. "So we could reconcile our differences and be reunited?"

"I doubt it," Martok replied humorlessly.

The man never had any grasp of irony.

"In the end, he knew he had been tricked. I think he wanted me to kill you."

"Somehow, I doubt that," Gothmara said. *Unless my hold on him slipped even more than I thought.* Gothmara unbelted her long cloak and flapped the long tails around herself. "It has grown very warm in here," she said distractedly, then turned her attention back to Martok. He held the Sword of Kahless before him now, ready for a trick, for a surprise attack. Ready for anything. *Almost anything.* "Morjod was my puppet even as you once were, my old lover."

"No," Martok droned, stepping forward. "Never. You

316

deceived me once, long ago, but never again. In the name of the Klingon people, I hereby charge you with treason and murder. You will accompany me back to Qo'noS to answer for your crimes."

Gothmara laughed. The man *was* delightful when he was full of himself. Reaching around to the small of her back, she twisted her hips as if loosening joints and removed a small vial from the inside of her belt. Pinching the top just *so,* she waved her arm before her and, concentrating, summoned her Voice. "Treason?" she asked. "All I have betrayed was a corrupt government. And murder? Who has died?"

"Who has died?" Martok sputtered. *"Who has died?* Thousands have died! You murdered my comrades, my daughters, my *wife!"*

"Wife?" Gothmara asked, her voice filled with confusion. "You are such a *simpleton,* Martok. Don't you recognize what's right in front of you?"

And even as Gothmara said the words, Sirella stepped out from behind a pillar. She wore a pair of manacles on her wrists and appeared disheveled, even underfed, but not too much worse for wear considering how long Gothmara had been holding her prisoner.

Martok blinked. Shook his head, but the figure before him remained the same. *Morjod must have beamed her off the ship just before it was destroyed. A trump card that he gave to his mother in case things fell out badly for her.* But he would not let the witch manipulate him. She had made her last mistake, taunting him, letting Sirella come within his grasp. Two steps, three at the most, and his love would once again be by his side; he would be able to protect her. His head fairly swam at the prospect of being able to make up for his past errors.

"Sirella," Martok said, and reached out to her with his right hand, the *bat'leth* hanging by his left side. "Stand behind me. We'll free your hands later."

"As you command, my husband," Sirella said, and moved into the circle of his arms.

As you command? Martok wondered. *What has Goth-mara been drugging her with?* But he could not resist the temptation to touch her, to encircle his wife in his arms and feel as if, even for a moment, he could protect her.

"My love," Sirella said, and brought her hands up to his chest. "I have missed you."

"And I you, Sirella," Martok replied. "But do not stand between me and that witch or she may . . . Oh."

As cold as he was, the knife blade sliding up into his midsection was by far the coldest sensation Martok had ever felt. A sliver of ice cut into his belly and now Sirella probed with it, searching for his heart so that she could freeze it. The shock rattled up and down his nerves, making his knees wobble and his fingers numb. His weapon was a dead weight in his hand, gravity too strong to defy.

Trying to turn away from her, Martok felt the *d'k'tahg* tear into his chest wall. Muscles quivered and he smelled a terrible odor that meant she had nicked his intestines. "Sirella?" he asked weakly, bending forward, unable to stand erect. Staring up into her face, he tried to ask "Why?" but was unable to breathe.

But it was not Sirella before him. He saw a dim gray outline, a flowing shape that danced before his eyes. A woman, yes, but not Sirella. She held something in her hand, but not a tiny knife. This woman held in one hand a simple wooden cup and in the other, something that gleamed brightly. He had seen this object before and, smiling, the woman tried to remind him of its name before she disappeared. When she vanished, Gothmara stood before him and Martok startled to awareness. *Ah, yes, a* bat'leth.

He raised the blade one-armed and swung. Just before it connected with her neck, Gothmara's eyes widened.

Martok overbalanced and fell on his back. *That's done it,* he thought before he passed out. *But Sirella will be very angry with me. . . .*

EPILOGUE

TWO MONTHS LATER

Martok awoke in his favorite chair, realizing that he had fallen asleep during the meeting with Admiral Ross. Once, he would have found this irritating and would have been profusely apologizing to the Federation officer, but he had been back on semiactive status for less than two weeks and everyone had been very decent about letting him occasionally have a nap. Besides, Worf was with him; he would be taking notes. *Many, many notes that he will want to review with me later. . . .* Martok sighed. This was the price for surrounding himself with conscientious operatives.

"Excuse me, Admiral. My mind was wandering. Could you say that last bit again?"

Ross paused, uncertain where to begin again. This was changing the rules, Martok knew. He was supposed to say nothing and let Ross finish. Then Worf would more or less repeat everything Ross and he had just said so that Martok would be caught up. The chancellor was tired of playing that particular game. He wanted to start a new one, a game called Paying Attention. Being feeble had lost its charm.

"I was saying, Chancellor, that Starfleet is satisfied with the new safeguards at our embassies. Not just on Qo'noS, mind you, but all of them. It *was* a rather outrageous gap in the security system." He glanced over at Worf. "And I assume you, Ambassador, will put all the embassies you visit to the test?"

"Of course, Admiral." The corners of Worf's mouth turned up ever so perceptively.

He finds the oddest pleasures in ambassadorial life, Martok thought.

"Excellent. Is there anything else, gentlemen?"

"No government business," Martok replied. "But how is Lieutenant Dax faring? We have not seen her since we held the groundbreaking for the monument at the Great Hall."

"Lieutenant Dax is fine, Chancellor, and sends her greetings. She's been busy as usual, though I hear through the grapevine that she has become fond of long, hot baths."

Both Worf and Martok laughed at the image. For days after they had returned to Qo'noS, the young Trill had done little but complain that she'd been left in the freezing armor so long that she could no longer feel her extremities.

"And you, Chancellor? How are you faring?"

Martok tried to sit straighter in his chair, but groaned where his bandages bound him too tightly. He had been putting on weight during the convalescence. Not nearly enough "physical" in his physical therapy. *Next week,* he decided. *Back into training.* He patted his midsection and said, "Tender, but surviving."

"And your son?"

Martok shifted uneasily in his seat. Drex had been out on the ice cliff for a long time before anyone found him. He would have, without question, died of exposure if someone had not wrapped him in a cloak. Drex suspected it had been Kahless, but no one knew for certain; nevertheless, Martok's son's fingers and toes were badly frostbitten and he had required extensive nerve and skin regeneration. Such procedures usually produced a certain amount of clumsiness, which the boy was finding difficult to endure. "He will live," Martok replied. "And he will relearn his warrior skills. Soon he will go to his new assignment aboard the *Gorkon.* Perhaps even with some added humility to guide him in the future. But he is still young, and so not always consistent." Martok smiled as he said that last part.

Ross nodded neutrally, every bit as much the diplomat as Worf and maybe a bit more. Finally, he came to the question that Martok sensed was most on the admiral's mind. "Any word of Kahless?"

Martok shook his head. This situation must make a Starfleet admiral very nervous. Where was the legendary emperor? Dead and buried in a mass grave on Boreth? Imprisoned by the new chancellor? Once again wandering the galaxy searching for the perfect Klingon warrior, seeing as his last selection was such a disappointment? "We have heard nothing, Admiral, but have no reason to assume he is dead. We keep the palace open for him and his throne awaits when he wishes to return to it."

"But until then," Worf said bluntly, "Martok rules the Klingon people."

"As it should be," Ross replied. "And as your people no doubt desire. That was quite a celebration, Chancellor, when you returned to Qo'noS."

Martok rubbed his nose and closed his eyes. He grew tired and the memory of the return to the First City was not a pleasant one: memorial ceremonies, receiving the families of warriors fallen in the empire's service, rebuilding what Morjod had destroyed, and the seemingly endless task of accounting for the lost, the dead, and the destroyed.

The Klingon Defense Force had sustained significant losses, both in troop strength and equipment. Finding and promoting those warriors worthy to replace Martok's lost allies had been challenging. Even reinstating the High Council—with the surviving poet-warrior *katai* taking a number of the seats—had proven to be a simpler task than selecting new generals. Finally, of course, there had been Martok's private ceremonies for Sirella and his daughters, as well as the start of construction of the memorial where the Great Hall had stood.

Some had wanted a new structure built where the old had stood, but Martok had asked for a garden to be installed to include a monument to his wife and Gothmara's other victims. Such was Martok's popularity at this time that none dared refuse any of his requests. An opera celebrating Sirella's life would be at the fore of the dedication ceremonies. *The Klingon people like a victory,* Worf had pronounced in an uncharacteristically sardonic tone, *but they will do anything for a tragic victor.*

"I don't remember much of the celebrating, Admiral, but they tell me the *gagh* was fresh and that the bloodwine flowed freely," he said. "Just one more question and then I'll let you go: Were you able to arrange for the payment to that Ferengi company?"

Ross snorted and said, "Yes, though it was hardly worth the effort. I think the transfer fees and 'handling charges' were more than the total amount you paid. Would you mind explaining now what it was all about?"

"It was," Martok said, "the current value of a vintage Federation vehicle called a Sporak."

"A Sporak? The big overland vehicles?"

"The same," Martok said. "I . . . rented one while I was on the run, but at the time I didn't have enough on me to cover the debt."

"Oh," Ross said. "This is one of those stories I'm not going to hear for a long time, if ever, isn't it?"

Martok nodded.

"Very well," the admiral said. "I have a few of those myself. I know what they're like."

"I'm sure you do, my friend. I'm sure you do."

They said their good-byes, leaving Martok and Worf to settle the outstanding business and drink a cup of bloodwine in relative quiet. They were sitting in the large office in the Emperor's Palace, which Morjod had occupied during his short tenure. Martok had, at first, despised the place even as he had understood why it was necessary to symbolically "retake" it; in recent weeks, since he had begun working again, he had enjoyed some of its pleasures, not the least of which were the large west-facing walls. Since Morjod's Hammer had fallen, the sunsets had been spectacular.

Worf and Martok sat quietly for several minutes and watched the western sky ripple and twist with shades of crimson, gold, and purple. Finally, as the room grew dark, Worf asked, "Do you think he'll ever turn up again?"

"Kahless?" Martok asked. "Doubtless. Unlooked-for and with some insane quest that needs to be fulfilled. Perhaps I'll even give him his sword back and tell him to be on his way. No more adventures for me. I have an empire to run."

"And that's not an adventure?"

"On the good days?" Martok replied. "No."

Worf laughed warmly, a sound that came out of him easier in these days. After a fashion, Martok was distressed not to have the old morose Worf around to tease anymore, but he found new pleasure in baiting the contented Worf, too. "No more visitations from Jadzia or any other women from your past?" Martok asked.

Worf shook his head and stared out the window. "Not a one. And you?"

Martok sighed. "Every night," he said. "But only when I dream."

"You should rest, my brother. You have much work to do."

"And you should leave my home and get some of your own work under way, my brother," Martok replied. "The Federation has been very generous to lend you to me for this long, but the people grow restless. They want to see their chancellor rule them . . ."

". . . And not the mongrel outsider."

"Don't say that so disparagingly, Worf. We're all mongrels here. It's what makes us great."

Worf rose and bowed slightly at the waist. "As you say, Chancellor. Perhaps I will try to finish up my affairs here soon. It does not sound like you have much more use for me."

"None," Martok said happily. "Go."

After his brother had left, Martok pushed himself carefully up out of his chair and walked slowly and gingerly out into the corridor, down the stairs, and outside the palace to a small garden he had asked to be constructed. This garden served as the model for the larger one being built on the site of the Great Hall in every way but in scale; in every way he preferred the smaller one.

During his long convalescence, this was the single spot where Martok had found peace from his thoughts. One of the gardeners, noting that the chancellor came here often, had arranged for a large, comfortable wooden chair equipped with thick cushions to be installed. Here, in this quiet place, he had long discussions with the many ghosts that drove him. He made peace with some of them. More than one early-rising (or late-to-bed) palace functionary had passed through the garden to find the chancellor muttering to himself, debating some arcane point. Eventually, to avoid being labeled a complete eccentric, Martok had commissioned a statue that had proved so popular a choice that a larger version would stand at the center of the monument garden.

The statue was a Klingon woman in a robe standing lightly on one foot as if she were either taking off or landing. In one hand she held a cup and in the other a *bat'leth*, as if offering one or the other to those who gazed upon her. Not both, though. This woman demanded a choice. The sculptor had given her Sirella's features, which pleased Martok no end, though not for the assumed reasons. *She is a goddess,* he thought in one of his long vigils, *for a people who do not fear the gods. But if the gods wear faces we know, we can learn to respect them as they should respect us. It is not too much to ask.*

Martok sat down in his chair, studied the statue, and smiled with private satisfaction. *And if in turn, in some future day, a new race of Klingons sees that the greatest and only goddess of this age wore Sirella's face, well, that will be all right, too.*

With that thought, Martok closed his eyes and slept.

And the chancellor dreamt.

ABOUT THE AUTHORS

Best known for his portrayal of General Martok on the television series *Star Trek: Deep Space Nine,* J. G. Hertzler was born into a family whose roots go back eight generations in the small Pennsylvania town of Port Royal. He was raised on various foreign and domestic U.S. Air Force bases, from El Paso to Casablanca—which may explain his lifelong philosophical confusion. J. G. was a college football linebacker and an antiwar protestor; he has canvassed for McGovern and strongly supported the men and women of our armed forces; he feels he has a gentle Amish soul inside a short-fused temper. In other words, Martok is close to his heart, and J. G. expects he always will be.

As an actor in the theatre, J. G. toured the rust belt with Roddy MacDowall in the 1996 National Tour of *Dial M for Murder,* held a shotgun on Holly Hunter in *By the Bog of Cats,* and had his severed head carried around by Irene Pappas in *The Bacchae.*

In television, J. G. has worked in countless episodics, mostly villains roiling with inner torment. A student of screenwriting, he's had three scripts optioned with no cigar . . . yet. Hope and rewriting spring eternal. *The Left Hand of Destiny* represents J. G.'s first foray into narrative fiction. It's been one helluva ride thus far, with a little help from his friends, old and new.

Jeffrey Lang is the author of *Star Trek: The Next Generation—Immortal Coil,* the short story "Dead Man's Hand" in the anthology *Star Trek: Deep Space Nine—The Lives of Dax,* and the coauthor (with David Weddle) of *Star Trek: Deep Space Nine—Section 31: Abyss.* He is currently working on a couple other projects, including more *Trek* and the graphic novel *Sherwood.* Lang lives in Wynnewood, PA, with his wife, Katherine Fritz, his son, Andrew, and Buster, who, no doubt, wants to go out for a walk right now.

Look for STAR TREK fiction from Pocket Books

Star Trek®

Star Trek: Voyager®

Enterprise®

Star Trek®: New Frontier

New Frontier #1-4 Collector's Edition • Peter David
  #1 • *House of Cards*
  #2 • *Into the Void*
  #3 • *The Two-Front War*
  #4 • *End Game*
  #5 • *Martyr* • Peter David
  #6 • *Fire on High* • Peter David
The Captain's Table #5 • *Once Burned* • Peter David
Double Helix #5 • *Double or Nothing* • Peter David
  #7 • *The Quiet Place* • Peter David
  #8 • *Dark Allies* • Peter David
#9-11 • *Excalibur* • Peter David
    #9 • *Requiem*
    #10 • *Renaissance*
    #11 • *Restoration*
Gateways #6: *Cold Wars* • Peter David
Gateways #7: *What Lay Beyond:* "Death After Life" • Peter David
#12 • *Being Human* • Peter David

Star Trek®: Stargazer

The Valiant • Michael Jan Friedman
Double Helix #6: *The First Virtue* • Michael Jan Friedman and Christie
  Golden
Gauntlet • Michael Jan Friedman
Progenitor • Michael Jan Friedman

Star Trek®: Starfleet Corps of Engineers (eBooks)

Have Tech, Will Travel (paperback) • various
  #1 • *The Belly of the Beast* • Dean Wesley Smith
  #2 • *Fatal Error* • Keith R.A. DeCandido
  #3 • *Hard Crash* • Christie Golden
  #4 • *Interphase, Book One* • Dayton Ward & Kevin Dilmore
Miracle Workers (paperback) • various
  #5 • *Interphase, Book Two* • Dayton Ward & Kevin Dilmore
  #6 • *Cold Fusion* • Keith R.A. DeCandido
  #7 • *Invincible, Book One* • Keith R.A. DeCandido & David Mack
  #8 • *Invincible, Book Two* • Keith R.A. DeCandido & David Mack
Some Assembly Required (paperback) • various
  #9 • *The Riddled Post* • Aaron Rosenberg
  #10 • *Gateways Epilogue: Here There Be Monsters* • Keith R.A. DeCandido
  #11 • *Ambush* • Dave Galanter & Greg Brodeur
  #12 • *Some Assembly Required* • Scott Ciencin & Dan Jolley

Star Trek®: Section 31™

Rogue • Andy Mangels & Michael A. Martin
Shadow • Dean Wesley Smith & Kristine Kathryn Rusch
Cloak • S.D. Perry
Abyss • David Weddle & Jeffrey Lang

Star Trek®: Gateways

#1 • *One Small Step* • Susan Wright
#2 • *Chainmail* • Diane Carey
#3 • *Doors Into Chaos* • Robert Greenberger
#4 • *Demons of Air and Darkness* • Keith R.A. DeCandido
#5 • *No Man's Land* • Christie Golden
#6 • *Cold Wars* • Peter David
#7 • *What Lay Beyond* • various
Epilogue: Here There Be Monsters • Keith R.A. DeCandido

Star Trek® Omnibus Editions

Invasion! Omnibus • various
Day of Honor Omnibus • various
The Captain's Table Omnibus • various
Double Helix Omnibus • various
Star Trek: Odyssey • William Shatner with Judith and Garfield Reeves-Stevens
Millennium Omnibus • Judith and Garfield Reeves-Stevens
Starfleet: Year One • Michael Jan Friedman

Star Trek® Short Story Anthologies

Strange New Worlds, vol. I, II, III, IV and V • Dean Wesley Smith, ed.
The Lives of Dax • Marco Palmieri, ed.
Enterprise Logs • Carol Greenburg, ed.
The Amazing Stories • various

Other Star Trek® Fiction

Legends of the Ferengi • Ira Steven Behr & Robert Hewitt Wolfe
Adventures in Time and Space • Mary P. Taylor, ed.
Captain Proton: Defender of the Earth • D.W. "Prof" Smith
New Worlds, New Civilizations • Michael Jan Friedman
The Badlands, Books One and *Two* • Susan Wright
The Klingon Hamlet • Wil'yam Shex'pir
Dark Passions, Books One and *Two* • Susan Wright
The Brave and the Bold, Books One and *Two* • Keith R. A. DeCandido

STAR TREK®

STARGAZER: THREE

MICHAEL JAN FRIEDMAN

WHEN A TRANSPORTER MISHAP DEPOSITS A
BEAUTIFUL WOMAN FROM ANOTHER UNIVERSE
ON THE *STARGAZER*, GERDA ASMOND SUSPECTS THE
ALIEN OF TREACHERY.

BUT SHE HAS TO WONDER—IS SHE FOLLOWING
HER KLINGON INSTINCTS OR SUCCUMBING TO
SIMPLE JEALOUSY?

GERDA NEEDS TO FIND OUT—OR PICARD AND HIS
CREW MAY PAY FOR THEIR GENEROSITY WITH
THEIR LIVES.

AVAILABLE AUGUST 2003